SIGNATURES IN STONE

A Bomarzo Mystery

SIGNATURES IN STONE
A Bomarzo Mystery

LINDA LAPPIN

Caravel Books
a mystery imprint of Pleasure Boat Studio
New York

ISBN 978-1-929355-90-7
Library of Congress Control Number: 2013934436

Design by Susan Ramundo
Cover by Laura Tolkow

Pleasure Boat Studio is a proud subscriber to the Green Press Initiative. This program encourages the use of 100% post-consumer recycled paper with environmentally friendly inks for all printing projects in an effort to reduce the book industry's economic and social impact. With the cooperation of our printing company, we are pleased to offer this book as a Green Press book.

Pleasure Boat Studio books are available through the following:
SPD (Small Press Distribution) Tel. 800-869-7553, Fax 510-524-0852
Partners/West Tel. 425-227-8486, Fax 425-204-2448
Baker & Taylor Tel. 800-775-1100, Fax 800-775-7480
Ingram Tel. 615-793-5000, Fax 615-287-5429
Amazon.com and bn.com

and through
PLEASURE BOAT STUDIO: A LITERARY PRESS
www.pleasureboatstudio.com
201 West 89th Street
New York, NY 10024

Contact Jack Estes
Fax: 413-677-0085
Email: pleasboat@nyc.rr.com

For Sergio, again and always

"Che ognuno v'incontri ciò che più gli sta a cuore,
e che tutti vi si smarriscano."

CONTENTS

The Angel and the Snake

CHAPTER ONE

Bomarzo, March 1928

We arrived in the evening after an exhausting drive along the sea through a land of silvery olive trees where innumerable dirty sheep dotted the meadows, and a rosy haze of blooms shimmered above low-lying peach groves. The Italian countryside looked sleepy and wet. Tenuous clouds, pinkish and plum–colored, streaked and feathered a lavender sky. And the light! Impossible to describe the tints of amber, ochre, bloodied tangerine. I was enchanted, but our artist friend Clive was too woozy to rhapsodize. He sat green-faced in the front passenger seat, clutching his Stetson on trembling knees, groaning at every curve. Determined to reach Bomarzo before nightfall, Nigel steered our gleaming Packard, fearless and expert, along dirt tracks, scattering chickens from the roadside, while I sat in the back, wrapped in a shawl, looking out at solitary oaks and ruined towers. Though I may have reached that phase of life dubiously called "a certain age" when women often cease to enjoy traveling, nothing engages my fantasy more than a long road trip with rapid changes of scenery, as in this undiscovered country called Tuscia.

About a hundred miles north of Rome, we turned inland to cross a marshland, then a succession of arid hills where broken bits of ancient Roman aqueducts stood stark against the twilight. Farther on, deep ravines gashed the terrain like unhealed fissures from which rose twisted masses of gray stone where ancient houses, domes, and grottoes were chiseled along the edges. Only a great turbulence from deep within the earth could have gouged out such chasms which appeared before us with hardly any warning as we rolled along. Flat meadows fell away into gorges where the road plunged, then laboriously wound up again. Thorny bushes scraped the sides of the car in narrow spots; jutting rocks thumped against the belly of the vehicle, causing Nigel great concern for his axel. God knows what would have happened if the car had broken down out there in the middle of nowhere. We might have been devoured by wolves, or by the ferocious white sheepdogs that pounced out of the brush to run alongside the car until their legs gave out, barking their heads off till we rounded the next curve.

Sometimes on a promontory we saw a cluster of houses, now all dark, or an isolated farmhouse with a yellow glimmer at the window or a curl of smoke above the chimney; sometimes a dilapidated church or hermitage nestled in a crevice along a cliff. The landscape was full of signatures, signs, and hidden meanings, I felt. An entire manuscript was displayed before my eyes, inviting me to decipher its alphabets, offering inspiration for the new novel I had come to Italy to write at Nigel's forceful insistence.

At last we were delivered to the forlorn town of Bomarzo built along the rim of a deep gorge where Nigel had leased half the *piano nobile* of an aristocratic old villa until July. The main attraction we had come from Paris to see was a sixteenth-century sculpture garden in a park appended to the villa, which until a few months ago, was so overgrown with briars and weeds that it had been entirely forgotten by generations of art historians. Clive had heard about it through an acquaintance who knew the tenant currently residing at the villa, an eccentric, American art-history scholar and retired college professor, working in great secrecy on a monograph about the place. Clive wanted to be the first modern painter to immortalize the park and its sculptures, and had convinced Nigel, his new patron and my publisher and old family friend, that he should contact Professor Finestone, the current tenant, and arrange to sublet part of the villa for a few months so that they could spend a holiday in Italy together and he could paint there. The idea was that Nigel would later publish Clive's sketches and watercolors of the sculptures in a book, perhaps as an accompaniment to the professor's monograph about them, which was rumored, according to Clive, to be of worldwide import—at least to the art world. These statues portrayed a series of monstrous, imaginary creatures—denizens of a pagan hell, or, perhaps, allegories of the seven cardinal sins. The place was known to local legend as "the Monster Park." That's all I knew about our destination, which had been explained during our journey down from Paris. As an author of mystery stories, I confess I found it all quite appealing.

Midway down a steep descent, we came to a gate behind which a somber villa illuminated by flickering torchlight waited at the end of a gravel drive. Lining the drive all the way to the villa were tall cypress trees, like hooded figures in the dusk. Beneath each cypress, a small oil lamp guttered. At the sound of Nigel's claxon, a man hobbled from the deepening shadows.

A short, stout, bovine fellow of about sixty peered into the window on the driver's side and mumbled a word to Nigel. I noted at once his canny black eyes beneath heavy brows, his beak-like nose and thick stubble of beard on cheeks shining with sweat. A coarse face, I thought, but not without character and rustic virility. Thrusting up a rigid arm to greet us with the Fascist salute, he turned to open the gates. Nigel nudged the Packard through and we drove on up to the villa. Trotting behind the car, the gatekeeper extinguished the lamps behind us one by one, snuffing them out with a heavy iron tool as we proceeded. When we reached the villa, the long drive behind us was almost completely steeped in darkness and you could no longer see as far the gate.

But the villa was ablaze with torches set along the monumental staircase and with lamps shining in the twenty or thirty windows on the upper floors. As we pulled over and parked near the foot of the staircase, I noted a stone archway with an imposing iron gate far to the right of the building. This, as we were to discover, was the entrance to the famous park which lay along the edge of an untidy lawn where the land sloped sharply down to be engulfed by an outgrowth of riotous vegetation.

I climbed out of the Packard, following the men, relieved to stretch my legs and smooth my stockings after so many hours on the road. I looked up at the villa from beneath the brim of my cloche hat. We had received a royal welcome with the dramatic touch of the lamp-lit driveway, but the villa itself, of yellow stucco with bluish-gray shutters, looked a bit run down. I noticed a couple of broken window panes on the third floor and a place or two where the cornice had crumbled away. My first thought was that I ardently desired a hot cup of tea, and I feared this place might not be able to produce one. My next thought was I needed a smoke, and I don't mean tobacco.

"This way! This way," spluttered a voice from behind me as the gatekeeper caught up with us. "Welcome. Welcome. I am Manu. I am keeper," he chortled, in between ludicrous bows. Unloading our bags from the car and piling them at the foot of the staircase, he ushered us up the gray stone stairs into a drafty, unlit hall hung with tapestries, where more stairs led to upper floors. Professor Finestone was not there to meet us, but he had apparently left instructions on what to do with his new housemates, for we were led directly into a dark kitchen opening off the hall, permeated by the smell of rancid grease and soot, where I was cheered to see a fire burning. In the middle of the room, four mismatched chairs were drawn up to a bare plank table. Huddled by the hearth sat a bony, blond slip of a girl wrapped in an apron.

Manu threw his chubby arm around the wraith's shoulder, "This is my Amelia!" he announced jovially, pulling the reluctant girl forward into the light shed by candles and oil lamps placed about the room. I saw then that her apron was dirty and her cuffs quite soiled and that she was not as young as she had first appeared. She was perhaps thirty years old. "She will cook, clean, wash clothes for you. Now she make tea! English people love their tea." Amelia glared at us, quite tongue-tied and unsure of what she was to do, until with a bearish growl "Vai!" *Go!* Manu pushed her to the stove where a kettle had begun to sing.

"Very good! We were hoping to meet Professor Finestone. Is he away?" began Nigel, with a slight clearing of his throat. I detected a bit of nervousness in his voice as he addressed the gatekeeper. We had wired the money for our rent to Finestone and expected to find him there. Suppose he had gone off without making proper arrangements with the owner of the villa? But Manu reassured us.

"No worry, no worry! Professor is in Rome. Back in few days. Till then, my girl and I look after you. We want that you feel . . . at home! Anything you need, ask Amelia. She will do. Is that not so, Amelia?"

Intent on buttering some slabs of bread for us, the girl did not answer. Unlike her father, whose command of English was surprisingly deft, Amelia didn't seem to understand a word of what was being said. I hoped my knowledge of Italian from my schooldays would suffice for me to communicate how I wanted my egg boiled, my chemises ironed, and at what time to serve my breakfast.

"Sit! Sit!" urged Manu, inviting us to the table with a clap of his hands while Amelia continued her preparations. "Tea almost ready." Now he turned to me. "Lady, come, sit near fire!" and as he seized a chair to offer me a seat, a little white cat that had been curled up there leapt to the floor with a yowl and crawled under a sideboard. Manu thumped the straw seat twice, as if to dispel fleas. "Lady! Sit! Gentlemen, Sit!" Clive and Nigel complied and I too sat down, after briefly inspecting the chair to make sure there were no insects. The three of us were too tired to talk and we waited in silence for our tea. I glanced at my companions to gauge their reaction to this rather rustic setting, which, I supposed, was not quite what any of us had been expecting.

The room with its red brick floor and charred ceiling beams looked positively medieval. Huge brass cauldrons dangled from butcher's hooks above a giant tiled stove. Lined up along rough wooden shelves were antique platters big as cartwheels, heavy enough to crush your toe if one should accidently fall on your foot. Cutting tools of iron and steel more suitable for display in a dungeon decorated the walls. Above the mantelpiece hung an oval mirror, its dim silvery surface finely gummed with grease and flyspecks. In every corner of the malodorous room, I noted thick skeins of spider webs, inhabited by large black things as big as a baby's hand.

Clive seemed to be observing all this through the wide eyes of an American ingénue to whom everything old and European, no matter how decrepit, is invested with quaint charm. But from the studied neutrality of Nigel's face and the stiff movements of his head as he gazed about the kitchen, I could see he was far from pleased and quite possibly furious. He was a creature of comfort who loved luxury even more than I, and we had already paid our full rent in advance. If the place should prove unsuitable, I rather doubted that we would get our money back. This whole trip had been arranged to satisfy Clive's whim—and now that he and Nigel had fallen out, on my account, well, I thought it likely Nigel already regretted our coming here. But I was in no hurry to head back to Paris, especially after accidentally setting my flat on fire, and running off leaving two months' rent due and no forwarding address.

Tea was served. As Amelia handed me a chipped but precious china cup that might have come from a museum, I noticed the edges of a nasty bruise on her neck, half hidden by the tired ruffle of her dingy white blouse. Her blue eyes slid sidewise to meet mine as her quick fingers rearranged the ruffle to hide her blemish. *"Sembrate stanca, Signora,"* *You seem tired, Signora,* she said addressing me directly. I don't know why but from the very first, I didn't like the sound of her voice.

The tea was passable and the food—ham, cheese, bread, olives—simple but filling. We drank and ate without further conversation. My mind was running ahead to when Clive and I would be alone again, hopefully after having a short rest. The drive had worn me out. A clock from somewhere, upstairs perhaps, chimed the hours. It was nine o'clock.

Manu had stepped out to bring the rest of our luggage in. Returning to the kitchen, he distributed candles, for there was no electricity anywhere in the house, and proposed to give us a tour of the ground floor before showing us to our rooms. Taking a lighted candelabra from the sideboard, he led the way—with Nigel right behind him, Clive following, while I brought up the rear. The draperies across the high windows had not been drawn, and pale moonlight shone in to help guide our steps through the villa, but the floor was uneven in spots; one had to be careful not to trip. The slim flames of our candles barely allowed me to gain a general impression of the place, but I could see, nonetheless, that it must have been in shambles for a hundred years at least.

The rooms were all dank and gloomy and smelled of must. Mildew and mold mapped the walls and mottled the tapestries blackened by centuries of dust. It didn't look as though there were a comfortable chair or sofa anywhere and it was also very cold—I could feel the chill of the marble floor through the soles of my shoes—but, admittedly, the ambience was intriguing. Lewd gorgons leered down, wagging their tongues, over doorways. Statue fragments and coats-of-arms were embedded in pock-marked walls where the flaking plaster was tinted in pastels: sky blue, pea green, ochre, lavender. Whenever we passed a mutilated piece of sculpture or a peeling scrap of frescoed wall where a detached head or arm were all that remained of an antique image, Manu would hold his candelabra higher to shed a patch of light upon it and say, "Very old painting," "Very valuable," or "Famous artist," with a touch of pride in his voice. A bleak warning immediately followed: "No touch, please."

Despite the dilapidated condition of the villa inside and out, one could see that the artistic treasures it housed were priceless. We groped along a gallery of Florentine-style portraits, their rich colors emerging jewel-like in our candlelight. All these paintings were clearly worth a fortune but the dampness of the place was hardly congenial to their conservation. I could see that several of the paintings had buckled from moisture absorbed from the stone walls on which they hung.

Clive, just two steps ahead of me, studied all this with great attention, pausing to poke his nose closer whenever Manu pointed out a painting or an *objet d'art*. Everything interested him intensely. As Manu and Nigel trundled along up ahead of us, he lagged behind, once to peek inside the drawer of a secretary along the corridor; once to terrify me by lunging out of a corner unexpectedly, grinning like a gorgon; and once to pinch my bottom and pull me behind some moldy brocade drapes, which only made me sneeze. I pushed him away. "Naughty boy! Not here, darling! Later!" Nigel knew all about us, of course, but I didn't want to make a show in front of a servant, partly because I was obviously much older than Clive.

At last we returned to the great entrance hall, now pitch black, where the fitful gleams of Manu's candelabra illumined an imposing staircase.

"We go up. Watch feet."

At the top, we came to a set of massive double doors decorated with gold stucco. From this hub, two wings stretched left and right into the dark. The interior of the place seemed even larger than it had appeared from the outside, and I imagined the villa must have incorporated structures from several centuries as various rooms and floors had been added on.

Manu indicated the ornate doors before us: "This is library.

Many, many books. Tomorrow you look." He thrust his cande-labra to the left. "Rooms of Professor," then gestured with the candelabra toward the right as dripping wax spattered the floor. "Your rooms that way. The Signora is next to library. The gentle-men just here and down here. Come along."

Across from the library, I noted a large painting set in a niche partly hidden by dark red velvet curtains. Curious, I stopped to have a better look while the others went ahead. Clive, noticing I had paused, retraced his steps to see what had caught my inter-est. Shoving his candle toward the niche, he intoned in an un-canny imitation of our keeper's voice: "Very old painting. Very Valuable! Famous Artist. No touch, please!"

I would have laughed, but when Clive pulled the curtains all the way open to reveal the painting in the niche, I was momen-tarily stunned. A lean, brown, handsome face emerged from its concealment to confront my own. Hazel eyes, keen and alive, bored into mine with a power of attention that took my breath away. The face belonged to a life-sized angel with rainbow wings in earthen tones—brown, beige, mauve, ochre, rust—like an ex-otic moth, standing guard in a boulder-strewn landscape. In one hand he held a scale; in the other, a sword pointed downwards, where it transfixed an ugly serpent with brownish-purple scales, by no means dead, the tip of whose tail coiled around the angel's left ankle. The snake's lidless yellow eyes were directed toward the viewer, glinting with the same vivid intelligence that graced the angel's brow. I think I gave a little gasp, and Clive grabbed my hand, he, too, fascinated by the angel and the snake. The two figures were not antithetical by any means; they seemed to make a whole, like a yin and yang.

Our contemplation of the painting was rudely cut short by Manu's intervention. "Lady! Sir! This way to rooms! I give keys." He had come to fetch us, and at the sound of his voice, I dropped Clive's hand. Manu reached out to tug the curtains closed, saying, "Ugly painting. Not valuable. Unknown artist.

You look tomorrow."

"Daphne!" Nigel now piped up from the dark. It was the first word he had spoken to me since our arrival. "I should very much like to retire now. You and Clive may stay up exploring, if you wish, and gaze at all the paintings you like. But I must get some rest."

"Of course, darling." As I turned away from the niche, the snake's amber eyes still burned into my retina, like the impress left by a bright spot of sun glimpsed on a cloudy day.

Manu handed out our keys, informing us that he would bring our luggage up at once and promising a kettle of hot water in the morning. Clive was conveniently installed in a room across from mine, Nigel in two large rooms at the end of the corridor. As we said goodnight, Clive wished me pleasant dreams. It was our code word to say I could expect a visit from him later in the night.

The lock to my room was rusty, and I needed Manu's assistance to turn the key. To my surprise, I found my accommodations much more inhabitable than the rest of the house had led me to expect. A fire had been lit in the great stone hearth, and several lamps and candelabras flickered on end tables and dressers. The room's chief glory was a giant double bed done up in red and gold damask with matching drapes shielding tall windows. I thought it would do very well as a boudoir. In an alcove was a dressing room with wardrobes, trunks, and even a zinc tub, but since, as Manu explained to me, the upper floors of the house were without running water, I imagined that bathing preparations would be quite complex.

I asked Manu to bring my things up at once, along with a nightcap of brandy and soda. As soon as I was alone, I plopped down on the bed over which hung an exquisite portrait of a lady, a minor masterpiece. I guessed it dated from the sixteenth century or so, judging by her costume: a lace-frilled crimson bodice snugly encasing a plump bosom, beneath which flowed a skirt of spinach green brocade. Nestled in the hollow of her throat was a silver locket. Her white fingers spread upon her breast displayed a ruby ring which I studied in detail as I adore antique jewelry, probably because I had to sell nearly all of mine years ago. Her eyes, blue hauteur and marble, gazed defiantly at the viewer and were met with her own disapproval in a full-length mirror hanging on the opposite wall. The lady looked so lifelike, I almost felt the need to beg her pardon for usurping her bed, where the fine linens were embroidered with the initial A.O., which I fancied must now refer to one of her descendants.

The fire had begun to smoke, so I rose to open a window, discovering then that behind the thick drapes was a door to a terrace to which both my room and the library next door had access. Taking a small oil lamp from the desk I ventured out and walked to the edge. From here, in daylight, one would enjoy a fine view of the countryside and a partial view of the park; but there wasn't much to see now, for a layer of clouds had rolled in to veil the moon. The night air smelled sweet of damp foliage and earth, though there was also a tainted smell of rotting leaves and bad drains. Leaning over the parapet of the terrace, I gazed out over the grounds. I could hear a faint bleating of sheep and tinkling of bells coming from the wall of the gorge rising behind the villa. As the moon slit the clouds, I noted dim white shapes moving in the shadows halfway up the gorge. At the top slept the town of Bomarzo, a cluster of stone houses cobbled together around a large villa, or perhaps, a former monastery, built of yellowish stone.

In the far right corner of the terrace was a narrow shelter resembling a sentry box, which I thought might hold a water tank, or, I hoped, maybe even a privy, for I hated primitive arrangements. Going to investigate, I found it was the entrance to an ingeniously concealed staircase with steep, iron rungs spiraling downwards. Regrettably, it was much too late and too dark to explore any further, but I promised myself I would do so the next morning.

I approached the door to the library, adjacent to my room, and peeked in—but the drapes were drawn. I then noted a third door giving access to the terrace on the other side of the library from one of the rooms in the wing occupied by the professor. It was chilly now and I had no wrap. As I stepped back inside, I found Manu in my room, oiling the lock on the bedroom door. My suitcase had been set on a chair by my writing desk, and a tray with my brandy and soda waited by the bed.

"Lady will catch cold." Manu put down his oilcan, went over to the terrace door, and banged it shut behind me.

"I did not ask you to close that," I said, annoyed.

"Lady does not want to get ill. Besides, there are bats, things that fly at night!" He pointed to the lamps on a small desk near the window. "They come to the flame. The Signora does not want bats in her hair."

"Nonsense," I said. That old wives' tale about bats getting in one's hair! Not a bit of truth in it. Still, glancing to the terrace, I did see a tiny bat flitting joyously in the night air. Its wings nearly grazed the windowpanes.

I dismissed Manu and before shutting my door, looked left and right down the long corridor and listened a moment, but all was silent. Retreating inside, I left the door unlocked for Clive then gulped down the brandy and got ready for bed, for I was too tired to do any writing that night. The wild spirit of Bomarzo excited and intrigued me, yet that first evening upon arriving, I felt ill-at-ease about the months to come, isolated, as it were, in the company of these two men, the younger of whom, most unexpectedly, had just become my lover. As the minutes ticked away and a clock somewhere down the hall softly chimed eleven, then midnight, I mused over the strange circumstances that had brought me here to this moldy old villa. I wondered if it had been wise for me to come on this trip after all, but I had not been in a position to refuse Nigel's proposal—especially after he had saved me from being burned to death when my Paris flat went up in flames. I had had only an hour to pack my bags and leave behind, quite literally speaking, the ashes of my former life. And now here I was, embarked upon a serendipitous liaison with an adorable younger man.

That fire in my flat back in Paris had been a very nasty business, and I wouldn't have come through had it not been for Nigel. I had been smoking. My lighted pipe must have tumbled from my hand as I sank into a reverie in which the floral trellises on the yellow wallpaper began to writhe like snakes. This intriguing spectacle did not in the least alarm me until one wriggled off the wall, dropping straight around my neck like a noose and I had no voice to scream. I lost consciousness to the hissing of serpentine tongues, which I later surmised must have been the steam issuing from the kettle I had forgotten on the stove. I was roused only when Nigel came knocking at the door and barking through the transom that he had just returned from New York and had missed me at the *Boeuf sur le Toit*, and was my first chapter ready? I moaned or laughed something in reply and suddenly the room was filled with smoke and there came an explosion. Nigel had kicked the door open and was flapping his overcoat against the flames which were demolishing one entire wall of my flat while I looked on dazed from the sofa where I lay surrounded by a pile of dirty tea cups, cast-off stockings and broken fruit plates. A tea cozy, it seems, had been left too near the stove, and catching fire, had first set a curtain and then the wallpaper ablaze.

When the fire had been put out, he looked at me, panting and red-faced, his high forehead beaded with sweat.

"Daphne," he chided, "had I not showed up in time, you might have burned to death like a witch at the Inquisition!" Noticing the pipe that had fallen to the floor where it had singed the rug, he reached for it and shook it in my face. "You promised me you would stop this!"

I closed my eyes and smiled vaguely while the room whirled around me, a carousel of cheap, broken furniture. "Thou shalt not escape thyself," I mumbled.

But the gallon of boiling bitter tea he poured down my throat set me on my feet again. The cold compress applied to my lids caused the blue pouches beneath my eyes to recede. When hunger returned against my will, he fed me spoonfuls of orange marmalade, the only edible substance in the cupboard, then placed a bundle of dollars on the table, which I contemplated with a blank stare. I was damnably sober again, damnably myself, damnably human and alive in this miserable world. Why had he not left me alone? He knew the money would tempt me.

"What is that?" I asked warily, pointing a shaky finger at the money, and noticing as I did, that it was high time I repainted my fingernails, though I didn't have the cash for a professional manicure. "A gift? A loan?" I resisted the urge to reach out for the pile, but I had already calculated at a glance how much would go to pay back debts, and how much was needed for rent, for food, for wine and other even more urgent necessities.

"You know very well it is an advance on your next book!"

"Hah!" I snorted, "then you can keep it!"

"You promised me another mystery. You have signed your name to that promise."

"And pray tell, who promised you, me or Marilyn Moseley?" Marilyn Moseley was my humble *nom de plume*.

"My dear, need I remind you that by whatever name you write your books, you are under obligation to me?"

"You are out of luck, old boy."

I then craved something stronger than tea to drink so I flung out a hand and opened a cupboard, looking for a bottle of whatever I could find, but they were all empty. I caught sight of myself in the mirror above the sideboard, then. Good God, what a hag! I ran a hand through my matted hair to tidy it.

"Marilyn Mosley is merely a figment of my imagination. She isn't real," I said as I continued to study my face in the mirror. Perhaps *I* wasn't real either. "Her promises carry no weight in this world. You had best forget her." Opening another cupboard, I found a bottle of absinthe with a tiny emerald drop at the bottom, but Nigel plucked it from my unsteady hand before I could put it to my lips.

"Of our imagination! Remember we are in this together."

Yes, indeed! We were in this together. He was my publisher. And now like the Devil himself, Nigel was here claiming his due. I hated writing those novels.

"But Nigel, darling, try to understand. After all that's happened, I am quite simply devastated. I have run out of ideas. I haven't got the strength, or the mental concentration, to write another novel. I don't know how I managed the last one. And I couldn't bear to be bashed about by those idiotic critics any more. I'd much prefer to write about daffodils and delphiniums for the *Lady Gardner* who are at least more punctual with their pay."

Nigel's thin lips repressed a grimace. He smiled as though a wire had been pulled through his gums. It had taken him two years to pay me my due for *Signatures,* my most recent novel, and I was convinced, despite his professed dedication to my family, that he had been dishonest in calculating my royalties.

"A contract is a contract," he intoned, then seized my hands in his. I looked at his long, pale, pudgy fingers. How immaculate the nails, how perfectly buffed by his professional manicurist. I had to admit that being touched by him still summoned up in me a strong, but not entirely pleasant sensation.

"Although the critics battered you a bit, your readers love you. They want another book from you."

"It is not me they love!" I protested, wriggling out of his grip. "They love Marilyn Moseley and Edna Rutherford, both of whom I find to be particularly detestable." Edna Rutherford was the name of my heroine.

"But Daphne, you *are* Marilyn Moseley and Edna Rutherford. And now, *Signatures* is to be published in America, and I have brought you your advance of one hundred dollars for Edna Rutherford's new adventure. And they are clamoring for more. Here," he said, thrusting his hand into his jacket pocket and pulling out a crumpled envelope. "The latest missal addressed to Marilyn Moseley, in praise of *Signatures* that has reached my desk, from a Mrs. Alice Ackroyd of Philadelphia." He tossed the letter at me. I opened it and read:

Dear Marilyn Moseley,
I have never written to an authoress before, but I want you to know that I am an avid reader of your books, which I obtain by special order from London. Your character Edna Rutherford serves as a shining example of modern British womanhood. I strive to follow her example in my daily life. You see, I, too, lost my husband in the war. Actually, I was wondering if my own life story might not provide inspiration for your next book . . .

I groaned, tilted my head back against the sofa, and closed my eyes. There was another hundred such letters—from England, Australia, India, in a hatbox in the cupboard—to which Nigel had ordered me to reply with a personable, hand-written note, enclosing a photograph signed "Marilyn Moseley," in each hand-addressed envelope. In actual fact, it was not a photograph of myself that was to be mailed to Miss Moseley's many admirers, but of Nigel's great aunt Mildred, whom he claimed looked more like a proper authoress than I. Nigel had had over five hundred pictures printed up for this purpose.

He knelt on the rug before me and took my hands in his again. If I hadn't had such a headache, I might have found the scene comic. Still I managed to say, "Nigel, is this a declaration?"

"Daphne," he said, pressing harder, modulating that irresistible tone of urgent appeal he knew how to manipulate so well. I had always wondered why he had never gone into politics. "This is better than a declaration. This is your ticket to success."

Ah . . . that word, "success" freshly delivered from the rough and ready streets of New York, with their stink of smoke and petrol, gin and vermouth and well-handled hundred-dollar bills. What had success to do with me?

"I know nothing can never replace Hawthorne Lodge or what it meant to you. . . ."

For a moment, my vision blurred with an unwelcome sting of salt and I clutched his hands tighter to keep from sinking into the abyss opening beneath me. I saw my home, Hawthorne Lodge, as it had appeared to me in childhood. A looming, benign, mysterious entity with its many corridors and stuffy rooms with low wooden ceilings, its scarred tea tables and shelves of musty books whose brittle pages broke off at the corners when you turned them. Its rows of white marble busts of Roman Caesars swathed in dusty red velvet, its broken spinet and moth-eaten maroon drapes—for family fortunes had been in decline for over a century. I saw a girl at thirteen in a white muslin dress, running across the turf toward the meadow where a single stone stood erect beside the old well, near a trough where ruddy horses drank. Then all was lost. Nigel Havelon, childhood friend and adult companion of my idiotic, indebted, and deceased brother, was the only human being left, and certainly the only human being in Paris, who knew where I had come from, what I had lost, what it signified. In his own way, I suppose he had tried to help.

"Daphne, are you listening to me?"

I nodded and repeated numbly, "Ticket to success. Never replace Hawthorne Lodge." I sighed, let go his hands and wiped aside my tears. The strong tea had made my brain begin to buzz and crackle. My headache had abated. The marmalade had revived the faint pulsing of blood in my veins. I took stock of myself and of my surroundings. The dreary and now scorched wallpaper; the little stove to feed with charcoal when one had money, though there was never enough of either charcoal or money; the sofa just big enough for one human body to lie on with its feet poking over the end; the battered table where I dined alone and scribbled out my poems and novels in the wee hours of the morning—this was my whole little world. A shelf of beloved books with unstitched bindings and a few items of clothing were practically all I owned. I was penniless—to all effects—loveless, without prospects, and with no friends in the world, it would seem, save Marilyn Moseley, Edna Rutherford, and Nigel. And the dreadful thing was that now that the stupor hadworn off and the sunlight pierced my reluctant eyelids, the body had begun to churn its unfathomable gears, and the will to walk and breathe returned.

"I feel responsible for you," he said, "I promised your brother on his death bed . . ."

His voice gave out. Speaking of Edmund still brought him to tears.

"Stop there!" I commanded and shot out a hand to restrain him. Why drag on with these stories of sorrow and failure? I looked around at the ghastly yellow wallpaper. "I suppose it's worth a shot. I'd much rather breathe my last in more congenial surroundings than be strangled by snakes in the wallpaper."

His eyes widened at my comment, but I patted his hand to reassure him, "I am speaking figuratively, of course."

"Very well," he said, " I have brought you this to sign," and he swept out a piece of paper from his pocket, unfolded it, and pushed it under my nose. Squinting at the fine print, I regretted not having ordered a pair of eyeglasses, which I had promised to do at my last birthday. Still I was able to read what it said. It was another one of his "standard contracts," offering this time, I was surprised to note, somewhat better conditions for the advance and the royalties than I had been given before. Then near the bottom of the document, I saw he had added a clause in very fine print naming himself as my literary executor. Perplexed, I looked up at him as I read it aloud. It did not seem to me that my literary estate was worth enough to be cited in a contract, and I told him so.

"We did discuss this, if you remember, and at that time you agreed."

It was true, we had discussed the issue after my husband Peter had died and *Signatures* had been such a success, bringing me for once, some financial reward. And at that time, I had indeed agreed to name Nigel as my literary executor. The war had made life seem very uncertain. It seemed the right thing to do at the time. After all, I was utterly alone.

"If you would prefer not to include the clause in your contract this time, we'll have my secretary type another copy, omitting it. But I can't leave you your advance until you sign, most regretfully."

I glared at the neat stack of dollars on the table, then back at the contract again. Nigel Havelon had just saved my life. Who else had I to turn to? I saw no reason not to sign, so I took the gold fountain pen Nigel held out to me and wrote my name at the bottom of the page.

"Excellent," he said, looking not only pleased, but relieved, as he smoothed back his glossy hair where a bit of telltale gray showed at the roots. Until then I had never noticed that he had begun to dye it. Perhaps he had started in New York. He clapped his hands and rubbed them together as if before a feast. "Now I shall take you somewhere where you shall write in peace."

"In peace? I doubt it."

"But without this."

He picked up my pipe again, snapped it in two, which must have taken considerable strength, and stuffed the pieces into his trouser pocket. Then he went to my writing table, rifled through a drawer until he found a sack of my hashish paste and pocketed that as well. Thank goodness, he did not know *all* my hiding places.

"Promise me."

"Promise you what?"

"That you will stop this nonsense before it kills you or coddles your brain."

I shrugged. "You want a book? I'll give you one. That's as far as I'll go."

"You'll go all right," he said, slipping on his charred overcoat and brushing off a few flakes of ash. "Be ready in an hour."

"Go where?"

"To Italy, of course, where else but to the land of artistic inspiration?"

And with that he was out the door. I went to count the money on the table, but it was gone. Nigel had taken every dollar of it back.

That afternoon before setting out for Italy, I had managed to reassemble myself in an hour and tossed a few things into my suitcase, imagining that in that country of pagan gods, I would soon be enjoying luncheons on terraces in Rome overlooking the ruins of the Forum, Venetian sunsets viewed from a gondola near the Zattera, and musical evenings in Fiesole. I packed a lovely dress for formal wear: a dark plum silk gown that set off my coppery hair, a dramatic black wool cape with a hood, which I thought would be just the thing for Venice; a black silk kimono; a bathing suit, hoping I might make it to a spa somewhere; and an emerald green silk negligee with matching peignoir. Not that I expected then to make a show of myself in bed for anyone, but I would have hated for the concierge to confiscate these items in my absence and sell them to a *marchand d'abis*, or worse, wear them to bed herself and burn them full of holes with her cheap cigarettes. They had been a gift from my late husband Peter. Nearly everything else I packed for morning or afternoon wear was respectably black, the nun's color of denial, except for a few pairs of white gloves and some white blouses. I also packed my little Florentine notebook and the only valuables that I still owned: a moonstone necklace and a topaz ring, my second favorite pipe, and a little stash of hashish paste in a silver box.

I looked around the room and said goodbye to my few remaining possessions then slunk down the stairs past the cubicle where the concierge lurked at this hour of the evening. Luckily, she was out somewhere on an errand. The tawdry paisley curtain of her cubicle was pulled shut and fastened with a safety pin. I was glad not to have to explain my departure. She had already warned me a few days earlier that I was two months late with the rent, and now there was the embarrassing question of the bashed-in door and the blackened wallpaper and curtains, which would have to be replaced at my expense. Nigel's plan to pack me off to Italy appeared to be an act of providence in some ways. I left her no forwarding notice for mail or bills. I had no idea how long I would be gone.

I had waited only ten minutes on the curb when Nigel drew up in his shiny black Packard just brought back from America. He was not alone.

Up front beside him sat a sunny-faced fellow of about thirty-five, with couperose cheeks and a shock of blond hair tumbling into not-quite-innocent eyes of intense blue. Nigel introduced him as Clive Brentwood, his new traveling companion whom he had met in New York. When Clive reached up to shake my hand through the open car window, I felt a jolt, as if I had just stuck a wet finger into an electric wall socket. But good heavens, he was at least fifteen years younger than I and, after my recent descent into hell, I must have looked at least ten years older than I actually was, and that is, old enough to be his grandmother. Clive was an American, from Texas, of all places, of which I had only a remote imagining. I adored his twang from the moment he opened his mouth.

The luggage rack on the rear of the car was already full, so Nigel put my bag on the backseat, where more bags were piled, including a leather portmanteau, an easel, and a wooden box of oils that smelled of turpentine. Each of these objects looked brand new, as though they had just been removed from a display window and had never been used.

"Clive paints," he said.

I climbed in and occupied the space between one of Nigel's gold-monogrammed leather traveling cases and Clive's painting equipment.

"By the way, Nigel, what has become of the advance I thought I was getting?" I asked as he shut the door and climbed into the driver's seat.

He patted his vest pocket. "Safely put away, my dear, for your traveling expenses. I shall dole it out to you as needed. But there will be none for any of your nonsense."

"How generous!" It dawned on me then that my advance might well be paying for the trip for all three of us.

I hadn't left the city in months, not even for a stroll in the woods of Fontainebleau, so as we made our way on through the cluttered environs of Paris and into the countryside, past fields and humble houses, a feeling of relief gradually settled over me. We hurtled along under an open sky slathered with soft gray clouds, scattered with migrating flocks returning northwards with the spring. Despite all, I was born a country lass, and when I breathed in the tang of warm rain on a newly ploughed field, something long asleep in me stirred.

Often ours was the only car on the road, though we encountered dozens of mules and oxcarts as we drove through the rural heart of France. Peasants out with their cows waved as we passed. Whenever we were hungry, we stopped at country inns to sate ourselves on hearth-roasted eggs and slabs of brown bread thickly spread with *pâté de campagne* and to quench our formidable thirst with heady *vin de pays*. I had forgotten how deliciously restorative country food and wine can be. Wherever we went in those rustic villages, we caused a slight sensation, perhaps because we were such a mismatched assortment. I, a mature lady of fashion with flaming hair and brightly painted Parisian lips; Nigel, the perfect, portly aristocratic Englishman in tweed; and Clive, a gangly American who wore checkered flannel shirts, a string tie set with a turquoise, and boots with pointy toes, just like a cowboy in the films. Fortunately, he had dispensed with his ten-gallon hat, as it attracted too much attention.

At mealtimes, Clive would regale us with funny stories about the land of Texas and the peculiar breed of Americans who live there, and I found him amusing enough. Nigel, I could see, was quite taken with him, and was on his best behavior: he was gallant, solicitous, and kind. At night, we slept in quaint *auberges* with open hearths in our rooms. I'd sit by the fire and smoke my pipe, grateful to be alone, while the gentlemen discreetly did whatever it was they were doing in their adjoining rooms.

Nigel and Clive at first had proved to be the perfect traveling companions on our trip down. There was no need for me to keep up appearances: to maintain a mask or to be entertaining, coy, or seductive, given the gentlemen's leaning. I could relax and be myself. No need to powder my nose surreptitiously, to pull up sagging stockings or rouge my lips on the sly, to refrain, for the sake of my waistline, from indulging in sweets or potatoes whenever we stopped for a meal, and it seemed I was always hungry. There was no need to chatter, for the sound of the motor and the wheels impeded all conversation. For them, the person in the backseat was a writer, not a woman, left to her own musings, and I had much to muse about. I thought of Marilyn Moseley, of Edna Rutherford, and how I would succeed in engaging their assistance once again.

These two harpies were actually not my creations, but my late husband Peter's. We wrote the first novel as a joke in three days while staying with friends in Cornwall. Edmund, my brother, showed the manuscript to Nigel, who ran a small publishing house, and who then decided to publish it. The reason our book was so readily accepted for publication was not because Nigel considered it a great work of literature. Nigel knew nothing about literature, really, although he was knowledgeable about painting. I always thought that he would have made a much more successful antiquarian than publisher.

The reason why he decided to publish it was because he owed Edmund money as my brother had given him a rather large sum to pay off a printer's debt. Publication of our book was intended as a sort of favor, or partial repayment of Nigel's debt, which in fact never was entirely repaid. Against all expectations, a thousand copies sold in ten days and Nigel was elated. He urged us to write another, and this was an even greater success, even though our royalties didn't amount to much in the end. Then the war came. First my husband, Peter, was killed, and shortly afterwards I lost the child in my womb—a daughter whom I would have named Persephone. Three months later, my brother Edmund died of influenza. After the war, I tried writing another novel, entitled *Signatures,* on my own, as a sort of methodic distraction for the numbness of grief. I also needed to make some money, since the war and the loss of Peter and Edmund had ruined me financially.

By then Edna had also lost her fiancé, just as I had lost my husband and brother. In *Signatures,* Edna's deceased fiancé intervened from the otherworld leading her to clues which would help her solve the murder of a young girl. The book was a success, I have been told, as it captured the desperate sense of psychic fragmentation we all felt after the war was finally over, and voiced our need to remake an intelligible vision of the world composed of meaningful signs. *These fragments I have shored against my ruins*, as Tom Eliot put it so succinctly. I had used that quote from *The Wasteland* as the incipit of my novel. I had even sent him a copy of *Signatures,* but he never bothered to acknowledge my gift.

As I pictured her, my alter ego, Marilyn Moseley, the author of my books, was a stout gentlewoman with a wattled chin who favored pink and blue tea gowns in the Georgian fashion, lived with her dogs in a genteel home, and entertained the pastor and the local commissioner at teatime. From their stories recounted over cream teas, she gathered copy for her novels and became acquainted with police procedures, poisons, and postmortems. A sober spinster, she enjoyed a generous glass of port after dinner, accompanied by a cigar, and as a hobby collected diaries of eighteenth-century gentlewomen.

The heroine of her books, Edna Rutherford, was quite a different woman from her imaginary author. Edna dressed in crisp white blouses with a mannish tie and trim navy skirts. She was an expert horsewoman, could drive and play billiards like any man, did not drink or smoke, and having lost her lad in the war, was determined to remain pure till the end of her days. Marilyn and Edna were my hidden selves, the ones who had found a place in the world where I had failed. What would Miss Ackroyd of Philadelphia say to learn that the aristocratic Miss Moseley was a fraud whose creator inhabited a coldwater flat in Paris and lived on absinthe and hashish? I now had the unenviable task of prodding Miss Moseley from her comfortable armchair by the fire, making her put down her cigar and pick up her pen in order to write another novel. What new adventure could await Edna Rutherford, I did not know. I also felt that they were as reluctant to encounter me again as I was to encounter them.

As we drove southward, I looked out at the changing landscape and dreamed, though when I tried to imagine a new plot, new characters, my head began to ache again, and so I simply allowed myself to absorb the scenery. Spring was just about to break in the Italian Alps, pink-tipped at sunset, where thousands of yellow crocuses peeked out from under patches of melting snow in the fields, and along the banks of half-frozen streams. Descending the Alpine pass guarded by the Hermitage of St. Michael, I lifted my face to the sun. How often in Paris had those rays been filtered through the gloomy splendor of Notre Dame, or through the emerald tints glittering in the bottom of an absinthe bottle. I was, despite all, quite grateful to be alive, and heading south.

Somewhere after we had left Turin, I looked up and saw two blue eyes peering at me in the rear view mirror with shy admiration. From village to village, the gaze grew bolder, more provocative, and I quite forgot about the scenery. I'd stare absently across a field or lake, then glance quickly back to the mirror, and there, reflected, Clive's inquisitive eyes flashed into mine with unmistakable intent. His sensuous mouth was set in the quizzical half-smile of someone who knows how to take his time to get what he wants, and how to savor every moment of delayed gratification. As for me, alas, those old coy impulses returned unbidden: the fluttering of eyelashes and the quickening pulse. I was too easy a prey for someone like Clive.

When we had stopped to lunch on perch at a lakeside tavern, Nigel left us for a few minutes while he combed the fishing village for English cigarettes. The young American and I had never been alone together until that instant. I gazed out at the blue lake barely ruffled by a slight breeze, at happy children in red boats rowing near the shore. Clive pushed aside his plate of fish bones and leaned toward me. The tepid March sun gleamed on the cutlery, on the wine glasses, and on his rather large teeth which he had just finished prodding industriously with a toothpick.

"Your lovely hair," he said without preamble, and I must have blushed despite myself. In my youth, this coppery mane had been my glory. Did it still have power over men? I had not yet had to take to henna, though for years my enemies in Bloomsbury had sneeringly accused me of such.

"I'd like to paint your portrait when we are in Italy. Would you mind?" he said dreamily, caressing the air in front of my face with his thumb in a painterly fashion. "You'd be a perfect model. You have such an aristocratic profile." He pulled a small drawing pad out of his breast pocket, made a quick sketch, presumably of my face, and tearing it from the pad, handed it to me. It did not resemble me in the least, and showed little skill, but I accepted it, smiled, and put it in my handbag. Then Nigel returned with the cigarettes. He paused before sitting down again, observing us sternly from above, and offered us both a cigarette. As he reached down to light mine, I couldn't help but note the tiny dimple of disapproval that had formed on his close-shaven chin.

Although Nigel was determined to reach Florence by midnight, the three of us decided to explore the town to stretch our legs before spending several more hours in the car. The sound of a barrel organ grinding out "Daisy, Daisy give me your answer do" from a side street led us to a flea market set up in the central square of the town. There at the base of a crumbling clock tower, ragged children, gypsies, and poor maimed veterans from the last war were selling trinkets and old broken bits of furniture, spread on dirty cloths along the cobblestones. Seeing those mismatched pieces of other lives made me melancholy. I imagined the families who had owned them, now disintegrated or dead, the houses from whence they had come, locked up and abandoned. I could just picture all the drawers, cupboards, and attics of a grand old house being emptied out into a heap of meaningless junk. Indeed since the war, Europe had become one vast flea market of meager pickings, and my own ancient family home had met this same fate.

Outside the door of a church, a one-legged man sat hunched over a crate bedecked with silver objects, foreign coins, and army medals. Feeling pity for him, we decided to buy something. Nigel noticed a handsome silver cigarette case with the name *Desire* engraved on the front. The price was very steep, but Nigel purchased it anyway, and promptly gave it to Clive who was very pleased to receive it. There was also a box of photographs, which I thumbed through—weddings, first communions, family portraits, grave aunts and uncles, and so many handsome soldiers. I cried out at the portrait of a lovely little blond girl, about four years old, wearing a white lace dress. She looked exactly like my mental image—the way I had always pictured her in my dreams and fantasies—of Persephone, my daughter, Peter's daughter, buried, unconsecrated, beneath the turf of Hawthorne Lodge.

"What is it?" asked Clive, astonished by my reaction, coming over to look at the photograph I held in trembling fingers.

"She resembles . . . a child I knew. The likeness . . . is startling."

He frowned, plucked the picture from my hand, and studied it with pursed lips.

"I'd say she resembles you, in a way," he said, returning the photograph to me. I was grateful for his discretion for he made no further comment, except, " Would you like me to buy this for you?" The modern solution to all loss or pain.

I shook my head. What would be the point of possessing such a photograph? Just more tears and remembered sorrow. I led them away from the stall to look at some tarnished silver trinkets spread out on a tarp along the ground.

Later Clive and I stood side by side on the water's edge, gazing out across the shining slate of water at the blue hills encircling us. Nigel had wandered off again to search for a telephone box, to call ahead to the next *pensione* and inform them we would not arrive until late in the evening. Clive took my hand, lifted it to his lips and caressed my fingers. Then, holding my hand before his nose, he squinted at the topaz flashing on my ring finger.

"That's a pretty little ring. A family heirloom?"

Delicately I withdrew my hand from his. "All that is left of a family fortune for centuries in decline," I explained, somewhat piqued. It would not do for him to imagine me an heiress rolling in money. It now occurred to me then that this mistaken idea might be the motive for his recent warming of attention. Vaguely I knew I should be on guard.

We walked along the bank and watched a boy wading out with a net to scoop up hapless minnows. Clive stopped abruptly, and grabbing my hand, kissed it with sudden rapture, saying, "I feel as though I have always known you. As though somehow you felt the same as me, inside." He clasped my hand firmly to his chest, where beneath his flannel shirt, I felt the thumping of a virile and seemingly reliable heart.

Who would not be flattered by such words? Something in me vibrated dangerously, but I shrugged off the sensation. Glancing aside, I noticed Nigel about a thirty yards away, walking toward us on the shore, pretending to read a newspaper as he shuffled along the sand. I had the immediate impression that he had been watching us. He must have seen Clive kiss my hand—with an impetus that went a little farther than mere gallantry.

"Well then," I said briskly, giving Clive's hand a friendly squeeze and promptly letting go, "that means you must be wanting your tea as well? Shall we see if they might give us some at that café near the boathouse? Oh look, here's Nigel," and I waved to him brightly. He returned the signal with a stiff flick of his fingers and stuck his nose back into his wind-blown *Times*.

Having a lover is a bit like being brought back from the dead. After so much loss, I just didn't expect any more love at my age. But two days later, in Florence, I didn't push Clive away that night when he stood in the doorway of my room at the Pensione Balestra, clad only in his American boxer shorts, and a calico shirt unbuttoned to reveal the golden furze on his chest. When he wagged a bottle of champagne, which I guessed had probably been bought with *my* money, before my nose, I knew what was about to happen. But I stepped aside, let him come in and ordered him to close the shutters above the murky, odorous waters of the Arno.

I hoped that Nigel wasn't too disappointed about the recent change in Clive. Observing the two men during the latter part of our trip down from Paris, while my intimacy with Clive had begun to flower, I dimly realized what sort of predicament I was getting myself into by stealing Nigel's friend. Seducing this young man had been the last thing on my mind when we set off from Paris on this journey, which was not even of my own choosing. I merely succumbed in my loneliness to Clive's ardent insistence. Indeed, who in my position could have resisted that ready smile? Those manly shoulders? The sleek flaxen hair and the electric touch? I could hardly believe my passion was returned. A boon better left uninvestigated, for the time being.

Later that first time in Florence, we shared a cigarette in my narrow bed at the *pensione,* beneath a bronze crucifix and a framed notice from the tourist police banning visits from unregistered guests. I asked, "What accounts for this change of heart? If not of sexual orientation?"

He laughed at my question. "I play *both* ways and in some you may never have even thought of!"

"Oh heavens! Well then, don't tell me! I'd rather not know! I am a bit old-fashioned, you know."

To this he did not reply, but just lay languorously beside me, toying with a strand of my hair spread out on the pillow, winding it tightly around his index finger, as if to keep me captive. I shrieked in protest as he tugged once—hard—at the roots.

"So this red stuff is real!"

"Silly boy! Of course it is!"

"It's so Venetian, so Titian. And you're such a *very* sophisticated lady. Nobody like you, back where I come from."

"You mean Texas."

"Yes ma'am."

The clock tower in the piazza struck two o'clock.

I sighed and caressed him. "Maybe it's time you returned to your room. Do you suppose Nigel heard you go out? Try not to make too much noise on your way in again."

"What does it matter?"

"Well," I reflected, still stroking the blond hairs on his chest, thinking somewhat regrettably that this amorous encounter had been a pleasant occasion unlikely to be repeated, "perhaps he wouldn't like it to know that you are here with me."

"Why should it bother Nigel to know that we are friends?" he kissed my hands.

I shook my head. "Nigel is a very . . . sensitive . . . person, and a very jealous one. He has always been possessive about his friends." God knows, he was very possessive about my brother.

"Nobody owns me, and certainly not Nigel. I belong to me," and giving me a devilish smile, he rolled over on his right side and fell asleep.

Next morning meeting Nigel at breakfast while Clive still snored in my bed and the maids clambered about in the corridor, banging open shutters and stirring clouds of dust, I bowed my head contrite before the man who fancied himself my benefactor and only friend.

Over rubbery eggs, cold toast, and tough strips of bacon, Nigel clipped, "So. Love has blossomed," and swilled down a cup of watery tea.

"Forgive me, Nigel," I hesitated in forming my apology. . . . Never had we broached the question of his "friends," not even when my brother Edmund died, though it was the suspicion of something between them that had broken my poor mother at the end. As a dear friend of mine once remarked: Oh, men's love for other men. It is truly the most jealous of human passions. Nigel stopped me cold with his curt remark.

"Best beware, dearest Daphne. The boy is winsome but he's callow."

I hated dealing such a dirty blow to Nigel by stealing his charming friend. After all, he had done so much for me. Looking back over the decades of our friendship, I felt guilty for betraying his trust, for not renouncing at once this newfound pleasure. And yet, Nigel Havelon had always called up in me rather ambiguous feelings. There was a time, many years ago, when my foolish mother considered him marriageable material for me. That was long before he had squandered his family's fortune in unwise business schemes in Kenya before turning to publishing. He was damnably handsome then. The unflattering jowls had not yet plumped out the sides of his face, giving him the corpulent, houndish look which distinguishes him today. As a girl, I had enjoyed his company for dancing and tennis and found him, yes, sexually appealing. I was older than Nigel by two years, and when I was twenty-three, we had had a brief liaison, very unsatisfactory, which ended with Nigel profusely apologizing and blaming the fiasco on the abundant champagne we had drunk all through the evening. I remember being disappointed at the outcome, for despite all, at the time, I fancied him.

It was then that I began to notice his interest in men, though I did not understand all its repercussions and observed in silence the evolution of his friendship with my younger brother, Edmund. I had not yet learned to interpret the unguarded looks that sometimes flashed between them, nor could quite guess what went on during their long evenings together supposedly spent "at the club" or their frequent escapes to Paris for which my brother footed the bill. God knows what sort of awkward triangle we would have made if I had followed my mother's advice and married Nigel. When I met my future husband, Peter Reynard-Simms, I had outgrown my silly attraction to my brother's bosom friend. Despite my mother's conviction that Nigel would not be averse to the idea of marrying me, which she had heard from his aunt, he had indeed never brought the subject up with me and most certainly had never proposed. Yet for a time after my marriage to Peter, I had the impression that Nigel's feelings for me had grown frostier. Then the war, my widowhood, and Edmund's death drew us closer in unexpected ways and now business interests bound us.

That first night in Bomarzo, I must have dozed off shortly after midnight as I lay waiting for Clive. After the long drive, he too probably felt exhausted and wanted to settle into his new room. My bed was comfortable enough, but the pillows and bedclothes felt damp, and I welcomed the warmth of the fire which brought a flush to my face, although my feet were freezing. Deep in the night, I woke with a start—half perceiving a bang or thump nearby, but the room was perfectly still. An animal on the terrace, I thought, a cat perhaps, remembering the white thing in the kitchen. Restless dreams followed; then I was wakened by a noise in the alcove, a tapping in the wall. I bolted upright, terrified there might be a rat in the wardrobe. Lighting a candle, I advanced to the alcove, where I discovered the noise was coming from the ceiling. I banged my fist on the wall, hoping to chase whatever it was—a big rat probably—away.

"Daphne, you're finally awake! Open up!"

"Clive? Where are you? " I could not tell where his voice was coming from.

"Up here. There's a trapdoor leading into your room! But I can't open it," he hissed. "See if you can open it from your side!"

I held up my candle to the ceiling where I noted a panel about four feet square disguised by an arabesque design. In the center of the panel was a small a brass ring.

"There's a ring!" I said.

"Well, pull it!"

The ceiling of the alcove was low enough to reach if I stood on a chair, so I fetched one and climbed up. I rather risked toppling off and breaking my leg, or worse, as I reached upward to grab the ring, but it wouldn't budge. I tried again, tugging for all I was worth, then inadvertently I must have turned it the right way and immediately set in motion a grinding of wheels. The panel shot open, and there was Clive, in his underwear, grinning down at me.

"Stand aside, baby. Let's see how this works!" I jumped off the chair and pulled it aside just in time, as he touched a mechanism and a folding stair slid out into the alcove.

Down he toddled in bare feet and swept me up in his arms.

"How did you get up there?" I asked in between kisses.

"There's a trapdoor in my room leading up to there, too. Great room for a studio with a skylight! I am going to set up shop there tomorrow."

"You don't think Finestone will mind? Might we have to pay more?"

"I doubt it. I mean, he gave us the rooms that were connected. He must have known we'd find out."

"Wasn't that wise?"

"Yes ma'am." And he carried me to the bed.

CHAPTER TWO

Clive must have snuck back to his room before dawn while I was still asleep, for I woke alone and with a slight headache, perhaps from the damp air or from the stink of ashes permeating the room. Manu had promised hot water in the morning, and out in the corridor, I found a tin kettle of cold water set outside my door—another one waited outside Clive's across the hall—evidently we were expected to boil the water ourselves! I brought the kettle in and poured some into the basin on the dresser in the alcove to wash my hands and face, wondering indeed when I would finally enjoy a long soak in the tub. I dressed and, before going downstairs, tapped on Clive's door, but the boy gave no reply. Wandering down to the dining room and across the hall to the kitchen, I found the place deserted. There was no sign of Amelia or Manu, but the table in the kitchen had been laid for three. To my horror, the little white cat stood on a counter licking a butter dish left uncovered. I flicked my hand at it and it leapt off the counter and out through an open window. There was nothing for breakfast except a pot of cold tea, which looked very much as though it had been made with the dregs of last night's brew, and a basket of buns as hard as stones.

An envelope addressed *To Our English Guests* lay near the teapot. I opened it and read:

Welcome to Bomarzo. My research has taken me to Rome for a few days. Everything has been arranged for your visit which I hope will be pleasant and productive. Amelia and Manu will help you with every need.

One thing I would like to ask of you is this: please do not enter the park gates until my return. This is mainly for your own safety—there are unmarked excavated areas into which you might stumble, causing harm to yourselves, and there are sculptures in need of restoration—they could be accidently damaged, or they could even cause harm to one of you if a loose piece should detach itself and fall. The whole area is also home to a very venomous viper which awakens in spring. Therefore I beg you all to refrain from exploring beyond the immediate grounds or visiting the park until I have returned. At that time, I will be delighted not only to make your acquaintance, but to show you the mysteries of Bomarzo and its "monsters," and arrange for you to enjoy access to the park during your stay, at your pleasure. Lastly, and please forgive me if this seems overly prohibitive, according to the wishes of the owners, taking photographs of the villa or park is forbidden at this time. You are of course free to make as many sketches and drawings as you like.

Cordially,
Jacob Finestone.

Vipers! That sounded like a lame excuse to me. What mysteries did the park hold which required such stringent secrecy? The effect of this prohibition was, of course, to sharpen my resolve to see the place immediately.

As I headed toward the park that morning, I learned that although it was off limits to us during Finestone's absence, it was not locked to everyone. I saw our maid, Amelia, wearing a ludicrous sun hat, with a basket on her arm, slip inside, followed by the little white cat, and lock the gate behind her. After both had disappeared amid the thick vegetation, I strolled over to the entrance. The massive black iron gate was over twelve feet tall, with a row of sharp spearheads along the top to discourage intruders.

I peered inside. The only sculpture I could see resembled the hindquarters of a lion or perhaps a sphinx half covered in vines, but through a gap in an unclipped hedge, I could make out a small army of workmen, uprooting stumps, clearing briars and weeds under Manu's supervision. There was no sneaking in as long as they were there. For the moment, I would have to satisfy my curiosity with other amusements.

There were many other things to explore in the villa and for the first day or two I did my best to become acquainted with them. There was the magnificent library which Finestone had adopted as a studio, where we were also allowed to browse. Stocked with hundreds of old leather-bound, musty-smelling books and decorated with many fine landscapes and antique maps and prints, it was a perfect place for a writer to dream. Cast-off curios from older days were crammed into crystal cupboards: seashells, embalmed reptiles, silver knickknacks, bits of pottery which looked like genuine Etruscan artifacts. In the symbolism of the Renaissance, the library represented the Mind of the Master of the house and the mind of the man who had created these collections was both commanding and fanciful: the range of interests displayed ran from instruments of navigation to alembics and alchemical equipment. I was sure I'd find some inspiration here.

I discovered passageways, concealed corridors, secondary staircases connecting unrelated rooms. Niches hid doorways which had been sealed centuries ago, or perhaps, only yesterday. A button touched by accident in the library opened a panel to reveal a secret chamber filled with dust and spiders, occupied by an abandoned broom and a bicycle wheel. All this delighted me. I imagined the love trysts, murders, escapes, and rescues which these now-forgotten spaces once made possible, the treasures or cadavers they might once have contained.

And then there was the villa's exquisite collection of paintings: portraits, landscapes, icons to study one by one. My favorite piece of artwork was the one Manu had so cursorily dismissed: the Angel icon in the niche across from the library. Its velvet curtains were always kept closed, I noted, perhaps to protect it from sunlight or dust. Was it more valuable than he wanted us to know? Or did the owners of the villa consider the gaze of the angel and the snake a bit too disturbing? Was that why they kept the picture partly hidden when foreign tenants came to stay at the villa? Did it hold some heretical meaning better hid from public view? Angels are usually shown slaying snakes, not conniving with them, as this one seemed to do. On my way along the hall, I would stop and move aside the curtain to peek into those eyes. What things they must have witnessed! If only those lips could speak.

With admission to the park denied for the time being, we settled down to the tasks we had come here for: I to my writing, Clive to his painting, and as for Nigel, he had decided to brush up his Italian and reread the *Divine Comedy,* a handsomely illustrated edition of which occupied an entire shelf of the library. But my good intentions came to naught. I sat blankly before my desk, pen in hand, lamenting the absence of a proper smoke, for I had consumed the supply I had brought from Paris, with no new ideas in store. Nigel didn't seem to understand that Miss Moseley and Edna Rutherford were produced by the pipe he had dashed from my lips. Without inspiration, I could not write. What was needed was a new batch of *signatures,* those curious messages our waking life sends us from our own unconscious, which I have come to see as promptings from the muse, and even as a spiritual guide for my own existence.

For this was the mystery I had discovered when I wrote my novel, *Signatures.* We are constantly immersed in a network of signs and symbols whose meaning eludes us, but which, if only we could read them, would reveal every detail of our past and even predict our future. Like anticipatory echoes, they tingle in our consciousness, building in crescendo until the event they herald becomes fully manifest. Afterward, they linger for a time before being drowned out by a new tide of signs rushing in upon us. Such signatures are everywhere—a glove dropped in the street, an unusual design of seaweed washed up on the beach, a picture postcard addressed to a stranger and slipped in between the pages of a borrowed book.

Signatures often take the form of odd coincidences, but we usually fail to notice when they present themselves. For example, on your way downstairs one morning, you nearly stumble on a toy boat left on the stairs by a neighbor's child. At breakfast an article on the front page of *The Times* catches your eye, telling of some catastrophe at sea. Stepping out to the street, you nearly collide with a delivery boy carrying a bucket of live eels to a nearby restaurant. As the day passes, you overhear snatches of conversation in which the words "water" or "island" are repeated. Returning home, you find the pipes have burst and a puddle has formed on the bathroom floor.

Now, the ordinarily inattentive mind will not pause to consider these coincidences. Many people would not even notice that they are connected one to another, as it were, thematically, to the concept of "sea voyage." But suppose the very next day, urgent business affairs oblige you to book passage to New York. These insignificant events occurring throughout the previous day may then be understood as a premonitory experience composed of dozens of minor "correspondences" or " signatures." Most likely, you will remember but a few fragments of the whole mosaic. *But* if you could piece them all together and properly interpret them, you would not only foresee your journey, but also the outcome of the business affairs taking you abroad. We are never attentive enough to what is happening around us. Mr. Ouspensky knew what he was talking about when he said, "There is no coincidence in a meaningful universe."

In my novel called *Signatures*, Edna's ghostly fiancé had communicated with her by scattering signs about her and leading her to their discovery: a book fallen open to a page where a tea stain called attention to a woman's name, the hands of a clock stopped on the stroke of ten, a letter delivered to a wrong address—all of which turned out to have a bearing on the case. For all of these events there was a cause explainable by the laws of physics. A gust of wind had disarranged the pages of the book; she herself had forgotten to wind the clock the night before; that day there was a new postman unfamiliar with the route. Yet behind all, there loomed a supernatural intelligence which had preordained that these signatures should manifest themselves to Edna at a specific moment in time, so that our detective could link them together as precisely as the elements in a mathematical equation whose final product was the murderer's name and motive. That supernatural intelligence was none other than her own unconscious mind.

The mind talks to itself not with *words*, but with scrambled symbols, pictures, fragments often severed from any literal meaning. If we wish to learn to read them, we must abandon the rational links of words to thoughts. Signatures are always there waiting for us, like unopened letters slid beneath the front door, accumulating after a long period of absence, written in a hieroglyphic alphabet we have forgotten. Perhaps the secret of reading the signs lies in a stimulated, heightened attention. But how may that stimulation be best attained?

Whenever I needed to stretch my legs after sitting unproductively for an hour or two, staring at an empty page, I used my "hidden passageway," the staircase leading down from the terrace, where, at the bottom, a door opened out into a narrow space behind the hedge where garden tools and tarpaulins were kept. The topiary of the hedge, trimmed in elongated rectangular and pyramid shapes, made a perfect camouflage and I loved the resinous smell of the bushes when they were thickly covered in dew. I would spy out from my hiding place watching hares or toads leaping in the wet grass and smoke a cigarette, staring at the locked gates of the park down at the end of the lawn. Sometimes I would listen to a concert by screech owls or nightingales. One evening my work was interrupted by the tinkling of bells, and sneaking down the staircase and out through the hedge, I found a herd of dingy sheep, grazing placidly on the huge lawn, blanching in the moonlight. Dozing on a stone nearby was their shepherdess, a child hardly more than twelve years old, while a dog watched over sheep and mistress. I suppose she kept her flock out in the moon all night in hopes of whitening their wool—a common belief amid country folk the world over.

After a refreshing pause, I would step back through the iron door, remembering to bolt it shut behind me, climb back up to my room and return to my desk. But not even a breath of chill air and a smoke would get my brain churning. The words refused to flow, and in any case, the schedule of Clive's visits quite put an end to my concentration. Way after midnight just in those hours most fruitful for my writing, he would scramble down through the trapdoor into the alcove and I would have to push aside my scribblings with a sigh, wondering how on earth I would ever manage to produce the book I had promised Nigel if things kept on this way.

Alas, the poor boy didn't turn out to be much of a painter. Although he claimed to have studied at Sargent's studio in Paris, it was clear he had no talent and little training in design, drawing, or perspective. Yet he spent most of the day up in his studio, or trudging about the grounds with a foldable American easel, which he would proudly display to anyone who demonstrated even the slightest interest. It folded up into a compact bundle of sticks which easily fit into a pocket or rucksack, and Clive seemed to think it was the cleverest device in the world. It had, however, one defect. Through so much repeated opening and closing, the screws of its joints had come loose, and tended to fall out and scatter on the ground. The latter part of Clive's demonstration of this novelty involved everyone picking through the grass or sand to retrieve them. This folding easel was the only piece of equipment he had brought from New York; everything else had been purchased brand new in Paris at a little shop in Montmartre where all the young painters bought their supplies. I recognized the shop label stuck on every piece.

Each day Clive worked away for hours, earnestly daubing globs of color upon his canvases, smudging his face, hands, and clothes with cadmium and vermillion. Whenever he embraced me, he smelled of linseed oil and turpentine and his nails were always edged in black and green. More than one of my chic black jerseys had been spoiled by little spots of paint after an encounter with Clive. Twice a day, right before lunch and then again in the late afternoon, I would climb through the trapdoor to his studio to see what he had produced. Timidly, he stood back from the canvas, begging approval for his handiwork. How to deny what was so easy to give? I tried to be encouraging.

I knew how eager Clive was to be considered as an artist. He loved to rattle on to us over coffee or a glass of wine about questions of technique, and if we were in a crowded café, he would slightly raise his voice and drop the names of " Cezanne" or "Renoir," until at least one head at another table turned in our direction. During our drive down from Paris, whenever we stopped at a *pensione*, he would write his name in the guestbook: *Clive Brentwood, painter, Paris -New York* and had even had a calling card printed in Paris, which he showed me, *Clive Brentwood, peintre*, with a Montmartre address. These he had left with the shopkeepers and with *patrons,* especially the *patronnes* of restaurants and taverns where we ate, if he liked the food, hoping I suppose to impress them or ingratiate himself with them so that at his next visit, he might be offered a free meal or at least a discount on the bill. Though I must say, the Italians we met did not seem to hold artists in high regard, or to take any special notice of them at all. How unlike France where artists and writers are universally respected and esteemed.

It was the artist's mystique and status he craved, the excitement of exhibitions and gallery openings watered with champagne, of provocative experiments sparking controversy and rage. Alas, *his* work would never set the Seine on fire. His pictures were arid splotches of paint, a glorified form of play and self-indulgence by a boy who refused to grow up.

To his credit, it must be said, however, that he had an extraordinary gift for grinding and mixing his own pigments. The knowledge he had of this technical aspect was the only thing that might suggest he had indeed frequented an important studio or school in Paris or elsewhere. Patient and painstaking as alchemist, he would stand by the window, blending his colors on a palette, his face hardened in concentration, his eyes narrowed, as he squeezed out his tubes, adding powdered specks of the most unexpected hues to create his final result. "There, you see, Daphne," he would say proudly, "this is the exact color of the pink in the lady's earlobe," or: "This is the shade of the moonlight in that landscape." I found it touching that this precision should be coupled with such a total lack of artistic talent in every other regard.

Those first few days, Nigel, deprived of Clive's attentions, moped around the house, and, frankly, I felt guilty. He clearly was uninterested in Clive's pictures now, which further wounded the boy's pride, but then, what else could Clive have expected after what had happened? Still, the fact that Nigel no longer took his work seriously was a blow to Clive's ego and they both took pains to ignore each other except when we met for meals. When weather permitted, Nigel would go off exploring our immediate surroundings, but I am sure he found the Tuscia countryside tedious. It held none of the civilized and quaint attractions of Tuscany or Liguria—it was craggy with overhanging cliffs, riddled with gullies, punctuated with dilapidated farmhouses, and populated by immense flocks of sheep. The inhabitants were as rough and obdurate as their landscape, and like Manu and his daughter, often shifty-eyed and unfriendly. I am sure Nigel would have bolted and headed off to Rome or Naples if it hadn't been for the lease, which had been paid to the full in advance. The three of us were rather stuck there, waiting for Finestone to come unlock the park and provide some entertainment or at least distraction, while the rains set in.

A gloom permeated the house in this bout of bad weather. The gray stone walls absorbed the damp like sponges. Threads of fine green moss crept across walls indoors and out, in between tiles and cobblestones, under the window ledges. One could almost feel it settling into the interstices of one's bowels and one's brain. As I sat reading in an armchair, writing at my desk, or while walking down the long, dim corridors, I would become aware of an unpleasant sensation: a prickling of chill in my left shoulder, which at first I attributed to the dampness of the villa, to its many airs and draughts. Soon it grew to be more than just a vague, half-unnoticed perception. It was as though my body had somehow sensed a movement just out of range of my peripheral vision, like the slight rippling of a curtain before an open window, or the flapping of dark wings. At times I would wheel around abruptly to see if there was something—or some-one—there. Of course, there never was. Sometimes, though, I would turn to lock eyes with one of the portraits hanging on the stairway or in the corridor. So life-like were they in the flickering candlelight, their pupils seemed to dilate, their eyelids flutter, their lips to twitch.

Dreadful storms woke us at night with the clattering of hail against the windows and terrifying explosions of revelatory light-ning. During the day, the rain poured ceaselessly down, staining the walls with streaks of damp where water seeped in through cracks in between the roof tiles and somehow trickled down to the lower floors. Nigel reacted to this situation by promptly catching a nasty cold that kept him confined to his room, dining off trays and comforted by whisky, with an armload of old books from the library stacked on his bedside table for amusement. Left to our own devices, Clive and I whiled away the hours doing what lovers do in similar circumstances to keep warm and pass the time. Indeed, we had no choice. In such miserable weather, the only solution was to crawl into bed where a bed-warmer, heaped with glowing coals, had preceded us. Clive's love-making was tender, boyish, but he was not particularly virile. Still, it was the solace for my fifty years, *une amitié amoureuse.* As those first few days of our affair progressed, we became quite close. During our long talks in bed as the rain battered the windows, he told me of his lonely childhood. Clive was the illegitimate son of a banker who had adored him and his mother, a saloon maid, thirty years her lover's junior. Unfortunately, the banker had failed to make provisions for them in the event of his demise, which, alas, occurred sooner than anyone had expected. He died peacefully in his bed, in the arms of his mistress, one afternoon, while Clive was at school. Afterwards, with the scandal ringing through the streets, the boy and his mother had literally been run out of town by the banker's widow. At the age of eighteen, he had left home when his mother took a new lover to support her, a violent man who abused her. Clive could not bear to see her weep or to witness their quarrels which always ended in his mother's being beaten black and blue. The only possible outcome would have been murder, he confessed to me—and since his mother refused to abandon her protector, by now her only source of support, with much regret, he had struck out on his own, worked his way eastwards and set sail for Europe on a steamer transporting timber to Cardiff. From there he had found his way to Paris, where he had met Sargent at a café frequented by artists. Recognizing his eager determination, the master allowed him to work awhile in his studio. He had recently returned to Texas to settle some "family business" there, for in the meantime his mother had died, and he was now all alone in the world. En route back to Paris, he had stayed a few weeks in New York, where he had met Nigel, and had returned with him to Paris.

At least that was the story he told me. I had no reason to doubt it was true. Yes, I admit, as he recounted episodes of his past and of his more recent life in Paris, I noted inconsistencies, and a certain reticence. What other people did he know in Paris, where had he lived, in what cafés had he spent his idle afternoons? Perhaps we might have crossed paths before? Right after the war was over, there were so many young Americans crowding the cafés and bistros of Montparnasse and Montmartre. Had he ever met my friends Virgil, the musician? Or Ezra, the poet? Had he ever been invited by Nancy, or by that formidable gray whale, Gertrude? But he would sidle away from any questions with an enigmatic half-smile, and pay me some compliment, such as, "And how could I have forgotten seeing your lovely head of fire," or some such nonsense, kiss me on the neck, and deftly change the subject.

I did not want to pry too deeply and could but feel for him. How much we had in common. Loss, humiliation, loneliness, homelessness, and financial hardship were no strangers to either of us! He would press himself close to me in the darkness, compelled not only by passion or appetite, but by a need for comfort. But he clung far too hard, I thought. I did not want him to be hurt. Then something happened which quite reversed our roles and set in motion the workings of a destiny none of us could control.

Ten days or so after our arrival in Bomarzo, I was awakened by an unfamiliar sound—a vigorous thumping accompanied by a shrill female voice singing in quartertones. The weather had turned, too, for bright sun filtered in through the chinks in my shutters. Donning a dressing gown and stepping out onto the terrace, I lifted my grateful face to welcome the return of the sun, then noticed Amelia in the yard below, beating out a pair of Ottoman carpets hanging on a line strung between two cypress trees. Clouds of thick dust billowed forth with every whack of her beater. Nearby Manu, wielding a small hand scythe, was shaping a topiary pyramid from a giant yew tree. I dressed and went down alone to breakfast. Clive and Nigel were either still asleep—which I doubted, for nobody could sleep through that ruckus—or were already up and about.

I marveled at the metamorphosis which had occurred in the villa overnight. The marble floors were not only swept, they sparkled under a coat of fresh wax. Brass railings gleamed and drapes were pulled back to reveal spotless windows. But the most amazing thing was the transformation in the kitchen where every surface had been scrubbed and polished, and delightful smells of roasts, pies, and sauces issued from a dozen copper pots bubbling on the stovetop and from within the incandescent womb of the wood oven. Tea and rolls with butter and jam had been laid out on the table, so I helped myself to breakfast. Going back upstairs again, I saw Manu bringing up the carpets on his shoulder and carrying them into one of Finestone's rooms.

These labors of housekeeping continued all morning and afternoon, not only in the villa and on the grounds but also in the park, where the men were burning huge piles of debris and rubbish. Neither lunch nor tea was prepared for us that day. Amelia left cold food for us in the kitchen, and I met neither Clive nor Nigel throughout the entire day. I had no idea where they were. I spent the hours reading, scribbling, mending a chemise—and by late afternoon was bored to tears. Slipping down the spiral staircase to smoke a cigarette in my favorite hiding place behind the hedge, I pushed open the iron door and hit someone smack in the face.

"What the devil!" cursed an angry voice. The person with whom I had just collided was Clive, accompanied by a bald, plumpish, gentleman with a bushy red beard tufted with gray. From behind thick lenses, the stranger's bloodshot, watery-green eyes inspected me with curiosity. He was dressed in overalls of coarse blue cotton and a collarless white linen shirt. In his hand, he held a silver-headed cane. I knew of course it could be none other than Professor Jacob Finestone.

"Clive, darling! I beg your pardon! I hope I did not injure you?"

"Not at all, my dear. Daphne, I was just talking about you. Please meet Dr. Jacob Finestone. Dr. Finestone, my friend, Madame Daphne DuBlanc."

The gentleman bowed stiffly and touched his lips to the back of my hand as we were introduced. His hand was cool and clammy, his fingers hirsute, perfumed, like his beard, with cigar smoke.

"The professor is just back from Rome."

"I came across this young man sketching on the lawn, and I guessed he must belong to the party of British artists who had arranged to share with me this magnificent villa. I hope you have found it comfortable, suitable, and above all, inspiring. I understand you are a writer."

I smiled at Clive and noted that he was not carrying any of his equipment.

"Yes," I said, "and I am most curious about the sculpture garden, the famous park."

"I have just told the men to fill in some holes, and to stake off unsafe areas. Tomorrow morning I will have the pleasure of showing you the park myself. You'll soon be able to visit it at your leisure. I believe, though, it is nearly dinnertime. Are you joining us, Madame, or are you out for an early evening stroll?"

I hadn't realized it was so late, and I wanted to dress for dinner, especially since our host had arrived. I renounced my cigarette, slipped back in through the door from which I had just come, and climbed back up to the terrace, with the gentlemen chatting behind me. I paused a minute to catch my breath on the terrace while Clive and Finestone, still engaged in conversation, went to the far edge of the terrace to admire the view. Then

Finestone gave Clive a little pat on the back and the two men turned and went into the villa by way of the library door. I noted to myself that it hadn't taken Clive very long to make friends with Jacob Finestone.

That night at dinner, the professor captivated us all with his intriguing banter, ranging from the present whereabouts of the Holy Grail (which he claimed was located in a sewer in Turin) to the qualities of aged pecorino cheese. I found him a genial conversationalist and by no means a pedant, as I had feared. He had a sort of fatherly appeal and I took to him at once. After dinner, we withdrew to the library, where Finestone showed us a portfolio of sixteenth-century prints depicting winged monsters, wag-tongued masks, and sundry gargoyles which he believed had been inspired by the bizarre menagerie of stone figures populating the grounds of Bomarzo. Before retiring to our separate rooms that night, he promised again to take us all on a tour of the park the next morning, but warned us we must be on time. He would not wait for us, if we happened to sleep late, for he had much work to do.

Clive and I were excited by the prospect of finally gaining admittance to the forbidden precinct of Finestone's mysterious research, but Nigel, who had at last recovered from his cold, deferred. He planned to go to Rome to see about some business. Besides, the dampness of the villa had been bothering his arthritic knee. Clive and I assured Finestone that we would meet him for breakfast at eight o'clock sharp, ready to visit the park.

Later that night toward one o'clock, Clive came to me. When we had done, I rose to rinse my face in the basin of cold water on the dresser, and stood before the mirror, brushing my hair a hundred strokes before bedtime, as I have done since my childhood. Clive lounged naked on the bed, with one knee drawn up in what could only be described as a lascivious pose, smoking, gazing dreamily at me. I was looking well, I thought, admiring my reflection, as the sparks crackled at the ends of my red mane, glad I had decided to pack this emerald negligee, though heaven knows I hadn't expected it to come in so handy. I had just slipped off my topaz ring and replaced it in its little velvet box in the dresser drawer where I kept my jewelry, makeup, and bit a of cash, when Clive said, "Let's go away together. Now. Tomorrow."

"But we *are* together, here in Italy, a lover's paradise." I daubed a spot of cold cream on my neck and tried futilely to rub away the wrinkles there.

"I want to be alone somewhere with you. Just the two of us."

I was touched by his urgency. "I can't go anywhere," I said, continuing to massage cream into my skin. "Nigel won't give me my money until I have given him a book. And I must confess, with all these distractions you have been creating for me, I fear it may take me much longer than I expected."

"To hell with Nigel!" he burst out, stabbing his cigarette in the ashtray.

I was surprised by this vehemence. I sat down on the bed beside him, took off my fur-topped mules and began to rub my ankles and the soles of my feet with cold cream. At my age, not even a new lover could keep me from my nightly rituals.

"Haven't you got any other money we could live on?" he asked.

I shook my head sadly. *Money,* then, was the real motive behind his ardor. "Neither have you, I take it?"

He did not answer this directly, but stared up at the portrait hanging over the bed. "Now supposing that little treasure were mine, I'd know just what to do with it."

"Don't tell me you are an art thief?"

"Haven't you noticed how many valuable little things are scattered all over this place, just waiting for someone to walk off with them? Who'd notice? Tomorrow we could be in rolling in dough, living it up in Paris or Berlin with our futures secure."

"A future secure behind bars! Don't even think of it, my boy,"

I said, shaking my head in stern disapproval. "And if you don't heed my warning, please leave me out of it. Besides, I thought you were here to immortalize the Monster Park with your paintings."

"I was only joking," he shrugged. "Never stole a thing in my life. I swear! Except you!" and he gave me that radiant smile.

"I would imagine Nigel has quite a different perception of who stole whom." I sighed and rubbed cream into my hands and cuticles.

"I love you, Daphne," he said so earnestly my whole body tingled. The words cut deep with their charge of joy and their throb of old, old pain.

I lay my finger on his lips. "Say you love my hair, my lips. Say you love the way I stir the sugar in my tea. But please, say no more."

Playfully he nipped at my finger with his teeth, which were surprisingly sharp. It hurt and I winced.

"Say you love me," he said.

"You know I adore you." I laughed at his petulance.

"Say you *love* me," he growled in a tone so menacing I might have been shocked had I had time to take stock of my reaction. But this I was not granted. He seized me roughly by the waist, threw me back on the pillows, and straddled me like a sheep at the shearing, with his knees pinning my hips to the bed. An insatiable kiss sucked my breath away, as in sweet delirium the room whirled round and round. I opened an eye at the center of this vortex to catch sight of the portrait reflected in the mirror. The lady pictured there seemed to be regarding me with a new sneer of disdain.

"Stop it, darling!" I gasped. "I can't breathe."

He tore another kiss from me and pushed my negligee up around my waist. "I won't stop unless you say that word."

There was no resisting the body's complicity to this game, to the little stabs of wild pleasure, the surge and shower of physical joy, until I cried out in sheer exhaustion the words he commanded me to speak: "*Love*," I croaked with what breath I had left, "I love you."

The moment I pronounced that phrase, he rolled away from me. Yawning, he stretched himself with a silly smile, pulled on his boxer shorts, and left the room. I lay there, a heap of overripe, overwrought, quivering flesh, dazed by the intensity of sensation and need he had awoken in this half-broken body of fifty-some years. *Lilacs stirred in the dead land.* I drowsed for a while in lazy expectancy, thinking that he had gone out to wash himself or have a smoke on the terrace, to snatch some bread or cheese from the pantry . . . those things men do after the act of love, when women crave to curl up in their arms and sleep. I was sure he would return, for we had slept side by side every night since our affair had begun.

While waiting, I caressed the impress of his body on the rumpled white sheet. Then I sat up and lit the lamp on the bedside table, smoked a cigarette and then another. I got up to tidy the bed, tucked the sheets back in, plumped and smoothed the pillows, and as I did so, found a long fine hair which I plucked with disgust from my lover's pillow. Examining it in the lamplight, I saw it was golden blond. Amelia! That girl should be more careful when making my bed. I would have to tell her that she must wear a cap while doing her chores. When I burned it in the flame of the lamp, it gave off a strong odor of singed chicken skin.

After an hour or so, I began to pace the room. The boy is exhausted, I thought to myself. He has fallen asleep on the couch in his studio, poor thing, and will awake with his neck out of joint.

I lay down but could not sleep and kept staring at the lamp till the oil burned away. My lips and nipples were bruised, my whole body ached, but I would have willingly submitted again.

His delayed return first annoyed and then alarmed me. Restless, I got up again, lit a candle, and pulled on a wrap, thinking I should go to look for him; but the chill touch of the brass door-knob stopped me as I was about to open the door. Once again I felt that prickling in my shoulder, a cold sensation, almost a cramp which I tried to relieve with a brief massage. I reflected it would not do to go to him now. I *must* restrain the impulse. I *must* give him time to return to me of his own accord. I went to my desk to write a note in my diary, but my mind went blank as soon as I dipped my pen in the ink. I rifled through the drawers, though I knew there was not a bit of paste left for my pipe. I had smoked the last of it days ago. I held my head in my hands for a moment and closed my eyes.

I must have dozed off in that uncomfortable position, for I soon became aware of a soft singsong murmuring in my ear, and I thought I recognized Clive's low, amorous whisper. I snapped awake instantly and looked around at the darkened room where the candle had gone out. I half expected to see my young lover sprawled in a seductive pose, but the bed was empty. I took a match from a desk drawer, lit the candle and inspected the room more closely. Clive had not returned. The murmuring had only been a dream, but it left me feeling unsettled, with a rapid, un-even heartbeat and a slight headache.

I sat there a few moments, listening to the silence in the house. The clock in the library next door struck four. Then, al-most in response to the chiming of the clock, an owl hooted outside. It sounded so near, as though the bird had alighted on the terrace right outside my bedroom.

I surmised it was the owl I had heard while asleep, which my dreaming brain had interpreted as a human, indeed as Clive's voice. If the bird was still there, I wanted to have a look at it. I tried to open the shutter without making any noise, but the latch was rusty. As I tugged and pushed, the shutter burst open and banged against the wall, and there came a loud rustling of wings as a large bird departed from the terrace with an eerie little shriek, giving me a bit of a start.

Candle in hand, I stepped onto the terrace. The air was damp and fresh and smelled of new grass and boxwood. It must have rained earlier in the night, for everything was drenched, but a cold wind from the north had swept the clouds away, leaving a terse black sky with a whorl of stars overhead and a bright waning moon near the zenith. I was surprised to see a very faint light glowing at this late hour in between the slats of the shutters of Finestone's room, which like mine, had access to the terrace. He, too, was still awake, and I did not want to disturb him. The light in his room explained the owl's presence on the terrace. I knew from my childhood in the English countryside that owls are attracted to lights burning late at night.

Walking to the edge of the terrace, and looking out toward the park, I was seized by the irresistible urge—or perhaps the caprice—to see it in the moonlight. I unhooked a lantern from the terrace wall, lit it with my candle, and hurried down my hidden staircase, out from behind the shrubs and on across the lawn toward the gate.

The lantern shone a bright cone of light on the ground as I made my way through the long dripping grass, crunching an occasional snail beneath my slippers as the rain soaked the hem of my dressing gown and bits of weeds stuck to my bare ankles. The stars seemed to grow bigger as I wandered away from the villa. Such a spectacle! I could make out *Cassiopeia* and *Ursa Major*. Behind me the moonlit villa seemed dwarfed by the shadowy mass of the ridge overhanging it where the old stone houses and towers of the town clung to the edge like moldering teeth set in a jawbone. The gate to the park was locked, of course, and tall walls of shaggy yew hedges obscured the view within. I peered in through the iron bars, but all I could see was a gray sphinx crouching at the head of a path vanishing amid the thick vegetation where boulders were visible beyond. Somewhere nearby a stream, or perhaps a fountain, bubbled noisily.

The night was chill. There was a feral tang in the air, left perhaps by a fox that had scurried by in the night, returning to her den. A lone anticipatory cricket chirped in a ferny recess, and then, with no prelude, a nightingale struck up her rich, thrilling song from the depths of the trees. I stood there entranced, pressing my face against the cold bars, tasting the rusted iron on my lips as I murmured my Keats to the night. *Thou wast not born for death, immortal bird! No hungry generations tread thee down!*

An inexplicable nostalgia welled up in me then. *Ah love, let us be true to one another.* How I longed to share this sight with Clive. I sighed like a schoolgirl, then had to stop and laugh at myself, and I pinched my cheeks to make sure these feelings were real and not a dream. *One must not cling to beauty or to joy*, I warned myself. Or one would find oneself in an untenable position. A position in which, I must add, neither Marilyn Moseley nor Edna Rutherford would ever be caught dead.

A movement deep within caught my eye, or maybe it was just a branch waving, followed by a rustling sound, made, perhaps, by the owl I had frightened away from the terrace or by some night-roving animal, like a cat or a weasel out on a hunt. But this was only a vague impression, and was immediately supplanted by a far more definite sensation. I heard a door open behind me, for sound can travel very far on damp nights, which caused me to whirl around. On the moon-washed terrace I saw a white figure exit from Finestone's room, where lights were still burning, cross the terrace and dart down the very staircase from where I had come; but instead of emerging onto the lawn, it disappeared into the ragged shrubbery to the side of the villa.

I had recognized the fleeing figure at once. Amelia had been visiting the professor! The door to his room opened again, shedding a wedge of light on the terrace, and Finestone appeared in his dressing gown, puffing a cigar. He waddled to the parapet on the far edge, craned his neck forward, looking out into the night.

I doubted that he could distinguish my shape in the darkness from such a distance, but for precaution's sake, I turned down the flame of my lantern and stepped into the shadows, shielding the light with my hand. I waited for him to finish his smoke and go back inside, which he did shortly.

So this was a discovery! Amelia provided other services besides cleaning, cooking, and laundry. I wondered if her father knew.

As I made my way back along the path, musing about the relations between Amelia and Finestone, I noticed a small white object gleaming in the tall grass. I crouched down to see what it was and found the half-crushed head of a china doll, the size of a tangerine, one blue eye gouged out. So cold to the touch was it after lying out in the dew, a shiver rippled up my spine as I plucked it from the ground to inspect it. No cheap trinket, this head was finely modeled with a pixie nose and painted with a cupid's bow mouth. It looked as though it had come from an expensive Paris toyshop. I felt a pang of melancholy as I stared into its one remaining eye, then, wiping it with my handkerchief, I slipped the head into the pocket of my dressing gown. I knew what I had found: the first signature of my Italian adventure. But a severed head was no auspicious omen. I poked about the grass for other pieces, but there were none.

Where had it come from? I had seen no children anywhere near the villa—except for the shepherdess who sometimes brought her sheep at night to graze on the lawn. Though she was not likely to own a doll with such a fine china head, she might have had a broken remnant of one picked out of the trash somewhere and may have dropped it while tending her sheep. Or perhaps a dog had dragged it here from a rubbish heap. I looked up at the villa all dark and shuttered and reflected that one reason the place seemed so austere was indeed its absence of any sign of children even in the past. No portraits of children hung in its picture galleries, no antique toys were on display. No primers or picture books or easy piano pieces were lined up on its library shelves. It occurred to me now that this was odd, for surely at one time there had to have been children in the villa. Generations of youngsters must have occupied the house, run shouting down its corridors and played hide-and-seek among the statues in the park. Why was there no trace of them? Puzzling this over, I mounted to my bedroom—and setting the doll's head on my bedside table, slid beneath the covers and was instantly asleep.

CHAPTER THREE

Next morning, I woke before dawn from an unquiet dream of shadowy figures glimpsed under water although my throat was parched. I lit a candle, and got up to fetch a drink of water, but tripped on the rug, nearly knocking something off the bedside table. That doll's head! It stared at me in an uncanny way with its one good eye, giving me, once again, a mournful feeling. I sensed it was somehow unlucky and decided to keep it out of sight, for I suspected it had influenced my nightmare. I always keep my "signatures"—all those odds and ends I gather while working on a new book—together somewhere and use them for inspiration when I run out of ideas. In a desk drawer I had found an old cedar box which seemed perfect for holding such a collection. I dropped the doll's head into it, closed the lid, and put it back in the drawer. Then I crawled back into bed and slept another hour or two.

I suppose it was the excitement of finally seeing the park that prompted me to get up and get dressed in time to meet Finestone at eight o'clock. Although the sky was overcast again, the weather was warm enough to sit outdoors, so he had arranged for breakfast on the terrace. It was only the two of us, however. Nigel had risen very early to drive into Rome as planned, in search of sunshine and amusement. Clive was still asleep after our exhausting night of love. I had knocked softly on his door, but had received no answer. Like me, he hated to rise before ten. I admit I was disappointed that he would not be joining us.

I found the professor standing at the parapet of the terrace, surveying the park, where we could see three young men industriously at work under Manu's supervision, hacking at the ivy with axes and scythes. Finestone looked like one of the workmen himself, for he was wearing blue overalls which starkly set off the gingery color of his beard. Tilted jauntily low over one ear was an expensive white linen fedora with a very broad brim, for he claimed to be sensitive to the sun, especially on cloudy days. I must say that like many Americans I have met, he had a rather unusual idea of style.

I sat down to the table where his breakfast had already been served on a silver tray: strong black coffee boiled up with sugar and a bundle of very brittle breadsticks, tasting of pencils and sawdust. The terrace was actually the roof of a building which must have been added on and attached to the rear of the villa in the centuries past, and which now housed the modern kitchens, pantry, and scullery, located right below us. The wide windows below had been flung open to the tepid air, and I could hear Amelia at work banging the stove door, dropping the iron stove rings to the floor with a clatter, and cursing as blasphemously as a Neapolitan sailor as she went about her chores. I smiled to myself, surmising that her foul mood was very probably due to lack of sleep, considering how late it must have been when she had finally crept off to bed. And I knew her secret. It would seem that this cold, drafty villa was really the House of Love and Pleasure.

As I waited for the girl to bring my English breakfast of poached eggs, toast, and tea, Finestone told me a little about the sculptures in the park. He explained that since the park had been overgrown and literally forgotten for so many years, except by tenuous local legends, there were almost no textual descriptions of it by visitors or scholars and very few drawings, prints, or other documents concerning it produced later than the seventeenth century. The sixteenth-century prints he had shown us the evening before were probably the only pictorial documentation in existence.

Sifting through the historical archives in Bomarzo and in Rome, he had discovered a few patchy descriptions of it in letters, diaries, and poems by the sixteenth-century nobleman, Vicino Orsini, who had first commissioned the park to be created, and in some legal documents and deeds relating to the lease of the land in the eighteenth century. That was all. There were no *modern* interpretations of its bizarre symbolism. Finestone's monograph would be the first, and he was convinced it would win him fame and recognition. He was working in great haste and secrecy, since he did not want any scholarly rivals from Florence or Rome to get wind of his research. From what he said, I realized it was a great privilege for us to be there witnessing the park's "unveiling," so to speak, day by day as the vegetation was stripped away from the statues and the paths.

"But antiquarians and art historians have been combing Italy for centuries, rooting out all its treasures," I objected. "How could such an important park containing such a huge sculpture garden, so close to Rome and Florence, have been ignored for so long? Why did its owners let it become so overgrown?"

"The answer to both those questions will become apparent to you as we explore it this morning," was his cryptic reply. "You may think of the place," he continued, "as a sort of *Divine Comedy* in reverse, a plunge from paradise to hell. Some of the sculptures you will see today may symbolize the emotional torments experienced by Vicino Orsini, who created the park as a memorial to his wife and had its statues sculpted by students of a local atelier. Others may be interpreted as a dream diary recorded in sculptural form of figures plucked from a lifetime of nightmares." He dabbed a pencil breadstick into his coffee and nibbled it efficiently with his small, yellow teeth. "Or there may be an even more esoteric explanation," he said casually, draining his cup.

Finestone had begun to intrigue me. The mind, not the man. I adore esoteric explanations.

"Indeed?"

"The park may conceivably contain an encoded message. Its statues and sculptures may spell out a formula for making gold, or for what gold symbolized to the alchemists: Immortality. Redemption. Eternal Love. Wisdom. Something of a sort dissimulated by private pictograms."

Signatures! I thought. The language of our inner gods.

"So the Monster Park is a sort of book," I ventured, "a book of emblems hewn in stone, conveying a message, telling a story, revealing an enigma."

"You mean *concealing* one," he replied with a patronizing smile.

Amelia arrived finally with my breakfast. As she exited the library and crossed the terrace, carrying a heavy brass tray in trembling arms, Finestone glanced at her in a manner which quite confirmed to me that it had most certainly been Amelia's lithe little shape I had seen scurrying through the topiary at four o'clock in the morning. That was no look of benign fatherly attention, but a searing flash of undisguised lust. It hit its mark, the girl colored. I saw then what had previously escaped me. With her hair nicely combed and that spot of pink in her pale cheek, she was undeniably lovely. I noted her pretty linen blouse with lacework decorating a tightly fitted bodice, her trim waist in a full striped skirt. Today her hair was clean and golden, recently bleached, I supposed, with chamomile from the kitchen garden or lemons pinched from the *limonaia*. Around her neck she wore a silver trinket bound with a black velvet ribbon. A gift perhaps from Finestone? Or had she pinched that from some bedroom drawer in the villa? Vaguely, she reminded me of someone, though I could not think who.

"Breakfast, Signora," she said primly, but a vain smile quivered at the corner of her pinkish lips as her hands unsteadily lowered the tray to the table. Though she was quite pretty, I found this girl's manners decidedly unpleasant. She had a way of mocking one on the sly. I glanced at her hands clutching the tray. They were the red and muscular hands of a thirty-year-old country woman roughened by housework, with bitten, discolored nails. They were certainly an odd contrast to her youthful face and her delicate pallor. I could imagine them very well moving across the good scholar's plump, hairy flesh. After depositing the tray, she scuttled away, and glanced back to exchange a coy look with Finestone. He gave a barely perceptible nod, which I interpreted to mean: "Later." Or maybe, "Tonight."

I lifted the lid of the silver serving dish on the tray, scalding hot to the touch, and gasped as it burned my fingertips. The lid flew out of my hand and tumbled to the terrace floor with a reverberating clang. I looked down at the food in dismay. The toast was scorched black. The egg yolk was runny and flecked with black crumbs of burnt toast. When I poured a cup of tea, out streamed a cold yellowish liquid.

Finestone stared at the disgusting contents of the serving dish, then grunted apologetically, "She's a good girl but hasn't yet perfected the art of the English breakfast," and offered to share the rest of his coffee and breadsticks with me.

"That's very kind of you. But I shall call her back and tell her to prepare me another breakfast."

Finestone squinted at his pocket watch. "It will be quite a wait, I'm afraid. She will soon be on her way to town. Today is market day." Looking from the terrace, we saw her hurrying out of the scullery with a wicker basket in hand and a wide-brimmed straw hat on her head. The little white cat trotted at her heels.

Finestone smiled. "Such amazing devotion in an animal."

We watched the cat follow Amelia for a distance, until she turned and spoke to it, at which the cat bounded back toward the villa. Mistress and pet reminded me of nothing so much as a witch with her familiar.

Reluctantly I accepted Finestone's proposal to share with him what was left of his breakfast and, once we had finished, we descended the spiral staircase from the terrace down to the lawn and headed toward the park. Finestone walked with a slight limp owing to a childhood injury when a gypsy cart ran over his foot, or so he had told us the night before at dinner, and he required the support of a cane when walking long stretches outdoors. Remembering the doll's head I had picked up from the grass along the way the night before, I scanned the ground for other broken bits of its limbs and body, but I found nothing.

When we reached the gate, Finestone produced a key from the breast pocket of his overalls and handed it to me. It was a huge iron key made by a blacksmith, weighing at least a pound, almost a potential weapon, and icy cold to the touch.

"Madame, I leave this privilege to you," he said, inviting me to unlock the gate.

What gallantry, I thought, as I turned the key and pushed open the gate. Before stepping inside, I held my breath for a second as a swimmer might do before a dive. Immediately I felt the air temperature drop a degree or two. A chill flickered through my knees, up my spine, and across my scalp, though there was no logical explanation for such a sharp change in temperature.

Finestone paused on the threshold, as if waiting to see my reaction, then stepped in behind me, seized my arm, and began my guided tour.

"In the mid-sixteenth century, when this place was created, parks and gardens were meant to offer more than just an aesthetic experience, a pleasant promenade in the shade or a showcase for flowerbeds. They were models of the cosmos and also tools for altering one's consciousness, possibly for changing one's destiny. Entering a place like this was like succumbing to a dream. Every detail was intended to produce a specific effect on the mind and body, to excite and soothe the senses like a drug. To awaken the unconscious self.

"The colors, textures, odors, and shapes of the plants, like yew and mistletoe and belladonna, all capable of inducing catatonia, nightmares, prophetic dreams . . . contributed to create such an impression, along with the tinkling of running water, and the cries and shrieks of exotic birds kept captive here in aviaries. All this was intended to catapult the visitor into a primordial state of awareness."

Closing his eyes, Finestone snorted in short gusts of air, like a yogi, as if to force oxygen straight to his brain; I too inhaled deeply the fragrance of the dew-drenched vegetation surrounding us. Clumps of laurel, rosemary, ilex, juniper, yew, pine, moss, fennel, rocket, and wild mint exuded their perfumes. Above our heads crows cawed in the treetops. It truly seemed an enchanted place.

A few feet away from where we stood, a trail snaked through the underbrush. He motioned for me to follow as he loped along with his cane. The path wove in between bushes and outcroppings of rock where ferns lashed out in our faces and thorns ripped our clothes. Picking our way through fronds and brambles, we reached the sphinx I had noted the evening before, situated in a small clearing from where an even narrower trail wound into the interior. Not far off we could hear the men working.

"This sphinx is probably a copy of a genuine Etruscan piece from Vicino's collection of antiquities. The surrounding hills and valleys are full of Etruscan tombs that must have provided an endless source of income to the duke. Such artifacts were prized highly by his aristocratic cohorts who used them to decorate their homes and sold them at great profit to English ladies of fashion. Many collectors and museums today would pay a pretty penny to add this copy to their collection. Here she crumbles beneath rain, and cold, and lichen."

Pensively, he patted the sphinx's haunches.

"Set here at the entryway, she suggests that this place is a riddle the visitor must solve."

An inscription, barely visible, encrusted with moss and lichen, was chiseled on the base of the statue. I deciphered the letters and read aloud, "*Tu ch'entri qui pon mente parte a parte Et dimmi poi se tante maraviglie sian fatte per inganno o pur per arte . . .*"

Finestone complimented me on my pronunciation.

"My brother and I learned Italian at school," I explained. "My family had a passion for opera."

I ventured a partial translation. "You who enter . . . tell me whether or not these marvels have been created through deceit or art."

Inganno o arte? Deceit or art? An intriguing proposition. Was the Monster Park a sort of "trick" or illusion? A flight of fancy only meant to entertain? Or did it artfully conceal a deeper meaning? "*Pon mente parte a parte . . .* ," I repeated. That was the phrase that I did not understand. "Literally, the words mean *put your mind side to side*," I said. I reflected on this. "Could it mean that the visitor must examine all sides? Or that one should stand outside oneself when making judgments?"

"Perhaps it is asking us to set aside the rational mind and not to make our final judgment until we have seen and pondered the whole." With a sweeping gesture, he embraced the park that lay before us, still immersed by copious vegetation from which emerged a few rough sculptures and massive boulders, resembling forlorn islands rising from a lake of green.

"But she is only the preamble to this eccentric representation of hell on earth, as you will see," he said, pointing to an area nearby where the men had succeeded in ripping off a tangled mound of brambles from a colossus. We wended our way toward it, waist high in weeds. Manu and the workmen greeted us deferentially when we reached them, withdrawing under an ilex tree several yards away, where a grinding wheel to sharpen their cutting tools was set up on a trestle. All the workmen seemed to hold Finestone slightly in awe, and admittedly he did cut a bizarre figure, with his ginger-colored beard, blue overalls, and scholarly air. Manu, I noted, kept glancing our way, as though to keep an eye on us as he sharpened the blade of a scythe on the wheel, sparks flying into the air.

"The horrific statues carved here may be viewed as fragments of consciousness itself, the residue of violent emotions."

The sculpture, at least twenty feet tall, crudely carved all of a piece from an enormous boulder, depicted twin giants in combat. Their thighs were as massive as tree trunks. The victor had seized his opponent by the legs and was dashing his head against the ground while tearing the poor fellow in two through the crotch and up through his torso. The features of their rough-hewn faces had eroded beneath scales of lichen, but those blank eyes and crumbling lips were still legible enough. The victim was screaming in horror and pain as his conqueror gnashed his teeth in the throes of a savage fury.

Placed so close to the entrance, this hideous sight seemed to serve as an introduction to what was to come. It was a statement, a challenge, a setting of the tone, the opening notes of an overture. It was meant to shock and warn visitors to the park, perhaps even, I thought, to terrorize them.

As if reading my thoughts, Finestone said, "The local peasants once believed that the statues came to life at night. Were they not held down and impeded by all these brambles and vines, they might break loose and go marauding through the town."

I pictured these two entwined figures, like some great golem, thundering down the streets, smashing windows and rooftops, wrestling and rolling in a deadly embrace. "So, I suppose that explains why the owners allowed it to become so overgrown? They were glad when nature reclaimed it."

Finestone smiled again and added, "After all, the ancient Egyptians knew how to breathe life into their statues of the gods, and performed special rites for this purpose. Perhaps this knowledge was preserved and transmitted to the Romans and then down to us through the Renaissance. Perhaps Vicino himself—or more likely the artist who sculpted them—knew the secret art of animating statues. Or perhaps this superstition arose in the local population because Vicino's clever sculptor may have invented devices, water works, or wind-driven mechanisms to produce sound or even the illusion of movement. Even in recent times, they have been known to roar in the night."

I shot a sidelong glance at the scholar. I could see he was teasing me, so I said, "And have you heard them roar?"

"Only in my dreams."

"How will the superstitious townspeople react now that you are rescuing the statues from oblivion, rendering beasts, like these two, potentially dangerous again?"

"After my monograph is published, tourists will come. Scholars and curiosity-seekers, students and painters armed with sketchbooks like our young Clive. Honeymoon couples will buy postcards and souvenirs at shops, and illustrious personages, like you and I, will sign the guestbook in the hotels that will spring up around the entrance. That will surely dissipate some of their destructive power."

I shuddered at the thought of such barbarization. "That is what has happened in England, too, with many of its old homes. My own for instance."

Finestone nodded. "The place is destined to become a beautiful cadaver trampled by hordes and picked by crows. It is the national destiny of the entire country, you might say."

"Will you not be contributing to this desecration by publishing your monograph and bringing crowds to this forgotten place?"

"Art historians are a species of crow, but a relatively harmless variety. I like to think my discoveries will bring prosperity to this poor, backward town."

"And to yourself as well, I take it."

He smiled, but made no reply.

We stood for a moment contemplating the sculpture. These naked, time-blackened figures carved from a single outcropping of stone and still partly imprisoned there called to mind unfinished statues of Michelangelo I had seen years ago in Florence: incomplete figures stirring to life, struggling to assume human shape within their rocky matrix. Finestone was right, there *was* a dreamlike quality about the place which immediately exerted an influence upon my imagination. With a flash of insight, I suddenly understood the sculpture's message. I knew exactly why it had been placed in that particular spot and what it meant, though I have no idea from whence my certainty had come. I suppose I had read its signature.

"It's a reversal. A very painful reversal," I said, staring up at the statue. "I believe it is saying: now that you have entered here, your perspective will be violently turned on its head. The resulting vision will make you mad. It will cause an inner division that will make you feel as though you have been ripped apart."

Finestone arched an eyebrow and nodded. His eyes glittered. I could see we were of a similar cast of mind. We both enjoyed guessing at emblems and riddles, as I had already realized the previous night at dinner when he had talked of the Holy Grail. We were two of a kind who find sermons in stones and personal meaning in the patterns of nature and art.

"And of course a rape, a violation," I continued. For through the loops of ivy clinging to their limbs, one could clearly see that in the process of tearing apart his victim, the giant aggressor seemed to be engaged in something else as well. The lower part of his body was pressed firmly into the buttocks of his victim. "It is saying: your most basic beliefs about yourself and the world will undergo violation. You must become impure."

"Perhaps . . . ," Finestone said, stroking his beard and squinting at the sculpture through his bifocals.

"What is your interpretation?" I asked.

"From the evidence I have gathered concerning the life of Vicino Orsini, it may represent his own anger and madness when his wife, Giulia Farnese, died. After her death, he wished to tear the world the pieces. Or perhaps instead the duke identified himself not with the slayer but with the victim lacerated by grief and loss. Or it may be warning in a Neoplatonic vein— "Passionate love leads only to madness." Or perhaps it says, "The body will be brutally sacrificed for the survival of the soul."

I said nothing in reply to this, but I did not agree in the least with Finestone's interpretations. They were much too meek and rational. Something far more basic and bloody was being enacted here. One could see why the local people found this sculpture so frightening, invested with a power that might come alive and wreak havoc in their midst. And what of the artist who had conceived this rape and these monstrous grimaces? Had he experienced such wrath or pain or had he only imagined them? Or had he tapped into the world soul where all emotions and all transgressions exist in potentiality?

"Tell me, Professor. You say the Monster Park is a sort of book or diary, that these statues are the residue of violent emotions and fragments of nightmares. You suggest they represent the patron's dark feelings and dreams, those of Vicino Orsini; but what about the artist who first imagined these forms? Might they also refer to his own life and experiences?"

"A very acute question, dear lady. If we knew for certain who the architect of the park was and the precise purpose for which it was designed, we might be able to answer that question more satisfactorily. But for the moment, you understand, I am not at liberty to disclose any of my findings, which are concerned with that very question; so, it must remain a matter of speculation, at least for the time being. Undoubtedly, these figures contain autobiographical references to the lives of both men."

I pondered this as I gazed up at the sculpture, and then I was disturbed by the buzzing of a bee around my ankles. I looked down into the nest of ferns and weeds where I stood—and there at my feet I noted a little white glimmer. Thinking it might be a piece of the decapitated doll, I reached down to the grass, but must have stuck my hand into an ants' nest, for when I pulled the object out of the tall grass my fingers were swarming with ants, which I brushed off in disgust. The tiny object I had retrieved proved to be a piece of mother-of-pearl, the face of a button or perhaps a cufflink. I glanced at Finestone's shirt where the cuffs were tightly buttoned, American style. This dainty decoration most certainly did not belong to him. It was small enough to have come from a child's shoe. Staring at the button, which seemed to burn into my palm like a small lump of ice, I suddenly saw in my mind a child's shoe dunked in water. I frowned at this impression, which had possessed me for a moment, then blinked twice to dispel it. Holding the button out to the professor, I asked, "Have you lost a button?"

Finestone checked his cuffs and shook his head.

"I'm no medium, but my guess is that this comes from a child's shoe and that it was torn off in unfortunate circumstances."

Finestone's eyes widened behind his bifocals. He went a trifle pale. "Perhaps. The daughter of the villa's owner met with a dreadful accident here about ten years ago."

"Oh?"

"She slipped and fell into a fountain, and was not found till it was too late."

"But didn't you say that the entire park has been overgrown for centuries? Wouldn't the fountains have gone dry in the meantime?"

"At that time, it seems, one or two had been rediscovered and put to use in a period of drought. After the child's death, they were allowed to be swallowed up again by the vegetation. At this latitude, it didn't take long for them to be covered over like the rest of the place."

My mental image of the child's shoe in water had been only too accurate. "I was struck by the fact that there is no trace of any children ever having lived in the villa."

"Everything was removed which might recall the tragedy to mind."

"I see." I supposed that explained why the owners of the villa had decided to lease it out to strangers, like ourselves. Having lost a daughter myself, I could empathize with their grief. It gave me an eerie feeling to think that the doll's head I had found might also be related to that sad event. "No foul play?"

He shook his head. "A dreadful accident. An act of fate."

"Do you know which fountain it was?"

"I believe it is somewhere near the in the middle, but I haven't located it yet. I expect it is quite large." He gestured toward an unbroken expanse of green. "Over in that direction."

I put the button in my pocket and mused on the story as we walked toward another area where some men were working. Finestone was absorbed in his thoughts.

When we passed a ferocious Cerebus, three heads snapping in all directions, Finestone seized the opportunity to introduce a new topic of conversation, one which he knew would appeal to me.

Amicably patting each of the hell dog's heads and caressing the tips of their fangs, he said, "These sweet creatures guarded the gates of hell, where you were allowed in, but not out again. Local legend claims these dogs are also guardians of a hidden treasure. If read correctly in the proper order, the statues in Vicino's park might guide the seeker's steps to where a treasure is buried. Although Vicino's descendants may not have given credence to such ideas, they may also have allowed the sculptures to become overgrown in order to prevent armies of potential thieves from invading the grounds with picks and axes, hoping to unearth treasure chests."

"That also sounds like a logical explanation for its abandonment," I said. "Do you believe there is a treasure buried here?" I did not voice my real thoughts: *Is that why you are here? To piece together a scattered map from these signatures or clues?* I thought it very likely.

Finestone laughed. "It depends on what you mean by treasure. When ordinary people think of treasure, they imagine precious stones or gold; a more cultured person may imagine some exquisite work of ancient art or an artifact which might be made from iron or bronze. Still they think of treasure in terms of something *material.* For a scholar like myself, "treasure" might simply be the confirmation of a name, a date, a mathematical formula, a missing word in a text. Then again, if a treasure exists here in any material sense, it may be an object which to an untrained eye may seem as dull and unremarkable as an old brick, but which to a person able to understand its meaning would represent a boon of inestimable value."

"Like the philosopher's stone, which allowed alchemists to transmute lead into gold?"

He laughed again. "Perhaps something less lucrative."

"Such as?"

He smiled but did not answer. I suppose he thought further revelations might compromise his research. Still, I was eager to know more.

"If there is a treasure," I suggested, "then aside from the clues represented by the symbolism or placement of the sculptures themselves, there ought to be a map. I mean, the sort of map one sketches in a book, or on a piece of parchment, or rolled up in a bottle, or stuck beneath a floor tile."

"That might make a good story for our novelist! Or it may be engraved on the bottom of a copper pot long since blackened by use, or painted on a wall destroyed by a fire or an earthquake. Or it may be encoded in the text of a poem, or it may have fallen into other hands and been transported elsewhere. To Rome. To Paris. To London. Or it may simply have been eaten by rats." He shrugged. "If there is such a map—or such a treasure—so far in my research, I have found no trace of it. But as I said before, the so-called treasure may be so apparently uninteresting that we may have it constantly before our eyes and noses, without even noticing it. For what better way to hide something than by keeping it in full view? In which case, a map would be useless, for even when face to face with the object of our quest, we would be unable to perceive it, and we might be persuaded that someone has stolen it, that it has gone missing in the night of centuries, or even that it never existed and is purely an object of fantasy. Remember, if there is a treasure in Bomarzo, it may also be something totally intangible, like an idea, a state of mind, an emotion or a dream."

It was my turn to laugh. "In which case," I replied, "there is no hope of finding it until it wishes to make itself known."

"Exactly. When we are ready for it."

We descended to a lower part of the park where the path followed a streambed chiseled in volcanic rock. No crystalline fount, the waters were sluggish and putrid, choked by dead leaves and rotting tree roots. A yellowish green scum clotted the surface, and frogs croaked from a patch of reeds. The path along the bank was slick with mud and I had to cling to the scholar's arm to keep from slipping.

Finestone used his cane to push nettles and briars aside along the path as we picked our way through the undergrowth, crushing wild mint beneath our heels. "Watch where you put your feet," he warned. "Be on the lookout for snakes. They sometimes come to the stream to drink."

"Poisonous ones?" He had made a reference to snakes in the instructions he had left us when we had first arrived, but I hadn't taken it very seriously.

"My dear lady, this is viper country. In spring they crawl up from their holes when the sun warms the ground."

I looked down in consternation at my little suede pumps and silk stockings to calculate how much protection they might offer against a viper bite.

Seeing my concern, Finestone laughed again.

"Don't worry, this will discourage them," and he brandished his cane in the air like a sword and then speared a dead leaf on the ground with its steel tip.

"I'm not afraid of snakes," I said tossing my head, "The woods around my childhood home were full of adders. We were always finding them in the currant bushes."

We walked on in silence. I stepped gingerly through the mud, eyes trained on the ground, wishing I were wearing a sturdy pair of boots of the sort that Edna Rutherford might wear, but I didn't own a single pair of sensible shoes. Life always seems to find me unprepared. I mused over the story of Vicino—how grief can trigger madness, how art allows us to express passions which we may never act out in the flesh, but which may be enacted by those who have been inspired by our poems, paintings, or thoughts. Thinking of passions and art led me to reflect on portraits, and portraits led me to the painting hanging above my bed. What passion did that glacial dame conceal? And who was she? I was sure Finestone must know, so I asked him.

"I believe it may be a portrait of Vicino's wife, Giulia Farnese."

"She seems to keep me under observation night and day."

He cast me a curious look and grunted in assent. "Probably by the school of Lotto, and worth quite a bit."

More than in the identity of the painter or the monetary value of the painting—which Clive had already suggested to me—I was interested in the woman whose death had moved her husband to create this astonishing park. I asked Finestone how she died.

"Murdered. Poisoned by her husband, perhaps. Maybe even in the very bed where you sleep, Madame."

"Really?" I said, a bit taken aback, but I thought this was probably a fabrication told for the benefit of the mystery writer who had come to Bomarzo to write a novel. But it was exactly the sort of detail I relish, which he must have guessed, so I laughed. "First he murdered and then he mourned her in madness. Very typical indeed of male perfidiousness. But why would he have murdered her?"

"Maybe she betrayed him."

"An excellent motive for murder, indeed." I agreed. "I think there is only one other motive that may outweigh it—money."

"That too might have played a part. She is buried there in that chapel." He pointed out a dome not far off.

"To whom does this property belong now?" I asked.

"It has returned into the hands of a minor branch of the noble Orsini family."

That explained the monogram on my bed linens. O for Orsini.

"So the child who died was an Orsini?"

He nodded, then changed the subject. Speaking about the child's death seemed to make him uncomfortable.

"Vicino and his wife did not live in the villa where we are lodged," he continued. "That was only a guest house for visiting friends and dignitaries who came to see his park, which was quite famous in his time. The duke and his wife lived in that palace up there on the cliff." And he indicated a massive yellow building with its windows all broken out, perched along the rim of the gorge wall directly above us. I had noticed it before, but had wrongly guessed it to be a monastery.

We had reached the next group of sculptures, where only one had been completely unveiled of its greenery. This was a giant turtle, bearing a trumpeting angel of victory on its back. In a way, it made me think of Amelia and Finestone.

"It illustrates the motto *Festina Lente*," he informed me. "*Make haste slowly,* credo of the Renaissance."

I took these words as a warning for my own situation. It certainly fit the circumstances for a person of my age and state.

Not far off lounged an androgynous figure with huge legs completely out of proportion. "I have seen this kind of distortion before," I said, " the typical hallucinatory effect one often experiences in dreams when under the influence of opiates."

Finestone snorted in agreement, "Or in the delusion of a prolonged nightmare."

From where we stood, two trails diverged. One led straight up an embankment to the chapel where Giulia Farnese's aristocratic bones lay interred. The other meandered along the stream, then steeply descended to a wooded area where more sculptures were still hidden beneath mounds of overgrowth. Here and there a huge hand or head stuck up from a nest of brambles and weeds reminding me of drowning persons caught in a vortex, begging to be rescued.

"Which way shall we go?" Finestone asked, pointing out one, then the other road with his silver-headed cane, "straight to the chapel or down through hell?"

The road to the chapel was a sheer vertical climb over slick muddy patches and jagged rocks. I could never attempt it in my dainty suede pumps. I'd never reach the top, and would only slide back down, ruin my stockings, and I dare say, break my neck.

"There's no guarantee I'll reach the goal," I said.

He chuckled. "Then we have no choice but to wend our way more comfortably to hell."

We rambled on to a clearing where a few smaller figures had toppled over obstructing the path, and we had to climb over them to proceed. At last we stopped to rest and sat down on a stone bench beneath an ilex tree. I turned my face to the sky, where a broad sunbeam cut through the dull clouds and shimmered on the green canopy above us. It was nearly eleven and the hour of Pan was approaching, but I could not feel the heat of the sun. Set deep in a gorge, the park was steeped in perpetual shadow broken only by the dappled effect of sunlight reflecting on the tiny leaves of the ilex and olive trees glinting in restless motion, stirred by the slight breeze. If stared at long enough, the ceaseless movement of foliage had a hypnotic effect, and after a few moments, I had to shut my eyes.

This was certainly the strangest sculpture garden I had ever set foot in. There were none of the flowering vines and bushes commonly planted for decoration in this temperate climate—no azaleas, hydrangeas, peonies, or camellias. Not even heather or dog roses. No attempt had been made to give the illusion of eternal spring. Nor were there any decorative plants to mark the cycle of the seasons with colorful berries, fruit or turning leaves. The only trees were evergreens—pines or cypresses, and massive ilex trees which also keep their leaves all winter, at whose gnarled roots grew a ragged underbrush of scrub oaks, ferns, nettles, and foul-smelling weeds in continual decay.

It struck me then that what was missing was the element of mind or intellect. There appeared to be no architectural design to the place at all. There were no *parterres* laid out in geometrical patterns; no logical arrangement of the figures to connect them in a meaningful sequence, from what I could see. They came at you helter-skelter, truly like images in a dream. Wherever a crest of rock or boulder protruded from the ground, there had the sculptor's chisel captured another frenzied spirit from the underworld. The author of this book of stone did not intend to tranquilize or soothe. This was not a park where one could hunt deer, make music, or have picnics. No place for play, meditation, or love. For what purpose, then, had it been created? In some ways, the random placement of the statues reminded me of the aftermath of an earthquake, or perhaps, of an explosion. Strewn around us were river gods, pouting putti, and lustful pans; ogres, nymphs and beasties; creatures shaken free from the bowels of the earth by some cataclysm, ready to sink back in at a moment's notice if the earth should heave again.

Since the days of the Ancient Greeks and Romans, philosophers of both East and West have held that the function of parks and gardens is to delight the senses, restore the soul, and bring a person back in harmony with nature and with himself. The Babylonians with their terraced marvels, the Japanese with their raked plots of gravel simulating water, the English with their wild rose and herb gardens all shared this aim, if achieved through different means. The creator of this place had had something else in mind. His garden was rough hewn rock and wild vegetation. Pleasure, sensual delight, order, harmony of spirit, or a meditative mood were very far from the mind of the man who had stamped such bestial faces upon these stones. Guilt, perhaps, and pain were foremost in his thoughts. Or a sort of perverse lust.

"*The Lady Gardener* would never approve of this," I ventured facetiously as we rose and made our way toward the gate. "They certainly would not consider it a proper garden."

"Neither did Vicino," Finestone replied flatly. "He actually never referred to it as a garden or even as a park, but as his Sacred Wood, his *Bosco Sacro*, and that is the term I suggest you use in thinking and speaking of it from now on."

I was puzzled that Finestone had not mentioned such an important detail before, but now that I had explored a bit of the place, this term *sacred wood* made perfect sense. It was not really a park or garden at all but an arena for some kind of initiation, as Finestone had intimated. An initiation of what sort?

On our way out, we passed a small fountain I had not noticed before, although we had walked right by it, just half an hour ago on our little tour. But that is how it was in the Sacred Wood. What you saw and understood was determined by your perspective, which was always shifting in relationship to time and space. You noted things only when you were ready to see them and if you were standing on a spot from which they could be properly seen. And each visitor saw something different.

The fountain was composed of three figures. Two creatures with moth wings and fishtails had grasped a third cherub-like figure by the waist. Holding him upside down, they plunged his head into the overflowing basin of water from which their fishtails emerged. One could not tell if the figures were playing a splashing game or committing a murder by drowning. The features of the cherub's face had eroded away. Was that mouth desperately sucking for air or emitting a laugh of delight? Or had the artist meant just that: to leave the scene ambiguous? Given the tragic story of a child's death by drowning in the park, it seemed to me a sinister signature indeed.

"Do you think they are playing or are they drowning that cherub?" I asked Finestone, pointing back at the fountain as we stepped out the gate. "Or might it be a sort of baptism?"

Finestone blinked behind his bifocals and locked the gate. "Some days I think one thing, some days another."

CHAPTER FOUR

Over two hours had passed during our visit to the Sacred Wood. Walking back to the villa, we noticed Amelia, who had returned from her shopping trip and was now in the yard doing the laundry. She was bending over a series of copper wash tubs lined up in a row, stirring and beating a wet bundle with a stick, then dumping it into successive tubs of rinse water. A flock of hens pecked about her feet. At the sight of the girl intent on this task, Finestone's broad face flushed with uncontainable pleasure. Not far off, amid a patch of bright daffodils, crouched the little white cat, mesmerized by the hens. At our approach, it crawled under a hedge.

The spot Amelia had chosen to do the laundry struck me as a most inconvenient place, considering the distance she need go to fetch water from the only tap in the house, which was located in the kitchen around to the other side of the building. It must have taken her several trips to fill up all those tubs, though I imagined Manu had probably helped her. Wrapped tightly in a pink apron, with her sleeves rolled up to the elbows of her well-turned arms, and her floppy-brimmed hat on her head, she attacked the clothes with a frenzy, wringing them out with enviable force and then laying them to dry along a boxwood hedge that skirted the front wall of the villa. Among the sheets and towels displayed along the bushes were several articles of feminine underclothes made of fine lace and silk, certainly not something a servant could afford to purchase for herself. I assumed these too were gifts from Finestone, or perhaps from some other admirer. Or did they belong to the lady of the house, the absent mistress, whoever she might be? Among the nightgowns, I recognized a few of Finestone's American striped shirts and several pairs of baggy undershorts which must have belonged to him.

I wondered if Clive had woken yet. I was eager to tell him about my impressions of the Sacred Wood, and perhaps take him on a tour myself to show him what I had just seen, that is if Finestone would consent to lend me the key. Looking up at the villa, I saw Clive, clad only in boxer shorts, with his hair all ruffled, standing at his bedroom window which faced out above the front lawns. It was obvious he had just got out of bed. I waved brightly, but he did not respond. In fact, I don't think he even saw me. It occurred to me that he was watching Amelia, which perhaps explained her presence in such an unlikely spot, far from the kitchen, right under the upstairs windows where she was in full display.

"Volete del pollo arrosto per cena?" the girl called, looking up from her washtub as we passed. *Do you want roast chicken for dinner?* She had a very unceremonious way of addressing Finestone, that's to be sure.

Finestone assented with a nod. I could see he heartily approved of the suggestion, for he was blushing again.

"Va bene. Ci penso io." *All right then! I'll see to it.* She finished wringing out a nightgown, draped it on some nearby branches, and wiped her wet hands on her apron. Then with an abrupt but nimble leap, she sprang at the nearest hen clucking about the hedge, clapped a hand over its eyes, immobilized its beak in her armpit and before the poor bird could give a valedictory squawk, she had wrung its neck before our eyes. A second hen fell victim to the same procedure.

"Energetic young woman," I said to Finestone, glancing up again to see if Clive had witnessed the murder of the chickens, but he was no longer at the window.

"And such an efficient housekeeper!" Finestone added appreciatively.

"Ecco, i vostri polli!" said Amelia, tossing her head. Grabbing the limp birds by their claws, she held them high in the air to show us. *There are your birds!* She thrust the birds under my nose as I walked by—*"Vi piace il pollo, vero, Signora?" You do like chicken, don't you, Madame?* and went off toward the kitchen.

Her words sounded to me like a warning, or at least a declaration of unclear intent, but I wouldn't find out until later that day what she was driving at.

Clive was not downstairs when we came in but I knew he was up and about, for when I mounted to my room, I could hear him at work in his studio. From my pocket I removed the pearl button I had found in the park and put it on my desk, then got out the doll's head which I had put in the cedar box. I reflected on the story Finestone had told me of the drowned child. Had the doll and button belonged to her? What might they be signatures of? How strange that I should share the same sad fate as the absent lady of this house: loss of a daughter. Gazing into that shattered eye, I speculated on what events it might have witnessed; then I put both head and button away carefully in the box and put the box in the bottom drawer of the writing desk. It has become a habit, if not an obsession, of mine, to preserve items like these randomly found on walks or in the street, as a collection of signatures that have come my way. I had a feeling these two pieces would sooner or later become eloquent.

I sat down at the desk and wrote until lunchtime, noting down my impressions of the Sacred Wood. Next door in the library, I could hear Finestone pecking at his typewriter. The tap tap tap tap through the wall nearly drove me mad. He seemed to be working on a very long manuscript and I wondered how on earth I would be able to concentrate over the coming days if he kept it up like this day in and day out.

While I was working, I heard Amelia go to up to the studio and announce that she had brought Clive some coffee. I had half a mind to ring and ask for some myself, but I got caught up in what I was writing, and the time simply flew. I was glad it passed so quickly for I was anxious to see Clive, who seemed to be in the throes of a creative spasm, at least to judge from the creaking of the attic floorboards. He was painting up a storm. Usually before lunch, he would tap on the trapdoor connecting his studio to the alcove of my bedroom, to let me know I should come up and have a look at his morning's work. Today, the signal did not come, and I was puzzled. Trying to make as little noise as possible, I climbed up on a chair and gently pushed on the trapdoor, but it was bolted from the other side. I began to suspect that my lover now wished to avoid me.

Amelia rang the gong summoning us for lunch. Clive appeared in the dining room ten minutes later, after Finestone and I had already been served our first course and had begun eating for fear it would grow cold. That day at table, it was only the three of us. Nigel had said he would be in Rome till quite late. I examined the young blond man sitting across from me at the lunch table, who, until that very morning, had witnessed countless dawns from my bed, every single morning for over a fortnight; and who, during the daytime, showered me with compliments and gallantries of all sorts. Yet in the course of a single morning, his manner toward me seemed to have altered beyond recognition, though the change was so subtle, or perhaps so inward, it was impossible for me to say precisely of what it consisted.

Though Clive was perfectly cordial to me throughout the meal, there was an underlying chill to our every exchange, from the passing of the salt to the dishing out of salad. His lips were frozen in a faint half-smile; his eyes, distant and blank, glanced aside when the three of us raised our glasses of *Est-Est-Est* in a toast. He had never treated me like this before, and I began to feel that dreadful panic that comes when one is unsure where one stands with one's lover. I cursed myself bitterly. These were emotions I thought I had outgrown with age, but it seemed I was as vulnerable as ever.

Finestone monopolized the conversation during lunch by describing Etruscan ruins in the vicinity, about which Clive demonstrated an uncharacteristically insatiable curiosity, for I had never known him to be even slightly interested in ancient ruins. He kept plying the scholar with more questions about Etruscan art and religion, so that Finestone's explanations became interminably more complex and verbose; but the second Amelia reappeared from the kitchen to whisk away dirty plates, refill our wine glasses or bring a platter of pecorino cheese, both men fell silent and observed her attentively as she moved about the room. I could see she warmed to their appreciation for she seemed to bloom before their eyes. In Clive's face I read the same shy yet ardent admiration that had so recently been turned upon me and then denied. In Finestone's, I read nothing more than a benevolent and greedy approval. He did not seem to notice the electric attraction flickering through the air between the young American and his adored Amelia.

After lunch, we withdrew to the library where we generally took our coffee after meals. Before the girl served the coffee, Finestone went briefly to his room to fetch a book on Etruscan art he wanted to show us, so at last Clive and I had a moment alone. As I sat down next to him on the sofa, my arm brushed his. Surreptitiously he shrank away from me just a quarter of an inch to distance himself from my touch. I was astonished by this change in attitude. Distractedly, he gazed about the walls, examining the landscapes and engraved maps hanging there. Then he got up and went over to one of the paintings, a romantic landscape of a mist-filled valley at dawn with a sky of billowing pink clouds. Pulling a magnifying glass out of his breast pocket, he inspected it inch by inch. I was surprised, for he was not the sort to carry such an instrument in his shirt pocket.

"Well, I'll be damned! I believe this might be a Turner although the signature is missing!" he announced. "Look at the technique in this pink mass of clouds. If only I could recapture it! What a brilliant painter of mist and fog. I'll have to go out at dawn one morning and see what I can do!"

I restrained a snort of laughter. Clive was more a painter of midnights than dawns. I had never known him to be fully awake or able to hold anything steady in his hand but a cigarette or a coffee cup before ten a.m.—much less a paintbrush.

"Clive . . . ," I began, trying to be patient. I went to him and touched his arm to summon his attention back to me, but just then, Amelia opened the door and brought in our coffee on a tray and Clive jerked his arm away. He watched her intently as she crossed the room, placed the tray on a table near the sofa, curtseyed to him and stepped out again, looking back at him from the doorway with that inquisitive coyness I had seen her use on Finestone, as if to say "When?" or "Well?" or "I'm waiting."

I slunk back to the sofa, but I had not yet resigned myself to the new state of affairs. I made one last attempt to engage Clive's attention: "Shall we have a walk after coffee? I could show you the Sacred Wood, which, by the way, is what Finestone says we should call the garden," I said, ignoring his rude rebuff.

"Yes, I'm in the mood for a walk, but I thought I would ask Finestone to show me some of the places he was describing today. I'd like to see those Etruscan tombs he was telling us about at lunch. We can see the garden tomorrow. I'm sure there will be plenty of time. Daphne, please pour the coffee before it gets cold. And remember two lumps of sugar for me, please."

He settled in an armchair across from the sofa and threw one leg across the armrest. Dutifully I obeyed: poured the coffee, stirred in the sugar, and handed him his cup, trying to keep my hand from trembling. I was in the throes of several unpleasant emotions which I had not felt in years.

"Ah, here's Finestone. Come have your coffee, Professor," said Clive.

Finestone bumbled in, dressed in white linen and fitted out in his walking gear: heavy boots, silver-headed cane, a small sheathed knife lashed to his waist, and, on his head, his wide-brimmed fedora. Under his arm he carried a large leather-bound volume, the book on the Etruscans Clive had wanted to see. He tossed his hat and cane on a hassock, then plopped into an armchair. I poured coffee for Finestone and myself. I drank mine bitter and black, hoping it might sharpen my wits, for I didn't quite like what was happening with Clive and I wasn't sure how to react.

While we sipped and chatted, Finestone showed us the book of Etruscan art, which Clive studied with unusual attention. I could see his interest was feigned; it was only an excuse in order not to speak to me.

When he had finished his coffee, Finestone rose from his chair and clapped on his hat.

"A constitutional after every meal aids my digestion," he said. "So, you have decided to join me on my rambles?" he asked Clive.

"I was hoping to convince Daphne to come along," Clive said turning to me. "You are looking so peaked today, my dear, I am sure it would do you good. With all the rain we have had since we arrived here, you can't have had much exercise."

Oh, can't I? I thought and smiled tautly. He was looking *very* good, an absolute picture of ruddy health. He had had quite a bit of exercise in the last few days, that's for sure.

"I'm afraid those shoes won't do for these trails," Finestone said frowning and pointing at my suede pumps with the tip of his cane. I had not changed my shoes after we had returned from our walk that morning. "They're all right for a stroll in the Sacred Wood, but not for an excursion up into the woods where we might have to ford a stream and climb a cliff or two."

"And doubtless encounter some of your vipers, I suppose. I am rather tired. I hope you don't mind if I stay here," I said, my eyes fixed on Clive's face. "I had a rather sleepless night." My remark brought not the slightest quiver of an eyebrow or twitching of the corner of his mouth. This seemed to me a very bad sign indeed.

On a piece of scrap paper retrieved from the wastepaper basket, Finestone drew a rough map of the trails he had discovered in the woods around the villa leading to an Etruscan site and then on to a neighboring village called Vitorchiano. That was the trail he suggested they explore, though they would not go all the way to the village, since it was a five-hour trek and it was already afternoon and the light would be waning soon. They would only go as far as the nearest Etruscan site, which Finestone described as a sort of altar in the woods. Still, it was too far for me to go and I certainly didn't want to tag along.

I watched them through the window as the two men set out on their hike.

I was puzzled by the friendship that seemed to have sprung up so immediately between Clive and the professor. I wouldn't have thought that they would take to each other at all. Clive was so facile, in a way, superficial, and not terribly bright, while Finestone was intellectual, subtle, and very learned. Yet they got on famously. I found myself wondering if they had ever met before. After all, it was through a mutual acquaintance of Clive's and Finestone's that Nigel, Clive, and I had come to this place and had arranged to sublet part of the villa from Finestone. However, I am sure one of them would have mentioned that they had met previously, if that were the case, and neither of them had, or at least it seemed to me. But now as I observed them, sauntering up the ridge, gabbing away, I remarked to myself how perfectly attuned to each other they seemed to be, like very old, fond friends. Then again, I thought, perhaps it was Finestone's fatherly demeanor that attracted Clive. After all the poor boy had had no real father of his own.

I finished off the coffee, smoked a cigarette, and thought I should take advantage of the afternoon alone to explore the old library, where I had never really spent very much time. During the day, Finestone often used it as his private studio. The four of us did gather there after meals, especially in the evenings, but I had never had the opportunity to poke about it alone. Finestone's Smith Corona was in proud display on a little writing desk, but his manuscript was nowhere to be seen. I presumed that he probably kept it locked in a drawer in his own room which gave on to the library.

Remembering our chat that morning of buried treasure and maps, I thought it very likely that if a map had been made showing the whereabouts of the hypothetical treasure of Bomarzo, the library would be a good place to look for it.

The room contained several old cabinets of pottery and shards, exotic seashells, ostrich eggs, framed butterflies, and even a viper preserved in a jar of yellowish liquid, as well as the usual seventeenth-century gold snuff boxes and china bric-a-brac. Among the musty books aligned along the walls were old herbals, bestiaries, religious tomes, books of emblems and coats-of-arms, and illustrated editions of Dante's *Vita Nuova* and *La Divina Commedia.* There was a print cabinet with many drawers, holding maps, engravings, and even old musical scores. I amused myself by examining all these papers and collections, but of course found no mysterious maps to buried treasure. Besides, I knew that Finestone had probably been over the villa, turning every leaf and tile. In any case, given that the legendary treasure of Bomarzo might not be universally recognized as "treasure," any map indicating its whereabouts was likely to be equally hard to recognize. What intrigued me most was the idea that the treasure might be a state of mind or an emotion.

At last I settled down on the sofa with some old tomes. I had been reading for nearly an hour when Amelia finally came to take away the coffee tray. I asked her politely in Italian to empty the ashtray and serve me some brandy, but she bounced out of the room as though she had not heard my request. I had to pour the brandy myself and dump the contents of the ashtray into the fireplace. Irritated by the girl's cheeky manner, I was determined to have a word with Nigel about her, though I doubted it would do any good.

I went on reading awhile then rang for the girl, for I had decided I wanted a bath before dinner. That was sufficient punishment for her impertinence, I knew, for it entailed hauling huge pails of hot and cold water up the stairs to my bedroom, for there was no running water in the upstairs rooms. The bell jingled merrily in the corridor but brought no response from the servants' quarters. After ten minutes, I rang again, waited impatiently a few more minutes, tapping my foot, then rose to go in search of her.

I found her in the kitchen, sitting on the hearthstone with a dead chicken in her lap, plucking out the feathers and tossing them into a basket at her feet. Her apron was streaked with blood. The little white cat, perched on the edge of a chair nearby, was watching her with keen attention, but the moment I stepped into the kitchen it gave an eerie meow, jumped off the chair, and slunk under the sideboard. My feelings about that animal seemed to be reciprocated.

"Did you not hear me ring?" I asked, but she only shrugged as her fingers worked the limp bird. Each quill detached itself from the dead flesh with a crisp snap.

"Would it be too much trouble to have a bath in my room?" I enquired.

"Non è a voi che devo rispondere." I need not reply to you.

Such impudence astonished me but before I could react appropriately to this outrageous provocation, Manu, in dirty work clothes, pounced in through the kitchen doorway. He must have just stepped in from doing some yard work, for his shirt was stained with grass and mud, and his hands were black with dirt. Yet he had to have been working close enough nearby to have heard us and to have appeared so quickly.

"Ubbedisci!" he growled. *Obey!*

Amelia tossed her head and went on plucking the chicken.

Manu strode to the hearth, grabbed the girl by the arm, and pulled her to her feet. The chicken tumbled from her lap into the basket of bloody feathers. Once more he ordered her to obey. Amelia, impassive, glared back in silent fury, and then turned her head to the wall. She did not even wince when he began to twist her forearm. From beneath the sideboard where it had taken refuge, the cat gave a pitiful almost human-sounding meow.

"I order you to stop!" I cried. I was as distressed by his violence as by her insolence. I did not want her to be injured on my account.

At my intervention, Manu let go her arm.

Amelia pulled her arm to her breast, rubbed it as if to soothe the pain. The fine pale skin of her forearm was mottled red and blue from Manu's powerful grip. She scowled at me. *"Va bene, Signora. Vi faccio fare un bel bagno subito!"* All right, Signora, I'll fix you a nice bath right now!

"Apologies, Signora," Manu said to me with a contrite nod, now removing his dirty cap. *"Stai attenta questa volta."* Be careful next time, he snarled to the girl, and then went out and resumed working in the yard, where I could hear the hiss of his scythe through the grass.

I had already begun to regret my request, but I could hardly change my mind at this point. With fierce industriousness, Amelia immediately began the preparations, stoking up the stove to heat the water in a huge copper cauldron and when it had reached a rolling boil, ladling it out into pails which had to be carried all the way up to my room. I watched her from the balustrade as she struggled up the steps, with two pails of water hanging from a broomstick balanced on her shoulders, careful not to spill a single drop or burn herself. There was a peculiar expression in her eyes that I cannot quite describe, mingling the determined stoicism of a Sisyphus with the pure hatred of a harpy. I could well imagine that my next request for a hot bath might be the prelude to homicide.

I heard a car drive up while the zinc tub in the alcove in my room was being filled. Looking from a window on the corridor, I saw Nigel returning, crossing the grounds in the company of a tall, dark, youngish stranger. A replacement for Clive, I presumed, and a very handsome one at that.

Meanwhile my bath was nearly ready. Gallons of boiling water had been carried up by our dauntless maid. These were then followed by canisters of cold water and all mixed in the tub with five gallons of milk, perfumed oils of juniper and thyme, and a handful of starch. Amelia leaned over the tub and stirred this brew with a long stick until the last lump of starch had dissolved. Then testing the temperature by plunging in her hand, she pronounced the bath ready and asked me if I needed anything else.

I said no and dismissed her—though getting into the tub unassisted was no easy maneuver as the sides were so tall and the wet zinc was so slick. Clutching the rim, I stuck one foot in and cried out in pain. It was far too hot to climb in. The girl obviously intended to boil me like a lobster. In just a few seconds of contact with the water, my toes had turned bright scarlet. There was no more cold water to add, so I just sat on the rim, stirred the water and waited for it to cool. It took nearly twenty minutes for the water to reach a temperature which humans might endure, but at last I got in and breathed a sigh of relief. It would soon be dinnertime and tonight, as a matter of pride, I intended to look seductive and refreshed when Clive and Finestone returned from their hike in the woods.

Lounging in the tub, I looked down at my poor naked body, the breasts still buoyant but beginning to sag, the red fuzz between my still muscular thighs. Useless to lament the loss of feminine charm. One clings as long as one can, but then the end of allure comes with all finality.

I traced the ugly scar splitting my abdomen where the poor dead child had been torn from my womb so long ago. Persephone! Did she watch me from the ether world as a medium in

Hampstead had once suggested? I had often sensed her nearby, a mild benign presence floating in the ectoplasm above this hostile world. But what sort of life could I have given her, poor darling, had she lived? There was nothing left after Edmund died and left us practically destitute. Hawthorne Lodge had been sold to pay off my brother's debts. The fields with their ancient, moss-encrusted stones where I had played as a child had been parceled off to the neighboring farmers, glad to see us fallen so low. The graves of my nearest and dearest now lay on land I no longer owned. All the books in the old family library where Byron had once sat for a stormy afternoon scribbling, waiting for a post-chaise; the letters to my grandfather from Southey; the Blake engravings that were my inspiration in childhood—all sold to an unscrupulous antiquary in London for a song. My income, reduced to a pittance! I must beg from lovers and strangers to pay the rent of a coldwater flat. Piece by piece, I had sold all the silver, all Mother's diamond earrings and pearl necklaces from India, keeping only the more insignificant pieces for memory's sake. And writing stupid novels to keep myself afloat. No, my dearest Persephone, far better you were never subject to the humiliation of all that, or worse, to the humiliation of what your mother has become.

I sighed and laid my head against the back of the tub in a very uncomfortable position, trying to keep the nape of my neck above the waterline, so as not to ruin my hair for the evening, and regretting that I had not thought to bring a small pillow. But I did not want to call Amelia and ask her to bring me one now. I closed my eyes. The starch was soothing to my skin; the oils smelled rich and intoxicating. Did I fall asleep then? Perhaps, for I heard again that strange rhythmic murmuring, resembling a wordless nursery rhyme, which inclined me to a sleepy mood until a very distinct noise roused me: the sound of a door opening behind me. Next came a sharp draft of chill air on my scalp. Someone had entered my bedroom! I drew up my knees, sat up in the water and tried to turn round to look, but the cramped space of the tub hindered my movements and the screen separating the tub from the rest of the room partly blocked my view.

"Clive . . . !" I called, and when no one replied, "Amelia?"

There was a rushing movement from behind the screen, a tin pail clattered as it was overturned, and suddenly my head was pushed down between my knees and my lungs were filling with water. I tried to push back up, but the force holding me down exerted such a strong pressure I feared my neck might snap in two. Abruptly it ceased, and I thrust upward with all my strength, and, grabbing the sides of the tub, gasped wildly for breath. I didn't have enough wind in me to scream. Catching sight of a dark shape in the steam-spotted mirror above the tub, I held fast to the rim of the tub, gulped in as much air as I could and rallied myself for a second attack.

A second passed, ten seconds, twenty. Nothing happened. The steam slowly cleared from the mirror and I saw that the threatening, dark shape was only the reflection of my dark silk kimono hanging on a hook by the screen. I scrambled out of the tub on wobbly legs, bundled my body in a towel, and dashed from the alcove into the middle of the bedroom, expecting to catch sight of my intruder, but the door was shut and nothing was amiss. I waited a few moments, chest heaving, listening to the silence, trying to ascertain the hidden presence of my assailant in the room, but everything was quiet. I peeked under the bed and in the wardrobe, but of course no one was there. I went to the mirror opposite the bed, examined the spot on my neck where the hands had grabbed me. No particular impress or unusual mark appeared on my skin, but my face looked swollen and blotched red as a beet.

Still shaking, I observed the room around me as I dried my dripping hair with a towel. My neck and left shoulder throbbed with pain. The skin on my nape was tender to the touch; my back ached from the strain of being bent forward. It had all happened so quickly: the sound of a door opening, rudely interrupting my reverie as I soaked in the bath; my head pushed down under the water; then the sudden release. Now nothing appeared out of order, nothing seemed to have been disturbed, except that one of the tin pails in which Amelia had brought the water up for the bath lay on its side behind the screen, spilling a small puddle on the floor. That might account for the noise I had heard, but the pail certainly could not have toppled over of its own accord. A gust of wind might have blown the door open and shut it again, but it could not have knocked a pail over, and in any case, the windows were all shut.

I took my kimono from the hook, slipped it on, went to the dresser and opened the top drawer. The little black velvet box containing my topaz ring and my moonstone necklace was safe in its usual place. The blue glass rouge pots and pink powder boxes were lined up in perfect order in the drawer. I reached for the small satin case where I kept my cigarettes, hoping a smoke would calm me. Opening the case, I discovered to my amazement the cigarettes were all gone but one, and the fabric felt slightly damp, as though handled with wet hands. My own hands trembled pitifully as I lit that remaining fag. Sitting down again on the edge of the bed, I stared blankly about the room, taking stock of my situation.

My attacker could not have picked a more propitious moment. Clive and Finestone, usually always around during the day in rooms directly communicating with mine, from which they might have heard me scream, were conveniently absent. The presence of a stranger among us in the villa, the young man who had come back from Rome with Nigel, introduced an unstable element into our chemistry. He would be a prime suspect, though the most logical and likely motive was lacking—robbery—since nothing had been taken but a few cigarettes. My valuable objects, plainly visible in the drawer next to my cigarette case, had not even been touched. Yet the aggressor had to be acquainted with the house, and well aware of the intended victim's—that is to say, my—vulnerability in that tub, hindered in all my movements, with my view obstructed and my back to the door. Every detail suggested precise timing and a calculated plan.

The evidence all pointed to Amelia. Why had she not finished the job when she might well have drowned me? Or had it all been a nasty little joke? And to whom should I report the incident, and in what terms? Should I step out into the corridor and scream bloody murder? Demand to report the incident to the police? Or discreetly have a chat with Nigel or Finestone, to warn them and try to arrange to have the girl sent away? My mind raced ahead, making connections. It dawned on me that she might be a homicidal maniac, and may even have been implicated in the drowning of the child in the story Finestone told me.

Had Nigel returned alone, I might have rushed to him at once to tell him what had happened. But I was loath to do so now, seeing that he was occupied with a new friend. As I sat on the bed, mulling this over, there came a scratching noise from under the dresser, and then a faint mewing. I got down on my hands and knees and peered under it, and there was Amelia's albino cat, glaring at me with its pink rheumy eyes. That cinched it! It was proof enough that the girl had been in the room when I was attacked. I banged my fist against the dresser to frighten the animal out of its hiding place, and off flew a fountain pen that had been left on the dresser top. The pen fell to the floor and rolled under the dresser. The cat mewed back at me but did not budge. I struck the dresser once again more forcibly and this time the cat shot out from under it and leapt toward the door, still closed. To my astonishment, it hurled its body against the door with a resounding thump three times until the latch lifted. The door opened a crack and out scuttled the cat into the corridor, leaving a trail of wet paw prints across the floor. I went to the door and bolted it, reflecting that if the cat was cunning enough to open the door to my bedroom, it might well have knocked over a nearly empty pail.

I crouched down again to retrieve my pen. It had rolled over to an almost inaccessible spot and I had to move the dresser away from the wall in order to reach it. The space behind the dresser was dirty with dust and cobwebs. Brushing away decades of filth, I seized my pen and was about to push the dresser back against the wall, when I noticed a brownish scrap of fabric or perhaps of parchment, sticking out two or three inches from behind the backboard of the dresser. In the bottom right corner, the wood had warped and buckled, and the glue had dissolved, forming a very narrow crack into which a sheet of something had slipped. Curious, I tugged at the scrap, but it held fast and I was afraid it might tear if I pulled too hard. So I took my nail file from the top drawer and began to pry the backboard loose. The wood was so thin and brittle, it splintered off into narrow strips, revealing a piece of parchment that had got stuck in this crevice God knows how many years ago. Gently I removed it and took it over to my desk to examine it in the light of the lamp. It seemed to be a drawing on parchment, mottled with dark stains and so thickly covered with gray dust as to be illegible. I blew a bit of dust away, sneezed, then wiped a corner clean with a hand-kerchief. A few words in fine black ink appeared, then a tiny drawing of human-like figures and of a length of wall. My hands began to tremble again as I realized what it was—a sketch—perhaps a map—of the Sacred Wood.

CHAPTER FIVE

For the rest of the evening until dinnertime, a wonderful smell of roast chicken with potatoes and rosemary wafted through the villa, of savory cheese pastries and fruit tarts. Amelia was on her best behavior as dutiful cook and housekeeper, and seemed to have set her mind to preparing us a feast. She may also have foreseen, I believe, that I would shortly be making some complaints about her behavior to Nigel.

I was in a strange contrast of moods given the bizarre events of that afternoon. I had of course examined the drawing, but could not make much of it. It would need to be carefully cleaned of its many layers of grime in order to be readable. I pushed the dresser back against the wall, wrapped the sketch in a sheet of newspaper and hid it beneath the blotter on my desk. That wasn't a very safe place for such a valuable find, but I did not know where else to put it. The parchment was too dirty to be locked in a drawer without soiling everything it touched. For the moment, I had decided to keep my discovery to myself. I did not intend to mention it to Finestone. After all, I am sure had he found it first, he would never have told anyone, until he had had a chance to decipher it and determine its authenticity and worth. That was exactly what I planned to do. I dressed slowly for dinner, donning my purple evening gown, a black silk jacket, my moonstone necklace, and a topaz ring. Then I doused myself with perfume and carefully applied my make-up—all the while thinking of Mark Antony arming himself before his last battle. I chose a special color for my lips—a rich, dark red with an under sparkle of bronze which I only use for elegant occasions. Oddly, the lid of my lip rouge pot was unscrewed. Amelia had been tinkering with my cosmetics, too.

At nine o'clock, a bit later than usual, the gong summoned us to the dining room where the table was laid with a white cloth and good china, lit with candelabras and decorated with lilacs from the hedge. Amelia wore a dress of black silk crepe, cut low in the bodice, and a frilly apron of San Gallen lace, so that she resembled many men's fantasy of the perfect governess. Clive couldn't keep his eyes off her, and Finestone blushed when her hand touched his while serving him an extra helping of roast potatoes. Why is it that intellectuals like Finestone always turn out to be such fools?

That night a stranger joined our merry band, the handsome Italian boy Nigel had met at the Pincio and had decided to bring home for his entertainment. The guest took a place of honor at the foot of the table, directly across from Nigel, who sat at the head.

Danilo was a flashy fellow, dark, sinewy, Caravaggio-esque, with curly hair and swarthy skin, darting black eyes, and a smooth but affable manner. He was the type that drives women, particularly older women, mad. I guessed that he was not yet forty. He was dressed like a gentleman but spoke like a Roman carriage driver. His English pronunciation was abominable, but we all pretended not to notice, and he had a fair command of the language. In conversation, Danilo revealed a practical mentality. Although lacking an education, he was gifted with a natural intelligence and quickness of response, which in America or India might have made him a success, but which in Europe tends to rot for the lack of opportunity. He had charm, intelligence, good looks, willingness to please, and I suspected that he willingly pleased persons of either sex as circumstances demanded. Nigel seemed delighted with his company and we all found him congenial.

Amelia instead seemed to have an outright aversion for the newcomer. As she took away plates and dished out drumsticks, she regarded Danilo with suspicion and contempt, giving him the smallest piece or scantiest portion or overlooking him entirely to show her disapproval. Danilo, in turn, looked down his long nose at her, but I could see he observed her as attentively as Clive or Finestone, although he masked his curiosity. I was watching her too, looking for telltale signs of guilt, but she glided blithely back and forth to the kitchen with the tarnished trays and serving dishes, as though nothing had happened.

Before the table was cleared for dessert, I reached for the breadbasket, clumsily dumping a pile of crumbs into an open handkerchief spread in my lap, which I then folded and surreptitiously pushed into the pocket of my little silk jacket. The crumbs would come in handy for cleaning the filthy parchment I had found behind the dresser.

It rained that evening and after dinner the five of us gathered in the library around the fire, which for once was blazing. I browsed through a book of emblems Finestone had recommended; Clive thumbed through a portfolio of phantasmagoric Piranesi prints, while Nigel and Finestone played chess. Danilo, with his long legs stretched out before him by the fire, was reading an English newspaper a few days old, reporting incidents of Fascist rallies in Rome on the front page. Every now and then I caught him mumbling the words to himself. One could clearly see he was a product of determined self-improvement.

Amelia's cat wandered in and attempted to insinuate itself among us. First it sidled up to me, but I shooed it away, and sent it scuttling over to Danilo where it rubbed insistently against his trouser leg. Our new guest would have none of it and pushed it away with a gentle nudge of his foot. Clive was much more direct when the cat importuned him, and taking the animal by the scruff of its neck, set it down firmly a few feet away, evoking a yowl. It finally found refuge in Finestone's lap. The professor caressed it absently while studying his chess moves. Grateful for the attention, the cat purred noisily. I plucked a few white cat hairs from my dress. It was a miracle we were not all covered with fleas. Never terribly fond of cats, being more partial to horses and dogs, I had taken a special dislike to this one.

Amelia entered the room to draw the curtains and rake up the fire. Her presence sent the air crackling and all the men snapped to attention. Dropping to her knees to one side of the hearth in a position that must have been quite awkward for the task she had purportedly come to perform, she gave a fine view of her low-cut bodice to Danilo as she swept away invisible ashes from the floor with a hearth brush. A strand of blond hair detached itself from her artfully untidy chignon. Clive watched her entranced as she paused to tuck it back up again, throwing out her bosom as she lifted her hands to rearrange her hair. Then, when Danilo's shoe inched dangerously near her broom, Amelia swept respectfully, if provocatively, around it. Suddenly she stopped, threw down her brush. *"Scusate, Signore, ho sporcato la vostra scarpa con le ceneri." I am sorry, Sir, I have soiled your shoe with ashes.*

"Puliscila!" He smirked. *So wipe it clean!*

She lowered her ruddy lips to his shoe, spat on it copiously, and then removing a rag from her apron pocket, obediently buffed it back to a shine, all the while gazing at him with a look which caused Finestone to turn red, Nigel to pale, and Clive to boggle his eyes, while Danilo remained perfectly impervious. At that point I decided to retire and go back to my room and write. Inspiration had finally struck for my new murder mystery; a homicidal plot was hatching in my brain. As I left the library, I heard them talking and laughing, Amelia's shrill giggle a piquant high note. Bolting the door to my room, I sat down to my desk and got to work. It was a chilly night and our haughty maid had neglected to light the fire in my hearth or bring in a brazier with coals, so my hands and feet were soon stiff with cold, but I was warmed from within by my imagination as an idea for a new book took shape. I always start with the murderer. And this new villain would be young, blond, female, unscrupulous, and the owner of an obnoxious little cat that would meet a gruesome end. I wrote for a while until my inspiration ran out.

Through the wall, I could hear the low murmur of the men's voices in the library next door, punctuated with Amelia's laughter. I was furious that Nigel and Finestone let her, a servant, go on in such a way. At last their voices grew silent. I heard doors shut, footsteps die away along the corridor. When I was sure they had all gone to bed, and there was little chance I'd be disturbed by anyone, including, alas, Clive, I slipped out the parchment and set to work cleaning it with the soft brush I used for applying my face powder and a handful of the crumbs I had collected from the breadbasket.

In the candlelight, I could just make out the figures and words scribbled in discolored ink—though I believed I recognized the twin giants and the chapel. There was also a sort of cave with a gaping mouth labeled *La Bocca dell' Inferno*—the Hell Mouth—located near the center of the drawing and, on one end, a leaning tower. The walls of the Sacred Wood were clearly delineated. The area outside the walls was filled in with skeletal trees, denoting a thick forest. Here were written the words *Le Madri in Lutto,* which means "the Mothers in Mourning." Several words were scribbled inside the walls. I managed to decipher *Il Viandante Eremita* and *La Sorella Scalza*—"the Traveling Hermit" and "the Barefoot Sister"—as well as the words *Coniunctio, Nigredo, Primo Bagno, Secondo Bagno, Terzo Bagno, Lussuria, Ferocia, Metanoia.* Dotted lines in no specific order randomly led to the center of the drawing occupied by a crude, bare-breasted female figure decorated with a scroll where the inscription read: *Innocenza, Il Desir del Cuor, Sophia.* "Innocence," "Heart's Desire," and "Wisdom." There was a funny doodle in the lower left-hand corner, which I made out to be a set of initials an "M" and an "I," followed by two other letters in faded sepia, which might have been a "BO" or perhaps a "BU" all blotted over by a very dark stain. Then again, the B might possibly be an R. Only the date was clear: 1560.

Some of these words I recognized as alchemical terms: *Coniunctio*—the marriage of opposites; *Nigredo*, the state of putrefaction that must be reached before gold can be created from lead; *Primo, Secondo, Terzo Bagno*—first, second, and third baths, also sounded as though they might be phases in an alchemical process. *Lussuria* meant Lust, one of the Seven Cardinal Sins. *Ferocia* might be a synonym for Wrath—another of the seven sins. *Metanoia* was the Greek word for *Pentimento* or Repentance. "The Mothers in Mourning" sounded to me like the title of a Greek tragedy. Instead, *La Sorella Scalza*—"the Barefoot Sister," sounded more like a character in a medieval allegory, or perhaps a comic figure. Remembering my conversation with Finestone that morning about the legendary treasure of Bomarzo, I mulled over whether this drawing might contain instructions on how to find it. In time, I thought I might share it with Finestone, once I had had the opportunity to study it thoroughly and penetrate its symbols. For the moment, it was totally incomprehensible.

Owls hooted out on the terrace. A branch tapped on the window. At last I put the map aside, undressed, put on a nightgown, and crawled into bed. I was in a melancholy mood, despite this exciting discovery. I suppose I missed Clive and was disappointed at having to get used to sleeping alone again. I must have fallen asleep around two o'clock, later to be awakened by a noise upstairs in the attic, a rhythmic squeaking of the sofa in Clive's studio. It took me a moment to understand what it was, then a picture flashed through my mind: Clive and Amelia locked in lewd embrace.

Served me right, I thought. I never should have let Clive lead me down the garden path. Certainly I was old enough to know better. I buried my head under a mound of pillows to muffle the offensive noise and had fallen asleep again when the murmuring began, a soft, low, breathy tone that pleasantly tickled my ear, cadenced like a nursery rhyme. Although I could not quite catch the words, they had the effect of soothing me instantly to sleep. Once again in dream I relived that wild night of lovemaking with Clive, which was so real I could feel his hands clutching my hips, the warm ooze of his seed between my thighs. I cried and moaned and laughed and wept in the sunless shining of flesh, while Clive kept repeating my name.

But that *was* his voice. This wasn't a dream. I shook myself awake. Through the pale dawn filtering in through a half-open shutter which I must have left unlatched, I saw Clive standing at the foot of my bed, shoes in hand. He must have come down through the trapdoor in the attic, since I had locked and bolted the door to my room before going to bed. I sat up with a start and reached to pull the sheet over my breast, thinking I was naked, then looking down saw that I was still clad in my nightgown. That evening's erotic encounter had only been a dream.

My next fear was that he might have seen the sketch, which I had left in full view on my desk.

"You were having a nightmare. I heard you cry out." His words were slurred and he was swaying slightly, holding onto the bedpost for support. "I came to see if you needed help."

"I'm all right," I said, propping myself up on the pillows. "What about you?"

As far as I could make out in the half dark, he didn't look well at all and from his tone of voice, I would have sworn he had been crying.

"I'm drunk," he said. "I can't get to sleep."

"Well, come here, darling," I said, and opened my arms. He tumbled into bed beside me. His hair was damp and his face bathed in tears. As my arms enfolded him, he began blubbering like a baby.

"I'm nothing to her," he said between sobs. It was final then. I had lost him forever.

"To whom, darling?" I asked kissing his hot little face and caressing the sweaty roots of his hair, feeling the tenderness one might feel for a feverish child. But I wasn't to have the sad satisfaction of hearing her name, for the moment his head touched the eiderdown pillow, he began to snore.

I got up from the bed, tiptoed in bare feet across the chill marble floor to the desk where I covered the drawing with a piece of newspaper and piled several books on top of it. I doubted Clive could have noticed it on my desk in the dark, but I thought I ought to make sure it was hidden in case he woke before me the next morning. I didn't want him snooping about.

The boy was still asleep in my bed when I went down to the kitchen where Finestone was having his breakfast. He had risen much later than usual, perhaps because it was raining heavily, not ideal weather for working outdoors. Amelia, busy chopping onions and carrots for a soup, seemed surprised to see me up so early. She greeted me with an icy glance which suggested that she knew exactly where Clive had spent the latter part of the night and that she did not approve. Finestone gestured for me to join him, and I sat down across from him at the rough plank table. The window was open despite the rain, perhaps to relieve the stink of smoke in the kitchen which smelled even worse on rainy days. Lilacs in full bloom frothed below the ledge, the sweet smell pungent with rain wafted in, mingling with the smells of soot from the fire and scorched bacon fat. Amelia had been unsuccessfully trying her hand again at preparing us a classic English breakfast.

The cat, perched on top of the sideboard, peered down, captivated by a strip of bacon sizzling and shrinking in a pan. That cat looked sick to me. Its eyes were runny. It was deplorable that a sick animal should be allowed in the kitchen. I watched the girl moving about, expecting her to make some subtle admission of guilt concerning yesterday's attack in the bath, but Amelia served me my breakfast of undercooked poached eggs and burnt bacon with her usual indifference. I saw that Finestone was still in her favor for she bustled back and forth, bringing him freshly brewed coffee, and he bashfully grunted his thanks each time she refilled his cup. That morning my tea was almost drinkable, for once, but the thick slabs of stale bread she had toasted for me were tainted with mold. I ate them anyway because I was famished.

Finestone, unusually pensive, did not seem to be in the mood for chatting. As I sat sipping my tea, absorbed in my own thoughts, I kept my eyes on Amelia, wondering if Finestone had any idea where Amelia had spent the earlier part of *her* evening. I also wondered what he would say if I told him I had found a sketch of the Sacred Wood, but that was something I had decided not to disclose, at least for the time being.

Now our maid was rolling out pasta dough on a marble counter, wielding a large rolling pin that looked as heavy as a cricket bat. Great physical strength is required to roll dough out properly and Amelia was obviously an expert. The sheaf of dough she held up to the window to inspect was as thin as paper and as translucent as parchment. As she cut it into long strips for *tagliatelle,* the knife scraped the stone countertop with a long, clean hiss.

When she had finished preparing the pasta, she came over to the breakfast table. Crossing her arms on her bosom, she asked me, "*Signò, il vostro bagno era abbastanza caldo ieri?*" *Was your bath hot enough yesterday?* and I almost choked on my tea. Sputtering, I covered my lips with my napkin and she turned her face away for a moment, but I caught her reflection in the mirror above the mantelpiece as she smiled in disdain.

I must not let her see that I was the least bit ruffled by her attitude, so thinking out the phrase carefully in Italian before I spoke, I cleared my throat and replied.

"Yes, it was delightfully warm, just the way I like it."

Her body stiffened at my words. I could see she was irritated by my aplomb.

She fetched more coffee for Finestone, who thanked her again, and remarked to me *sottovoce,* "What a gem of a girl," and I nearly choked again.

Finestone rose, saying that rain or no rain, he was on his way to the Sacred Wood, which he had promised to show Nigel's visitor. The two men had already had their breakfast and were waiting for him in the library. He invited me to come along, but I declined saying I intended to do some work that morning since I had finally gotten started on my new book.

"Ah, yes, your new novel. Your last, *Signatures,* was an interesting proposal. At any moment the arrangement of objects around us can spell out future events or solve enigmas of the past."

I was delighted, of course, that he had heard of my novel, but I guessed that Nigel or Clive had told him about it. He was not the type to take an interest in mystery novels.

He flung his hand out toward the table at the remains of our breakfast. "And what would this scene be the premonition of?"

I looked at the tea and coffee dregs in their stained cups, the breadcrumbs and bits of eggshell scattered across the rough wooden surface, the splatter of dried egg yolk, the thickly coated butter knife and a blot of spilled coffee on my napkin, exactly the color of old dried blood. There was no doubt in my mind that the scene spelled out murder and perhaps more than one. But knowing Finestone would never understand me, I smiled and said, "Only that we have just concluded breakfast and the table needs clearing."

He must have appreciated my wit, for he chuckled and went out. I sat in the kitchen awhile longer, savoring a second cup of tea and watching Amelia intensely, thinking here we are: murderer, victim, and a room full of potential weapons. What will her next move be? A jab in the ribs with the knife lying on the counter? Or boric acid stirred in with my sugar? A blow on the head with the iron griddle or the rolling pin? Too obvious, I thought. Suffocation with a musty pillow while I slept was more likely.

Amelia did not seem to like being observed, for she moved about the kitchen nervously, dropping things, never once catching my eye. When she set a plate of meat scraps for the cat in a corner, it leapt from the top of the sideboard to the table, nearly knocking the sugar bowl into my lap, then down to the floor where it ravenously attacked the food. Amelia watched her pet gobble the meat, then knelt down to fondle it when it had finished. "*Povera bestia,*" she murmured, *poor beast*, lifting it to her breast and wiping the rheumy encrustations from around its eyes with a corner of her apron. Her devotion to the animal was touchingly sincere. Perhaps it was the only really human thing about her, but her knowledge of hygiene was appalling. When she came to clear the table without washing her hands, I got up and left the kitchen.

I intended to see if Nigel was still in the library. I rather doubted that he had accompanied Finestone and Danilo to see the Sacred Wood. He hated gamboling about in the rain because of his arthritic knee. Ever since he had fallen out with Clive, Nigel had become bored with Vicino's Sacred Wood, and I thought it was likely I'd find him mulling over a copy of last week's *Times*. I wanted to tell him what had happened to me the day before. How I had almost been *drowned* and *strangled* in the bath by our servant girl, whose comment—*Was your bath hot enough?*—was to my mind the admission of guilt I had been expecting. I wanted his advice, his help; above all I wanted him to *do* something. But I didn't want to discuss this with him while Amelia was around, even though I knew she couldn't understand English. Or at least so I presumed, but I also thought she might be cunning enough to pretend she was more ignorant than she actually was. I thought I had better wait until she had set out to do the shopping before going in to talk to Nigel. I went upstairs and lingered by the tall windows in the corridor, peeking out from behind the dusty velvet drapes until I saw her heading up the drive, shielding herself from the rain with a large black umbrella. Turning from the windows after I had made sure she was gone, I saw that the curtains of the niche housing the angel icon had been left open, and I swear, in a strange quiver of the light, that snake round the angel's ankle seemed . . . well, not to move, of course, but it leapt out at me in a peculiar way. It conveyed a shocking emotion. I went over to examine the painting more closely, searching for the artist's signature, but found none. Then, not wanting to dally any longer for fear Nigel might go out and I might miss my opportunity to speak to him, I stepped into the library, where I found him sitting by the hearth, drinking tea and reading through his correspondence.

Looking up toward the double doors, he hastily shoved his letters into a drawer as I entered the room, making me curious what demanded such cautious privacy, for an alarmed expression had flashed in his face and then subsided. He coughed twice and bade me good morning, nervously running his fingers through his hair, where the roots had recently been re-dyed, probably during his last trip to Rome. Settling in a worn leather chair across from him, I told him the story of how I had been attacked in the bath, but he seemed distracted. When I had concluded, emphasizing a second time that I was sure that Amelia had been my assailant, he only shook his head and sighed. Laying a hand on my arm with gentle pressure, he asked quietly, "Daphne, have you been smoking again?"

Blood rushed to my cheeks. "You mean you don't believe me?" I tore my arm away.

"It's not that I don't believe you. Sometimes you . . . exaggerate. All women and all writers exaggerate. Embellish the truth. I can't blame you for that. You wouldn't be such a damn good writer of mysteries if you didn't."

"I haven't touched smoke since you threw away my pipe in Paris!" I lied.

He lifted an eyebrow. "Sometimes when one has a history of using certain substances, when one ceases to consume that substance, the lack of it may alter one's perceptions."

Though he had chosen his words carefully, their import was not lost on me.

"It was no hallucination that our maid tried to drown and strangle me in the bath and I think everyone here in this villa ought to know about it. And moreover, you should do something before something more serious occurs."

"From what you have said, I gather that you did not actually *see* Amelia attack you. Can you be absolutely sure that you just didn't . . . ummm . . . fall asleep in the bath, and then slide down so that your head dropped into the water, at which point you woke in the throes of a sort of panic? I mean, drowning people do have delusions of different sorts . . ."

"No, I am absolutely sure that is not what happened!" I bristled, rising to leave. "I *know* it was she who attacked me! It was no delusion!"

"Don't take offence, Daphne. But this *knowing* of yours doesn't hold water, I'm afraid, if you'll pardon the pun. One can't go around accusing people of attempted murder these days, without proof. I am asking you to reason with me about what has happened, about what you *imagine* has happened. Sit down, please and let's reason it out together."

Reluctantly, I obeyed, though I perched on the edge of my chair, ready to spring.

"The girl's a hussy," he conceded, "who probably belongs in a brothel, but I doubt she would have the strength to drown you in a bath."

"She's stronger than she looks." I said. "Have you seen her wringing out the laundry or rolling out pastry? To say nothing of strangling chickens."

"Why would she want to drown you in the bath? Think about it. These people make their living by working for English tourists like ourselves. It doesn't make sense that they would murder their source of income. The police would find out immediately and they'd go to jail, or be hanged, or whatever they do to murderers in this country. She'd have to kill us all and hide us in that bloody sculpture garden, and that would be a messy business, especially with all the work going on there not to bury but to unbury as much of the place as they can. Murderers generally have sound and solid motives for their actions, as you yourself know well. Why on earth would she want to kill you when she never saw you before in her life and isn't likely to see you again once our stay here has terminated?"

I did not want to say *jealousy* and bring up the delicate matter of Clive. Besides, it was not necessary for her to murder me in order to wean the handsome Texan from my affections. That had already been achieved. Was pure visceral dislike a sufficient motive for murdering a stranger? But maybe her gesture had only been a warning. A way to say I—or perhaps all of us—were under her control.

"Homicidal maniacs do exist, you know."

"Daphne, this isn't one of your novels."

"And besides there was a previous drowning here some time ago. Maybe she was to blame for that, too."

He peered at me quizzically and I promptly continued. "A child drowned in the fountain."

To this Nigel replied with a groan.

"Don't you understand that we are in danger?" I could hear my own voice growing hysterical, but could not control it.

"I understand that you sincerely believe we are. I know, Daphne, you have been under quite a bit of strain, which is why I brought you here to Italy in the first place, after that little episode in your flat."

I stared at him in puzzled silence.

"I know how distraught you have been, and how fragile you are."

Then I got what he was driving at: "I am in perfect possession of my faculties, thank you, Nigel. That afternoon in Paris, well, it was just an unfortunate accident. It has nothing to do with this."

"Indeed. . . ." He paused and cleared his throat. "I should point out to you, however, you did not actually see the girl; all you saw, I'd like to emphasize, was a cat!"

"But don't you see? The cat's the proof that she was in the room. You must have noticed that it follows her everywhere."

His nostrils flared with sudden impatience. "Most importantly, Daphne, you were not harmed."

"Not this time, but that doesn't mean there might not be a next time, for me, for you, or for any of us." I was truly exasperated by his nonchalance.

He sighed again. "Well, we can't send her away. She and Manu come with the place. And if we call the police, what shall we tell them? That you *think* someone tried to strangle you in the bath and you found a damp cigarette in your drawer and a cat under the dresser? Moreover, dear girl, we really are stuck here. I . . . we have paid a rather large sum to stay in this villa, and it wouldn't be returned, I am afraid, should we decide to leave before our contract runs out. Finestone is a jolly enough fellow, but I don't think he'd be pleased if we pulled out now. I have signed a lease, you know. And where would we go? We can't afford suitable lodgings in Rome or Florence, to say nothing of Venice. When I went to get my mail at Thomas Cook's yesterday, I found a very disturbing letter from the bank refusing to advance the money I asked them to wire to me. So we really can't go anywhere else. I suggest you have as little to do with her as possible, if you find her so detestable, and get on with your new book. By the way, at what point are we?"

I confessed that I had only just started conceiving the plot. He was clearly disappointed by this news.

"Just a friendly reminder, my dear, you are here to write a book."

I nodded woodenly, amazed by his refusal to take my worries seriously. All he was really concerned about was getting another book out of me.

"And another thing, Daphne. Don't . . . I wouldn't say anything about this story of yours, being strangled in the bath. Gossip can lead to ugly consequences, especially if, as in this case, you have no proof of your accusation. Though it *is* a good detail, especially the cat! Put it in your new book. Your readers will love it." He patted my knee and poured himself another cup of tea, insisting that I join him and I did. I don't know why, but Nigel has always had this stifling effect on me. He always manages to get me to do what he wants.

Inwardly fuming, I sat and sipped, gazing distractedly about the room, then noticed something odd, which, alas, I did not consider important at the time. Outside the drizzle had stopped and the sun had pierced the clouds for a moment, shedding a beam of light upon the wall and upon the picture that Clive had been admiring the day before, illuminating the very detail of clouds and mist he had pointed out to me. In the warm sunlight so sharply contrasting with the gloom of the library's wood-paneled walls and ceiling, the painting appeared more vivid. The yellowish patina of age seemed to have vanished in the night from the surface of the canvas. It was if the painting had shed its skin. The colors looked very fresh, almost, I would say *damp*, and I could swear I smelled a whiff of turpentine mingling with the scent of Nigel's sandalwood cologne and the smoke from the fire stoked with pinecones. But this did not occupy my thoughts for long; I had other much more serious things on my mind. I put it down to a trick of the light on a cloudy morning.

I returned to my room and mulled over what we had said. It was true: I could not prove that Amelia had been my attacker. I could not even prove that I had been attacked. And it was strange that I had no mark, no sign upon my delicate skin, which chafes even at the touch of rough wool. There were no bruises, broken capillaries, or broken skin. Did that mean perhaps that my assailant had worn a special pair of gloves? I rejected outright Nigel's conviction that this experience had been a panicked dream or a hallucination. My aching neck was the proof of that. Why was he so eager to dismiss my fears? And what of the financial question to which he alluded at the end of our conversation? We were indeed living on my advance, as I had imagined, and Nigel at present had no funds of his own.

I decided I should keep an eye out and watch the girl even closer and, as luck would have it, over the next few days, I encountered her far more frequently than I should have liked, without ever having a direct confrontation with her. She deftly avoided a face-to-face clash with me, and yet seemed to have become ubiquitous. Turn a corner, and there she would be, slinking down a stairway with a mop and pail, followed by her albino familiar. A scent lingered when she passed, like sweet peonies rotting in a vase. Something mysterious and impalpable seemed to signal her passage through the rooms, a stirring in the chill air, soft footsteps approaching then retreating, a candle gleam reflected in a brass doorknob or across a sequence of darkened window panes. Quite unconsciously, I began to identify this feeling of her presence with that odd sensation I sometimes felt when I wandered the corridors alone—that tingling in my neck and shoulder—the slight perception of movement in the shadows glimpsed from the corner of my eye. The unpleasant suspicion of being watched, of being stalked, abided with me day and night.

How she managed to tread about so stealthily in those wooden-soled shoes of hers, I had no idea, but often she appeared in the upstairs corridor, as if out of nowhere. I could tell when she had been in my room on the pretext of dusting or mopping a floor. The objects on the dressing table or on my desk seemed to be arranged at sharper, more aggressive angles. A penknife or letter opener out of place would be positioned like a dagger ready to fly through the air and strike someone in the throat. Or while rambling about the lawn, I'd look up at the sound of a shutter opening and there she would be, with a rug beater in hand, savagely thrashing a carpet, and causing great clouds of dust and grit to drift down on my hair. As I ducked out of the way with a cry of protest, she would call down a lame apology, but the next morning the episode was likely to be repeated. And once, right after I had passed under Finestone's window, a terracotta pot of geraniums toppled off a ledge.

"Attenti!" Look out! she shouted as it smashed behind me.

I glanced up to see the tip of a white tail disappearing from the ledge back inside through the open window.

Manu, who was working nearby in the yard tying up a rose trellis, heard the crash and promptly came to investigate. Seeing the broken pot on the ground, he cursed.

"Ne ho avuto abbastanza! Stai attenta, ti ho detto!" I have had enough! Be careful! I said—he bellowed beneath the open window, shaking his fist, but the girl closed the shutters with a bang. "Such accident will not happen again," he apologized, sweeping up the shards with a broom, but I shook my head and walked off without reply. That girl was incorrigible.

That night at dinner when Amelia served us at table, I noted that both her wrists were black and blue. I winced to see the marks of her father's violence on those dainty arms. Both Clive and Finestone had noticed too and I could see they were upset, but I was secretly glad she had been punished for her wicked little joke. *True,* she had waited till I was out of the way before she knocked the pot off the ledge, and *possibly* it might have been a movement of the cat's which had dislodged the pot and caused it to fall; but I doubted this, simply because the animal was so scrawny and fragile and the pot must have weighed twenty pounds at least. It would have taken a good shove to move it. In any case, if I had suddenly stopped or turned round for any reason, I might have been struck directly on the head. The impact would have been fatal.

I had had envious rivals before, of course, and had always dismissed them with a shrug, a smile, and a toss of my head. The very thing was preposterous—to be challenged by a servant girl—and yet I could not deny the very poisonous feeling she created in me, not just dislike, but pure unmitigated hatred, tinged, I admit, by fear, one of the few emotions I was not used to indulging. I knew I was not safe as long as she was in this house, and yet there was nothing I could do to protect myself except lock my door and keep on my guard. Nigel thought my fears were the product of a hashish dream, and both Finestone and Clive were so smitten by the girl they could not see the truth about her. Danilo was a stranger in whom I could not confide. Under these circumstances, I was forced to keep my misgivings to myself and remain ever vigilant, ready for anything.

I soon realized that I was not the only one who watched the girl. Manu kept her under surveillance even more closely than I, and this, I slowly came to understand, was why he always managed to appear so quickly whenever there was damage to repair or apologies to give. He organized his chores so that he was often within hearing distance of wherever she might be, that is, when he was not needed in the park with the workmen. While she was in the kitchen, he would be in the vegetable patch right outside the back window, hoeing a row of beans or harvesting cabbages or turnips. When she did laundry in the yard, he'd be pruning hedges or raking leaves not far away. When she was busy doing the rooms, he might be somewhere in the upstairs corridor, stacking bundles of kindling, fixing a shutter, oiling a hinge. His prompt response and ubiquity were not reassuring. Rather he made me uneasy. I had no idea where he lived, for he was always about the villa or the grounds from sunrise till midnight. I presumed he had a cottage somewhere on the edge of the park, or up in the town. Amelia slept on a cot in a dank spare room off the kitchen.

His close supervision of the girl deepened my suspicions that she was mentally disturbed and needed to be kept in check, though I had no proof of this. I had convinced myself that she was somehow involved in the drowning of the child in the fountain. All I knew of that event was what Finestone had told me, and when I later pressed him for details, he changed the subject. In any case, I felt it wise to keep an eye on both Amelia and her father.

Manu was a burly fellow, stout, with a paunch protruding from his rough hand-woven shirts permeated with the smell of old sweat. His shaggy black hair, threaded with gray, was combed straight down over his forehead, partly hiding the bushy eyebrows that met above an impressive beaked nose. The huge callused hands with blackened nails looked prodigiously strong. In the shed behind the topiary, he kept an arsenal of tools: giant rusty shears, bludgeons, picks, rakes, shovels, sickles and scythes which he handled with expertise. I could only admire him as I watched him hacking at the hedges and shaping the topiary with a hand-scythe, forming cones, spirals, and rectangles from box-wood and cherry laurel bushes, with no need of a yardstick to attain geometrical perfection. I would not have wanted to meet him on a dark London street with his tools in hand, but it must be said he was generally perfectly civil to all of us, and obedi-ent whenever his services were required. Yet there was nothing servile about him. He was unscrupulous, canny, resilient and tough, rather like the Tuscia landscape itself. Indeed, these were the only qualities he and Amelia seemed to share. Her pallor, her willowy physique, her more refined features seemed to belong to another race altogether. Impossible to imagine how he had fa-thered such a creature. Perhaps her mother had not been a saint.

With a house full of men, among whom she had captivated first Finestone, and then Clive, Amelia made a point of parading about wherever they would be most likely to see her. Even Nigel, despite his professed dislike of the girl, seemed struck by her, and as we lounged on the grass, reading newspapers and drinking coffee in the morning when the weather permitted, he would put down his copy of *The Times* to watch her striding across the

lawn, inevitably followed by her little white cat, balancing a basket of wet laundry on her head on her way to hang up sheets on
the clothesline strung up in a sunny spot. She did have a graceful
carriage, and with her head held high, her blond hair streaming
in the gentle breeze, the willow basket perched unwaveringly on
her head, she looked like a figure in an antique cortege bearing
gifts of sacrifice to a god. Clive would stare at her in rapture as
she passed, then slip a pencil from his pocket and make a few
incomprehensible sketches on a notepad, sigh at them and put
them away.

The only one untouched by her charm was Danilo, but her
attitude toward him had changed within hours of his arrival.
The more he ignored her, the more disdainfully he behaved, the
more she craved his attention. He seemed to take especially cruel
delight in pointing out the social gulf between them, though
they might have shared a touch of complicity, as countrymen
among foreigners. After all, Danilo too had been born into the
lower classes. But he was Nigel's special guest and companion,
while she was merely a servant. It seemed to be his arrogance that
fired her attraction to our Roman friend. When in his presence
she smoldered, trembled, paled. She thrust out her bosom and
chewed her lower lip, but he remained singularly, nobly oblivi-
ous to her. These attitudes were communicated solely through
glances and gestures, which I as a novelist, love to study: a shrug,
a pinching of the lips, a nervous movement of the hand. I rarely
heard them speak, unless it was Amelia enquiring, *"Altro caffè,
Signò?"* or *"Volete ancora delle patate?"* More coffee, sir? Another
helping of potatoes? To which Danilo would mumble a curt, in-
articulate reply. That Amelia was infatuated with Danilo did not
mean, however, that she disdained the favor of her other admirers—Finestone and Clive—and his haughty demeanor did not
prevent him from watching her from the corner of his eye. For
he did.

After Clive's recent visit to my bedroom, albeit in a state of inebriation, my hopes for a revival of our previous intimacy remained unfulfilled. Polite and patronizing, he treated me with vague indulgence, the way you might humor a now tiresome but once favorite aunt grown senile. No rejection could have been crueler. I sought detachment, pondering the mutability of our affections which had been transformed in so short a time. Clive had deserted Nigel to seduce me, then had dropped me to pursue Amelia, who in the meantime kept him and Finestone teetering on a tightrope, while panting after Danilo. Bomarzo had somehow brought out the fickleness of our souls.

Colder too was the mute hostility that had arisen between Nigel and Clive. I could see that Nigel could not bear him now. Everything about the boy grated on Nigel's nerves—the scuffed, pointed toes of his cowboy boots; his nasal vowels; the devil-may-care pose he always struck, which I had learned was merely a pose; his pervading presumptuousness. Pretending to be a painter, an artist, when he was really just a boy who had never grown up who liked to draw pictures. Moreover, our young American friend had proven to be an artful sponger—a parasite, who got his living through his charm. Even his friendship with Finestone, I realized, could be viewed from that perspective, for by consolidating his relationship with the man from whom we were subletting our rooms, Clive had made sure that he had an ally outside our tight little threesome. Even if Nigel wished to send him away, and I had no reason to doubt this, Finestone surely would have allowed him to remain. And yet Clive was unconcerned with Finestone's reaction to his infatuation with Amelia, which was gradually becoming more and more visible to everyone. I had no doubt that soon Finestone, too, would be forced to open his eyes.

One night I was wakened by a strident caterwauling, a moaning and scratching from the library next door. That cat again! I heard a sputtering and ripping of rotten fabric, then the crash of glass shattering on the floor. Two cats in heat must have got in there and were now wreaking havoc among all those old fragile objects. First a thud and a crash, then a bang, and a yowl! At last I could bear it no more, and as another object smashed to pieces on the floor, decided to intervene, much as I dreaded a confrontation with two furious felines. I lit a candle and stepped out to the corridor. One of the double doors to the library was ajar and a light was burning within. Finestone, clad in long red underwear, stood in the corridor, looking toward the library with such an imbecilic look on his face, I thought he might be walking in his sleep. "Those cats!" I hissed. "I have had enough!" Finestone mumbled a timid warning in reply as I dashed the doors all the way open.

Shards of glass on the floor glinted in the gleam of my candle. Books and papers were strewn about the room. The heavy red velvet curtains had been half pulled from the rods, and a couple of chairs overturned. In the middle of this mess, Amelia, stark naked, lay stretched face down on the desk, gripping the edge while Clive mounted her from the rear, riding her wildly to ecstasy. With his head thrown back and his face mottled purple, gasping for breath, he collapsed as he climaxed, crumpling forward on top of her with a thud. She turned her face to the door, saw me, yawned and then smiled—a lascivious, annihilating smile of triumph that might turn a man to wax and a woman to stone. I backed out of the room and shut the door—turning round I saw that Finestone had retreated into his own room.

I had no doubt that this little show had been performed for my benefit, and, of course, also for Finestone's. By using the library for their tryst, Amelia had chosen a room from which neither of us could fail to hear them, but where Nigel and Danilo would not be disturbed. The following night I heard them upstairs in the attic, in Clive's studio, and thus it continued night after night. In a way, I admit, Amelia's victory was partly a relief to me. It must be clear to all now that I was no rival to her, and with so much nocturnal activity, surely she would have little energy left for mischief, and certainly no motive for it, at least toward me. I hoped now her spiteful jokes would cease and that I would be left in peace.

Such a definitive closure with Clive put me back where I had started at the very beginning of our trip to Italy: an aging writer in need of consolation and inspiration. What I required was idiot's distraction—the sort of play that rests one's mind to allow one's creative forces to recoup. Finestone at least had his research in the Sacred Wood; Nigel his Danilo; Clive his Amelia and his dreadful paintings. I, too, needed a hobby of some kind. I turned my attentions upon the parchment I had found, determined to unravel its mysteries.

The more I studied it, the more fascinated I became, and the more remote grew the possibility of concentrating on anything else, such as the novel I was supposed to be writing, for instance. Some of the images haunted me: *La Sorella Scalza*—the Barefoot Sister; *Le Madri in Lutto*—the Mothers in Mourning. It was uncanny how these enigmatic epithets seemed to hold veiled personal references to my own life. They sounded like signatures intended for me.

Aside from its resonance for my interior life, I tried to reason out the function the drawing might have had, the intentions of the artist who had drawn it. Could it be the sketch of a stage set for an opera, play or ballet that had at one time been performed in the Sacred Wood? Could it have been the instructions for a game, a sort of Snakes and Ladders once played in the park by Vicino's friends, who moved among the statues according to a roll of the dice, to be rewarded or punished as the dice decreed? The many inscriptions sounded like fragments of an incantation or a spell. Could the drawing be a sort of magic diagram for conjuring spirits? Several of the inscriptions contained alchemical terms. Did they hide a formula for making gold, as Finestone had hinted? What did MI BO mean? Could it stand for a person's name or a place name? Words came to mind:

Milano–Bologna. Or even *Mio Bosco,* My Wood. And what of the date, 1560? Surely Finestone could solve these mysteries, or at least offer informed speculation, but I wasn't ready to share my discovery with him yet. Vaguely, I thought it might be used for the framework of a story or as images for a poem I might write. But I couldn't grasp the connections between the figures, words, and pathways. The fact that *I* had found the parchment, and not Finestone, and the fact that I had found it so easily was, I believed, another signature. Through some strange quirk of destiny, *I* was intended to find it; it bore a message specifically for me which I must decode. At the moment, however, I hadn't a clue as to its meaning, but I thought that if I spent more time in the Sacred Wood, familiarizing myself with its statues and random trails, I might stumble upon a key.

§ § §

Outside the gates of the Sacred Wood, the surrounding hillsides were ablaze with yellow broom and luxuriant lilacs of lavender and white, but inside there was no spring. An indefinite season reigned of monotonous evergreens and weeds which never bloom. Still, with the milder weather, it was pleasant to be outdoors, and after breakfast I often accompanied Finestone through the Wood, where he inspected the previous day's labors and gave instructions to the men. Each day a new colossus or group of statues emerged from the tangled vegetation in the Sacred Wood as a hundred years or more of vines gone wild and rotting tree stumps were ripped out of the ground and burned away. The gardeners were not working systematically by clearing off an area completely before continuing on to the next one. They shifted from one spot to another, creating bald patches in the greenery from which the statues emerged, still covered in dirt and lichen which then had to be carefully brushed away.

Finestone claimed he had discovered only about a third of the statues which he believed the Sacred Wood contained. Many of the major figures, descriptions of which he had found in letters written by Orsini to his friends, were still to be located. I soon noted, however, that when giving orders to the men, the professor unfailingly seemed to know which hump of ivy and briars hid a statue and which concealed merely a mass of unshaped stone. I began to wonder if he was in possession of his own map with precise indications as to where the sculptures were situated. "Over there we will find a life-size elephant," he'd predict at breakfast. Or, "That will be a fountain of three graces." And inevitably, by the end of the day, when the workmen had thrown down their scythes and axes and had gone to rinse off their grime and sweat in the stream, those very figures had been identified. Once I asked him how he knew where to look, and he replied, "My nose."

As we roamed about the Wood together, Finestone gradually took me more into his confidence, allowing me to glimpse a bit of what his research consisted in and even engaging my assistance. One important task I helped him with was cleaning the inscriptions. For near every statue an inscription was usually found, sometimes chiseled on a crumbling patch of wall, sometimes etched on a nearby boulder. These had been placed here supposedly to guide the visitor in interpreting the gaping gorgons and winged monstrosities peopling the Sacred Wood. My task was to clean the earth and lichen away from the inscriptions with a wire brush, stain the carved letters with crushed beet juice so that they would stand out more clearly, then copy them down in a notebook. Like the statues themselves, the inscriptions teased my mind and often bore the unmistakable resonance of a signature attuned to my current situation: ANIMUS FIT QUIESCENDO PRUDENTIOR ERGO, said one.

"But what does it mean?" I asked, for I had forgotten much of the little Latin I once knew.

"Contemplative life tames the soul," Finestone explained with a sigh, and I suppose it was good advice for us both after the defections of Clive and Amelia, each of whom, however, at least during the daytime, had become unusually discreet about their liaison. I rarely saw them exchange a single word now, though whenever she was near, Clive watched her with a bedazzled, hangdog expression. Sometimes while I was working with Finestone, I would see them in the Sacred Wood, but never together. Amelia might be treading through the long grass with a basket on her way to gather wild asparagus or chicory which grew along the stream; Clive, after ten o'clock in the morning, might be setting up his easel near a statue. I thought it very likely that they might have a clandestine meeting place somewhere in the park, beyond where the men were working. Our other companions, Nigel and Danilo, never visited the Sacred Wood at all, at least as far as I could see. They preferred jaunts through the countryside in Nigel's Packard, which Danilo had learned to drive.

Another task I helped Finestone with was measuring the statues, not only their height and their maximum and minimum diameter, but also the distance from nose to mouth, or elbow to fingertip. These measurements were carefully noted down and from them Finestone made abstruse calculations which I did not understand at first. He explained that the proportions of the figures might be one of the keys to the identity of the artist who designed them. I realized that if I could learn more about Finestone's research, this would help further my own enquiry into the meaning of the drawing, but he was careful never to give away the name of the artist he believed had conceived the sculptures and their overall setting within the Sacred Wood. Sometimes I felt he intentionally led me astray, suggesting now one, now another school or artist—Vignola, Leoni, Salvati— who might have been responsible for the original design of the park. For each name, Finestone supplied an argument in their favor, only to rebut it completely.

"In any case," he went on, "not all these statues were made by the hand of a master carver or his pupils." He pointed out a nearby group of the three graces which had recently come to light. At first glance, with their hefty behinds and crude facial features, they certainly belied their name. "Those figures, for example, are obviously the work of unskilled beginners—perhaps even of slaves."

"Perhaps," I mused, "but there may be another interpretation, too: Those ladies may be a protest against the canon of physical beauty of his era with which he did not agree. Or, it might be a warning: don't be fooled by a pretty body and face. True grace may not always lie in a harmonious body and an attractive face. Or maybe he didn't like women's bodies."

"An interesting thought," he conceded.

We walked in silence for a few moments. " I believe," he said, "this Wood was an esoteric school for sculptors in which local students of diverse talents learned to carve with differing degrees of success. The school was probably presided over by a great genius of the period, who surely designed, if not sculpted with his own hand, at least three or four of the statues here and breathed his own life and spirit into them to make them immortal. Or at least left instructions on how that could be done. This accounts for the enormous psychic energy the Sacred Wood and its figures exude."

I supposed he was referring once again to the ancient Egyptian art of animating statues. It was a thrilling idea that such knowledge might have been passed down through the Renaissance and Baroque eras to us today. He had never spoken before of his theories in such detail and I was fascinated. "Will you share with me the secret of his name?"

He smiled. "I assure you it is an illustrious name and a momentous discovery. After I publish my findings, backed up by irrefutable evidence, the whole history of Renaissance art will have to be rewritten. The Sacred Wood is his most complex work, his spiritual testimony, his manifesto created near the end of his life. The statues you see here were the custodians of his most intimate thoughts, dreams, and emotions. And of course, of his demons."

We had discussed this previously, and I had not then received a satisfactory answer to my question, either. "And not those of his patron, Vicino Orsini? Didn't you say before that the statues might illustrate and commemorate events in Orsini's life?"

"That merely formed the pretext. The artist who sculpted these forms surely drew them from the depths of his own soul."

"It was, I'd say, a tormented one." I was thinking of the wrestling giants, trying to relate them to what I knew about the lives of the great artists of the Renaissance. Reflecting on Finestone's studies of proportion, I considered the possibility that Leonardo might be the artist he had in mind. But Leonardo had produced no sculptures that I had ever heard of, and probably was long dead before the first stones were carved in Bomarzo. From what I remembered of art history, the dates did not coincide. Moreover, the place was much too dark and perverse for the likes of Leonardo.

I wondered what bearing the parchment I had found might have on Finestone's research.

During his long stay at the villa before we had arrived, he had had time to inspect every drawer and cupboard, to study letters and other documents in the archives, analyze the sculptures' stylistic features and proportions, and match all this with the chronologies of artists' lives. Had he really found all the evidence he required? The drawing now in my possession might contain a clue to corroborate or refute his theories. Was I ungenerous in not wanting to share it with him? If indeed Finestone's discoveries were as momentous as he claimed, and if that drawing should offer significant proof of those claims, then it could be of great value, at least to him. Just how much might it be worth? While my mind was fiddling with these calculations, a sudden cry filled the mild spring air, and a workman came running toward us through the tall grass, waving his cap and shouting. "*Professore! Professore! La Bocca dell' Inferno!*"

"The Hell-Mouth?" I asked, recalling the figure on the drawing.

Eyes ablaze, Finestone grabbed my arm and hastened after the workman, his cane thumping along the ground.

Before us rose a steep flight of eroding steps carved from a single mass of rock, thickly carpeted with moss, leading straight into the flank of the hillside. Midway up, we could make out an opening, like the mouth of a cave, still partly curtained by tendrils of ivy and honeysuckle. Three men on ladders were at work chopping at the vegetation with hatchets and ripping off vines, slowly revealing a grotesque, ivy-bearded mask carved in the rock face splotched with large patches of moss. From inside came the echoing of voices as other workmen hacked away at the briars choking the entrance and filling the interior of the cavern.

"*Attenti! Una Vipera! Ammazzatela!*" Watch out! A viper! Kill it! cried Manu's voice from inside, and his shout of alarm was followed by the smash of a stone against the ground.

A hand reached through the ivy and tossed the snake out through the entrance and down the stairs where it landed precisely at our feet. I screamed.

"That's a viper all right," said Finestone bending down to inspect it through his bifocals. "A big one, too. A bite would kill you in minutes."

I stared, mesmerized, at the reptile. Its short, thick, ugly body with jagged brown markings and its triangular head certainly resembled the specimen preserved in a jar in the library. Then to my horror, I saw it writhe and attempt to rear its damaged head.

"Heavens, it's still alive!" I shrieked and stumbled back nearly slipping on the mossy trail.

"*Attenti! Attenti! Non vi muovete! Colpirà!*" Watch out! Don't move! It's about to strike! warned one of the men on the ladders, but before he could scramble down to our rescue, Finestone with unexpected promptness impaled the reptile with his cane. The snake writhed once more and then was still.

"Bel colpo, Professò!" cheered the men—and it had been a good shot, indeed. The snake was most decidedly dead. I gave a sigh of relief.

Fintestone withdrew his cane from the viper's body, kicked it aside, and showed me the tip of his improvised weapon, where a bright steel blade flashed, sharp as a razor. He squeezed the silver handle of his cane forcibly and the blade retracted with a snap.

"I told you this was good for discouraging snakes. I never go anywhere without it."

I must say I was surprised. I would not have thought him the type of man to carry a weapon far more deadly than any viper.

Enough ivy had now been cleared away from the façade of the cave so that the mask beneath was visible in its entirety. A hideous, giant, brown face with arching brows and eyes a-goggle observed us, more in astonishment than in wrath or horror, to have been awakened from his vegetative sleep. I was awed by the sight, of course, but I was even more amazed by the fact that I had already seen such a face before. In Paris. There is an artists' cabaret in Boulevard Clichy called *L'Enfer* where the façade of the building is shaped like a giant's mask similar to this one. To enter those smoky premises where all pleasures and transgressions may be sampled for a fee, you pass through a laughing mouth beneath bared teeth and gloating eyes. The artist who designed that façade could not have seen this Hell Mouth in Bomarzo, but might have seen sketches inspired by it, or even dreamed it. With one subtle difference. This mouth was open not in laughter, promising pleasure of the flesh. Like a vortex, the perfect O of its lips was designed to suck you in and keep you there.

A head poked out through the entrance. It belonged to Manu. "Safe to come in, now," he called to Finestone, "We kill the vipers in their nest."

Finestone offered me his arm as we climbed the slick stairs

and stepped over the threshold into a narrow chamber, illuminated by a torch fastened to the wall. The men crowded to one side so that we might view the chamber unencumbered. I shuddered at the sight of a small heap of dead vipers among the uprooted weeds and brambles near the entrance.

The first time I had entered the Sacred Wood with Finestone, I had felt a sharp drop in temperature, as though the sun had momentarily withdrawn its warmth and had cast me shivering in the shadows. This time standing in that dank chamber, I felt a similar chilling sensation, though an octave more intense: a sinking, cold, unredeemed feeling, an oppression accumulating in my breast. I felt I had been turned into a lifeless piece of clay.

My expression must have belied my extreme unease, for Manu asked if I were all right or if I wanted him to fetch a chair for me, which I declined.

This was most certainly not the first time I had visited a tomb or a crypt. I had been in Egyptian and Greek tombs before, which were darker, more claustrophobic, and far more suffocating than this, but they had not disturbed me in such a way. Nor was this dismal mental and physical sensation produced by anything one could see in the tomb, like moldering piles of bones or skulls one often finds in crypts which are certainly not cheery to contemplate. The Hell Mouth was empty except for a stone table, or perhaps it was an altar, this too covered in moss. There was no other decoration, furnishing, or inscription. The chamber had been hollowed out of a huge rock set in the flank of the hill and formed a perfect resonating chamber. Finestone hummed a note and the place vibrated eerily, lifting the hairs on the nape of my neck. He turned to me expectantly, as he did whenever he wished to sound out my reactions, but all I wanted was to leave that place immediately and return to the light of day. I turned back to the entrance, telling the professor I needed a bit of fresh air, and after a moment he followed me out again.

Outside the men had succeeded in clearing away the

remaining vines from the façade, where above the mouth an inscription was exposed. OGNI PENSIERO VOLA, meaning *Every thought flies.* I pondered this: Thoughts fly in time and space. Was this a confirmation of telepathy? That thoughts live outside the body and may be communicated across time? I had no ready solution. I imagined that the Hell Mouth must represent something special to Finestone, perhaps the proof he sought. Gravely, he surveyed the face and scribbled a bit in the notebook he always carried with him. I guessed he was studying the proportions of the features.

I was sure of one thing as we made our way down the stairs and back out of the Sacred Wood: The giants had promised us that our perspective would be turned upside down and that we would become impure. The turtle told us not to force or race, but to plod our way with our angelic burden. The ugly graces told us not to be dazzled or fooled by appearances. And now the Hell Mouth promised a deep plunge into the depths of our own ambiguity.

The Hell Mouth

CHAPTER SIX

We all have our shadow sides where the sun rarely penetrates, where shame, fear, guilt, and wrath lie concealed, rather like the statues of the Sacred Wood beneath their cancerous overgrowth of green. It is curious how some people and situations serve as catalysts to bring them to the fore—to expose them to the brutal but healing light of day. Thus was it with Danilo and myself.

At first our young Roman friend proved to be an amusing and soon useful addition to the household. Danilo never stayed more than two or three days at a time, and was always going back and forth to Florence or Rome and sometimes as far as Naples for his work, the nature of which was never disclosed to us. I assumed he had a roster of wealthy persons requiring his company or his services as "guide and driver," and he seemed to be paid very well for them. He wore well-cut suits, a gold watch, and an opal signet ring. His teeth and hands were beautifully kept and his shoes came from the best shops in Florence. He had mastered a smattering of French and German, though his accent was dreadful, as it was when he spoke English.

After dinner, Danilo would draw me into long discussions about art, religion, or politics, the point of which, I soon gathered, was to increase his knowledge of these subjects and enhance his vocabulary and English conversation skills. He would ask me to recommend books or plays for him to read, and after he had begun to trust me a little, he would ask me the meaning of a particular word or phrase he had come across while reading an English newspaper. Despite his profession, he was by no means extroverted and sociable, but rather reserved, which I appreciated.

Theater and opera were among his favorite subjects for conversation. We discovered that he had a nice tenor voice, and the two of us sang a few duets in the evenings; sometimes Finestone chimed in with his gruff baritone. When I learned that Danilo was intimately acquainted with the world of actors and artistes, I thought that as a frequenter of backstage doors and café concerts, he might be able to help me obtain certain substances to fuel my writing. After I made my request he was glad to oblige, though with each new delivery of hashish or absinthe, the price predictably increased and I began to run up a debt. To convince Nigel to dole me out bits of cash, I would claim I needed to send Amelia or Manu on an errand in the town or to go myself to buy stamps or send a telegram.

"To whom, my dear Daphne?" he would enquire when I used the latter excuse, and I would have to say that my senile aunt Melissa was having a birthday or a surgical operation.

He always complied without further questions and handed over a small bundle of bills, though he never gave me enough to repay my accumulating debt to Danilo.

Our arrangement was that when he returned from Rome, Danilo would leave a little cloth sack for me somewhere in the Sacred Wood, where no one was likely to find it. Sometimes our hiding place was behind a loose stone in an ivy-covered wall, sometimes deep in the recess of the mouths of Cerebus guarding the pathway, sometimes in the hollow of a rotten tree trunk. It was like an Easter egg hunt. I would surreptitiously retrieve the packet on one of my strolls through the Sacred Wood where I liked to come alone at odd hours: right after lunch while the whole villa snoozed, or late at night, lighting my way with a lantern. Now that the weather had improved and the days were longer, the gate to the park was generally left open during the day, so that we could all come and go at our leisure, but it was locked at night to discourage intruders. Finestone had given me my own key, but he had warned me to beware of stumbling into holes if I wandered there after dark. Another key was also left at the disposal of our whole little group in a desk drawer in the library, so Danilo could enter the Sacred Wood whenever he wished to deliver my packet even when the gate was locked.

During my solitary rambles, I learned all the byways and secondary trails weaving through the Wood: the grove where the workmen rested at lunchtime, sitting on stones beneath a giant oak, wearing little hats folded from cast-off newspapers to protect themselves from the sun; the grotto where they kept their tools along with a demijohn of wine with which they refreshed themselves; and a pool fed by the stream where the men came to wash, well hidden in the ferns. There was also a plot of medicinal herbs tended by Amelia, growing in a secluded, sunny spot and encircled by tall hedges of juniper and yew, where devil's weed bloomed profusely, alongside scrubby rue plants, rows of stinky valerian, nightshade, hemp, wormwood, and tobacco. It was a poisoner's delight.

Yet the Sacred Wood awakened my senses without the addition of drugs or wine. As I roamed at twilight about the *bosco,* I would meditate on the statues denuded of their greenery at the end of the day, pondering their link to the enigmatic phrases on the drawing I had found, trying to understand what meaning they had for me—and at the same time, seeking fresh ideas for the novel I was supposed to be writing. Each new statue suggested a perversity of mind and a certain savagery of temperament I thought might inspire the villain in my new novel, though the plot had not quite congealed. I let those grotesque images of lust and violence work upon my imagination. I was haunted by something Finestone had said: that the Sacred Wood might be the model of the artist's mind; the statues transmitters of thoughts, feelings, nightmares which might in turn influence our own moods and actions. Might that be the meaning of *Ogni Pensiero Vola?*

I was not the only visitor to the Wood in those in-between hours. On my evening walks I heard snuffling noises, creaking branches and whispering leaves, shuddering wings and scampering hooves. I thought it quite likely the place might be infested with wild boars and foxes or prowling tomcats from the town. At other times I caught sight of shrubs moving and treetops swishing on windless nights, where perhaps owls roosted, their eyes invisibly beaming forth in the night to locate their prey. Sometimes I caught the scent of burning leaves. Once I believed I saw the gleam of a cigarette through the bushes or smelled tobacco smoke. I knew I should be on my guard, and I was aware that someone else, besides Finestone and myself or the Wood's natural inhabitants, also wandered there in the evenings.

My former failed assassin, Amelia, left a slew of evidence behind her: small footprints in the mud, accompanied by feline paw prints; scraps of paper; the gold tips of my own cigarettes she had filched and smoked on the sly, for doubtless her father would have beaten her if he had seen her smoking. Once I found a pick covered in rust, which had been left out all night in the rain, hidden under a hedge. I took that as a warning, a signature, that I must be careful. The Sacred Wood would be a perfect setting for a murder in case she wished to fulfill her aborted attempts on my life. Another time I found a shred of plum-colored silk caught in a blackberry vine. The threads certainly looked as though they had been torn from my dress, but when I went back to my room to inspect the dress itself, I could find no sign of damage. I made notes on all these clues and added the threads and paper scraps to my box of signatures, thinking I might use them as material for my novel. I wondered if Amelia had followed me to the Wood to spy on me. Had she discovered my pact with Danilo? But as it turned out, she had her own reasons for frequenting the place, and these proved to be quite unrelated to me.

I would observe her watering and pruning the plants of her medicinal garden, picking prickly pods of devil's weed or digging up mayapples, plucking more innocuous boughs of bay laurel or tearing off handfuls of juniper berries to fill her basket. Sometimes she fed the stray cats that inhabited the park, leaving scraps of old spaghetti in a sheet of newspaper; or she sprinkled pocketsful of breadcrumbs on the ground for the birds. She never seemed to notice that she was being watched and I was careful to keep out of sight, for I feared retaliation should I be discovered. It soon became apparent that her real reason for being there was to meet someone in the bushes. But it wasn't Clive. Whoever it was spoke fluent Italian.

I never saw his face or shape. I only heard his voice indistinctly, arguing, pleading in a tremulous tone followed by her cruel, caustic replies, occasionally a slap, a thud, a groan, a cry, footsteps running down the path, sighs, imprecations. His or hers? I could not say. Once or twice, peering out from behind the bushes, I glimpsed her face as she darted back toward the villa—furious or desperate, horrified or disgusted? . . . It was impossible to tell anything except that she was in the throes of a strongly negative emotion.

It gave me a feeling of power to know that for once I had the advantage over her. I might be able to discover her secret and betray *her*. I was even in a position *to ambush* her if I wished, to repay her for her nasty little tricks! I was curious, of course, to identify her interlocutor. From the rapidity of the exchange I had overheard, he had to be Italian so that ruled out Clive, who could only stutter a few basic phrases—he relied on other forms of communication—as well as Finestone, who spoke Italian correctly, but slowly and tediously. Nor could it be Manu, for the voice was high-pitched, unlike Manu's raspy baritone. I could never make out the words, for they spoke too quickly. At first I presumed it must be some fellow from the town, or even one of her father's workmen to whom she gave assignations before returning to the villa where Clive would eagerly receive her favors. I had often noticed the young bare-chested gardeners watching her as she strode across the lawn with her laundry basket balanced on her head. Then one evening I found a shred of finely woven dark gray gabardine snagged in a bush and realized the man she met there was probably no workman but someone from town.

After Amelia had quit the scene, I would linger awhile before stepping out of the hedges, always too late to catch sight of him. He always managed to escape by means of a hidden path toward the exit, and I was left alone with my thoughts. With my little packet in hand, I would return to my room and, late at night when the others were asleep, I would open the window wide, so that no one would smell the smoke—luckily Nigel's room was down at the end of the hall—and prepare my entry into the kingdom of my muse. I was convinced that my imaginative powers would be strengthened by the nourishment Danilo had provided. Alas, I discovered this no longer was true. Once the delicious passivity had invaded my body vein by vein, I lay on the bed in a dream-like state, in which I was, however, by no means asleep for my brain flickered with colors, light, strange images. Who came to me then was not Edna Rutherford, or any other character from my next book, but Clive with his inexorable request. Again and again, I relived in dream our final night of love together. The body that pressed and prodded and sucked was as solid as my own. We soared, we whirled, we tumbled through a space illuminated by fiery gleams. With each downward swoop to earth, I lost consciousness as his body slipped away from mine.

How many nights did I relive this ecstasy before it became a nightmare? A dozen, I suppose, though with each descent to sleep, I found myself gasping for breath, each parting kiss a suffocation. When I woke hours later, my throat ached and my legs felt cold and heavy, and it took me a good half hour before I had the strength to climb out of the bed and stand before the mirror, where the first glimpse of myself for the day was always a brutal shock, far worse than the day before.

One morning a sound stirred my brain before the dream had subsided. My eyes were still closed, and I was afloat in the ether with the throbbing heat of my lover's body weighing upon me. I was ready to sink back to earth. But this morning I was at once aware of my own body in the bed, of the room where I lay and the position of its furniture around me. Birdsong intensified in the trees outside my window as the dawn crept across my eyelids. The act had just concluded but our bodies were still fused. I must have lived a thousand moments like this one in the past, that drowsy moment when you want to curl into the comfort of your lover's warmth and sleep till noon.

The villa was silent, but I heard the clock in the library next door strike six times, nearly time for Amelia to be up and about her chores, for Manu to begin splitting logs for the stove outside the kitchen door. Perhaps I murmured the name "Clive—" or of some other man from a more remote day—and it was the sound of my own voice that brought me back to myself.

My hands rested on my lover's haunches. Idly, I caressed the small of his back, my fingers grazed, then clasped more firmly an appendage sprouting just above the cleft of his buttocks, which certainly should not have been there. Thick, muscular, covered with a fine fuzz like the antlers of a young buck, the consistency and diameter of a tennis racquet. There was no mistaking what it was. Good God, *a tail!*

As my eyes shot open in astonished horror, my gaze was absorbed into the preternatural glare of two amber pupils boring into me. I did not or perhaps could not see the face itself. I cannot describe what I saw in those depths which drew me in as to a vacuum. At the very bottom lurked a blackness like the unquiet waters of a northern sea at night, where I might very well drown within seconds, engulfed by overwhelming pain and sorrow. Then a burning tongue, sharply pronged as a cake fork, stabbed itself between my lips till blood trickled from my mouth staining the pillows. How I managed to free myself from this incubus, I do not know, but with effort I disentangled myself from it. I watched it rise from the bed, stretch its dark, luxurious wings, then with a muffled whirring sound, it was gone. Where it had gone, I cannot say, certainly not out the window, for the shutters were closed.

I woke hours later, my whole body numb. My ears roared; my throat was scorched. A painful cold sore had formed in my mouth. My fingers felt like wax or rubber until I finally managed to rub life back into them. Half-dazed I tried to sit up and take stock of myself. The immaculate bedclothes were unruffled, the unstained pillows as perfectly stacked as though for a queen in her coffin; but my silk negligee was glued to my body with sweat and I was shivering with fever. I swung my legs over the side of the bed, pushed up on wobbling knees, but could not stand up. The dresser, the desk, the window, whirled round and round as the portrait of Giulia Farnese, reflected as a multitude in the mirror opposite the bed, stared down at me in a chorus of sneers. I collapsed groaning back into bed.

I realized I had caught a flu and possibly an ear infection upsetting my balance, and the fever had brought me a delirious and hideous dream. I furiously rang the brass bell on my bedside table, doubting that anyone would come, but to my amazement five minutes later Amelia opened the door, bearing a tray with a pot of tea. She was almost smiling.

"Avete dormito più del solito, Signò." You've slept even later than usual, she said, in a surprisingly civil tone, setting the tray down and going to open the shutters.

The bright light hurt like hot stones pressed against my eyelids. I tried to sit up, but couldn't heave myself up. I asked her to bring the tea to the bedside table, but she ignored my request, and removing a rag from her pocket, went about dusting the furniture as though I were not there. She stopped, bent over to retrieve something from the floor and held it up to the light streaming in through the window. It was a large, dark feather.

"Rather big owl must have come down the chimney," she said, and was about to slip the plume into her apron pocket.

"Leave it be," I croaked, remembering my winged lover. "Put it on my desk."

Hesitating, she glared at me, but then shrugged and obeyed. "It's only a feather from a dirty old bird. What good is it?"

"Now bring me my tea," I said, "I'm ill." And for once the girl did as she was told. She assisted me, rather ungraciously, and helped prop me up on the pillows, then set the tray in my lap and left the room.

I downed the boiling brew without sugar in one gulp, the best remedy I know for a painful throat. It cauterizes the tonsils killing all germs. Then I sipped a second cup with plenty of milk and sugar meditatively, letting my fingers draw warmth from the heat of the cup. The horrors of the nightmare had slithered away and I was able to reflect on them more objectively. I feared I was on the brink of a new crisis, or would be soon. Danilo's supply was tainted with some poisonous substance, that was clear, which could possibly be fatal if I kept on consuming it.

Those night flights had become riskier and more terrifying, and now I had discovered the true nature of my hallucinatory partner and the cause of his arising. Could I bear to be engulfed again by the bleak waters awash in those pitiless eyes? In a searing glimpse, I had seen the pain of the world in which my own pain was but an infinitesimal drop—and yet it was unbearable in itself. It seemed to me I had heard the cries of the damned, the lost, and the abandoned who had succumbed to those depths. It would be so easy to close my eyes and join them, sinking into that morass. And yet the faintest voice, more an echo than a voice, more an intuition than an echo—Edmund? Peter? Persephone?—urged me to resist.

A ray of light warmed my eyelids and my chest, stirring in my bosom an animal gratitude. Curiosity was not yet dead in me. Nor was the desire to see Amelia put in her rightful place, two reasons that might still make it worthwhile to get up and face the day.

The tea and sugar had revived me. I managed to get out of bed and go to the desk where I examined the feather. It was nearly a foot long, brownish purple, tipped with a zigzag trim of white, not unlike a feather from a turkey's wing. It seemed odd that the feather from the wing of a supernatural and possibly demonic being should look and feel so much like a common turkey feather. Still, it had an odd metallic sheen to it, and when for a moment I caressed my cheek with it, a shiver rippled up along my spine. I wrapped it in a piece of paper and put it in my box of signatures which I kept in the same drawer where I had hidden the drawing of the Sacred Wood.

After breakfast I dragged myself on very weak legs next door to the library. Among the shelves, I had previously noted several books of engraved plates illustrating the local wildlife of the Tuscia and Cimini Hills, and I thought I might have a peek through them to see if I could identify the bird from which this feather had come. I lugged a few volumes back to my room where I lay in bed, examining the plates, though the little clouds of dust released by every turn of the page made me sneeze dreadfully. There were many fascinating species: hoopoes, mute ducks, swans, herons, owls and vultures—all pictured amid craggy gorges and ruined towers; but the feather I had found did not seem to belong to any of them. The effort rather wore me out and I pushed the books aside. I slept until dinnertime when Amelia brought me a bowl of broth and some sort of creamed fowl on toast, tasting, I must say, very much like turkey.

CHAPTER SEVEN

The fever lasted three days and quite cured me of the desire to smoke any more of Danilo's hellish mixture, at least for the time being, or to drink any more of his dubiously distilled absinthe. My throat felt raw, my lungs scorched and ached as I shivered and sweated beneath a mound of moldy eiderdowns. Amelia dutifully brought me broth and tea, boiled eggs, toast, and tisanes. I suppose I should have been afraid of being poisoned, but I was too weak to resist. Against my expectations, I recovered quickly, while Clive, Nigel, and Finestone left me alone and kept out of harm's way, fearing, I suppose, that I might infect them. Edmund, after all, had died of the Spanish flu and Nigel had a horror of communicable diseases. Only Danilo came to see how I was, once to bring chocolates, another time a bouquet of pearly pink peonies. I suppose his conscience bothered him for selling me that deadly paste probably adulterated with paint thinner or some other household poison. When I was well enough to get up again, the good weather had finally come to stay, but the atmosphere in the villa had changed.

I immediately noted that Finestone was looking gray and unshaven and was always grumpy at mealtimes. He no longer chatted with me pleasantly over coffee on Neoplatonic themes or told amusing tales about the Etruscans, and his relationship with Clive, once so fond, now seemed strained. He spent much more time alone, and the typing in the library had become more intense as he pounded his Smith Corona for hours. It was not hard to guess that the reason for his ill humor was Amelia's total defection in favor of Clive. She had ceased to show the scholar the special courtesy he had previously enjoyed and no doubt had put an end to her nightly visits. She had even abandoned her daily routine of chores for him: his shirts looked rumpled, cuffs grimy, his trousers unbrushed, and his socks mismatched. In the morning, I would sometimes find him in the kitchen, making his own coffee as Amelia had neglected to prepare it for him, and once I saw him washing out socks and underwear under the kitchen tap.

Nigel, instead, appeared to be in the best of spirits, and spent most of the days out on drives through the countryside, either alone, or in the company of Danilo on his visits up from Rome, which had now protracted into longer periods of several days at a time. Only Clive seemed unchanged, always undaunted, always content, locked in his studio painting up a storm and making love to our servant all night in his attic studio. Amelia, it seemed, clearly had him in thrall.

I tried to get back to my book, but I felt too listless to hold the pen for long and yearned to spend time out of doors in the blessed sunshine, which I am sure was indeed what the doctor would have ordered, as long as I did not take a chill at night or overexert myself. Nigel and Danilo obliged me by taking me with them sometimes on their excursions, and occasionally both Finestone and Clive tagged along. Thanks to his previous employment as a guide for rich foreign tourists in Rome who wanted to explore the outlying areas, Danilo knew every nook and cranny of the Tuscia countryside—palaces built by popes and grand old Roman families, statuary gardens with luxurious displays of azaleas and magnolias now all in bloom, boxwood labyrinths to tread. We picnicked at the base of dilapidated towers in the middle of the woods, and rattled in the Packard along the cobbled streets of quaint villages that looked as though they were about to tumble off the cliffs on which they clung. One day we went as far as Tarquinia to visit the famous Etruscan tombs occupying the flank of an arid hill near the sea. It was a relief to see the dancing Mediterranean again. I felt I had been landlocked or forest-bound too long in Vicino's gloomy Sacred Wood.

Right outside the entrance to the tomb area in Tarquinia stood a low cottage where a lazy yellow dog tied to a post lay curled up asleep. Nearby, a few sad-looking sheep grazed on a stubble of grass. As we made our way toward the tombs, the dog woke barking and a little boy ran out of the hovel to greet us, babbling in a mixture of German and English, and shaking a ring of rusty keys in our faces. This was the caretaker's son who agreed to take us down into the tombs in exchange for an exorbitant fee. The Etruscans seemed to be even more in vogue than ever. Hence they had become more expensive to visit.

The boy led the way across a vast, barren field where dozens of small-roofed structures stood, rather like sentry boxes. These were the entrances to the tombs, which were accessed through shafts cut diagonally in the rocky hillside. Each entrance was closed by an iron door and a padlock. Our guide opened the first one we had come to and shone his lantern into the narrow entry where steep stairs disappeared into the blackness. Stepping in from the bright sunlight, one was quite blinded at first. The drop in temperature inside the dank entryway brought a shiver to my bones.

The boy distributed candles to each of us to light our way down. As we descended, he chattered on in broken English about some English tourists he had recently accompanied by the name of Lorenzo and Brewster and wondered if we knew them, which we did not. At least on the first ramp of stairs, we were aided by the light streaming in through the open doorway behind us; but midway down we were plunged into darkness, except for the dim gleam of our candles and of Finestone's white jacket which almost seemed to glow in the dark. Every now and then, Finestone paused on the stairs to brush a spiderweb from his sleeve or from the crown of his hat. I thus gathered that he disliked spiders as much as I did.

At the very bottom, we found ourselves in a womb-shaped chamber hollowed out of the rock. The boy lifted his kerosene lantern to illumine the burial rooms. Stone couches plastered with lichen lined the walls which were painted with eerie scenes of the underworld. The frescoes were in a pitiful state, peeling and scabby, yet in a few striking ones, the figures and the intent of the artist who had conceived them were still sharply visible. Red dancers whirled around a banquet where men and women lounging on couches supped cheerfully and drank from brimming chalices. Solitary travelers took leave of their families to begin a long journey toward the realm of forgetting, the door to which was guarded by a pair of blue-winged devils.

Some were single tombs, others had multiple chambers. The boy warned us to stick together and not to venture alone into any of the corridors leading off and concluded with the unpleasant story of a German tourist who had disobeyed this suggestion and fallen down a shaft and broken his leg. It had taken more than half a day to hoist him back up again.

After we had visited four or five tombs, I began to grow tired. They all looked and smelled the same, it seemed to me, of dank and moldy earth and stone and not terribly healthy for my lungs given my recent recovery from the flu. Many of the frescoes were too damaged to make much of in the faint light of our candles, though admittedly they could be richly imagined. It was also a perfect environment for bats, spiders, and scorpions, to say nothing of rats. I was still feeling a bit fatigued after my illness, and while the others went on ahead to explore a tomb with several adjoining chambers, I sat down on one of the stone couches to rest and rub my heel, where an annoying blister had formed. I was well in sight of the iron stairway, so I would be able to join them for the extenuating climb back up the moment they had finished their tour. I could also hear them nearby talking in the next chamber. The echo of their voices was quite audible underground as an indistinct murmur in the midst of which I recognized intermittently the tones of Finestone's and Clive's voices.

I don't know how long I sat there; one loses one's sense of time in such places. I let myself go in a state of reverie inspired by the tomb paintings we had seen: the river of forgetting, the journey of the dead. I thought of my dead loved ones, dwellers in an underworld, their mouths full of darkness and dust. The Etruscans perhaps revolted against the classical concept of the afterlife as a sunless, joyless realm. For them with their spinning dancers and wine cups, death appeared to be one endless party. Yet the solemn feeling in these tombs belied such a belief.

A noise nearby, only half perceived, perhaps the soft thud of a stone falling to the ground, must have jostled me from these melancholy thoughts, and I realized I couldn't hear my friends' voices any more. Yet not more than a quarter of an hour could have passed since I had sat down to rest. Nervously, I called out to them but no one replied. I got up, a bit puzzled as to why they hadn't come back for me. Then I heard the murmuring of voices again, farther away, and relieved, but still anxious, I decided to follow them.

There came a distinct sound from one of the side rooms. It was more like the flapping or rustling of cloth—not like the noise made by bats or rats, but more like the sound of someone shaking the crumbs off a tablecloth or sand from a blanket after lying on a beach. Immediately in my imagination, I pictured Finestone vigorously sweeping the dust and spider webs from his sleeves, which I had noted him doing several times as we were making our way down the stairs.

"Professor Finestone! Here I am!" I cried, and I stepped into the room where my candle caught the gleam of two amber eyes. I lifted the candle higher and made out the virile, muscular form of a giant winged being. As those yellow eyes locked on mine, I felt the life force being sucked from me. Then something or someone touched me, or rather scratched me on my shoulder. I screamed, dropped the candle, and found myself in total darkness.

I sank to my knees and felt the ground, searching for the candle, but my hand only found a heap of soft feathers. Thinking I had touched some living or dead creature, I cried out again, expecting, I suppose to be bitten by the thing on the ground or perhaps struck down at any moment by whatever it was that had touched my shoulder, but moments passed and nothing happened. With uncharacteristic presence of mind, I remembered I probably had some matches in my pocket, and digging out the little tin box, I struck one. In the bright flare, I saw that the yellow eyes had changed their position and were now staring at me from the opposite wall. I also saw that they were firmly embedded in the round, fluffy face of a rather large owl who winked at me once before the flame went out. The flare from my next match allowed me to locate my candle which had rolled into a corner. I lit it with my third and last match.

I examined the creature depicted on the side wall of the tomb, tracing the bold lines of its design with my tiny flame. Though the frescoed face was half scratched away and eroded by lichen, in the magnificent muscular form that remained, I recognized the winged semblance of my nocturnal lover. I had to laugh at myself then, momentarily relieved of my fear of a supernatural aggressor. At his feet lay a pile of plumage, probably the carcass of a bird dragged in and devoured by a fox. The heap of feathers seemed to be of the same coloration as the feather I had found in my room—dark with a jagged white tip, so I plucked a few plumes from the heap and put them in my handbag. Then I decided it was high time I returned to the staircase and found my way back up to meet the others outside. They were surely wondering what had become of me. Sheepishly, I remembered the fate of the hapless, disobedient German.

The room seemed larger now as the darkness expanded

around me, and the floor was treacherously uneven, so my progress was slow. Groping along the walls, looking for the opening through which I had entered, I realized that I had lost my bearings. I discovered not one but three doors leading out of the chamber where I now found myself. From which one had I entered? I tried them each in turn, but none of them was as close to the stairs as I recalled. As the minutes ticked by and my candle burned low, the anguish of being lost down there in the tomb intensified. At last I found the iron stairway, which was not at all where I remembered it being, and made my way up as quickly as I could. Midway up, I saw that the door to the outside had been shut, and I was seized with real terror then, for I feared I had been locked in. I bounded up the stairs, though God knows from where I summoned the strength to do so, for at this point, I was exhausted.

To my great relief, when I reached the top, I found the iron door unlocked, but it took another great burst of strength, especially considering my debilitated condition, to push it all the way open. Outside, I was astonished to see that twilight was falling fast. Purplish clouds shot with gold curdled the horizon. Our little party had arrived at the tombs shortly before midday, and I had calculated that no more than three hours had passed, including my misadventure, which was, indeed, completely my own fault for disobeying the guide's instructions. I looked about for the others, though the field was deserted. All the doors to the tombs were closed. A chill wind was rising and crows swooped low, casting long, jagged shadows on the beaten earth. The place looked unfamiliar somehow, and I understood then that I must have exited from a different stairway from the one we had originally descended. I could not see the boy's cottage from where I stood, or even the road where we had left the car, both of which were clearly visible from the entrance to the last tomb we had visited. Convinced that I had been left behind, I frantically began to run in among the tombs shouting for help, and I nearly twisted my ankle, stumbling on a stone. The barking of a dog far away was the only reply, and I headed, limping, in that direction, remembering that I had seen a dog tied up outside the caretaker's cottage. It seemed to me that I could smell smoke in the wind and the odors of food cooking.

At last, two figures appeared in the distance and began to run toward me across the barren turf, and moments later I was sobbing in Nigel's arms. Danilo trailed behind.

"Daphne! Darling! Are you all right? You look shaken. What on earth happened to you? We have been fraught with worry!" Nigel looked distraught and I felt so immensely comforted by his concern that I cried even harder.

"I was afraid you had left me here," I sniffled.

"What nonsense!"

Nigel handed me his silk handkerchief, which I gratefully accepted. I wiped my face and blew my nose.

"We were beginning to think you had stumbled into a hole like the proverbial German tourist. Finestone was so worried he was about to go fetch the police, so Danilo and I decided to make one last effort to find you. We have been wandering around these tombs, looking for you for hours. You must be dying of hunger! We certainly are. The people at that cottage have prepared us some food."

My teeth chattered as I sobbed, overcome with relief. My illness had rendered me emotionally very vulnerable, and I felt dreadfully cold, too. Those hours in the dank tomb had chilled me through and my bones were aching. Seeing me shivering, Danilo immediately slipped off his jacket and put it around my shoulders. We made our way toward the cottage now, which was a good half-mile walk. I hobbled along, leaning on Nigel's arm, amazed that I had managed to wander so far from the others. I had had absolutely no sense of the distance I had traveled underground, no sense of the time passing.

Clive and Finestone were sitting at a table set up beneath

a wisteria pergola in full bloom out front of the little cottage. Nearby a bonfire blazed and lamb chops were grilling, sending up coils of thick, fatty smoke. Our little guide's family had spread a banquet for us on a homespun cloth: rounds of pecorino cheese ranging from fresh to well-aged, flasks of red wine, hunks of coarse brown peasant bread. From the pile of gnawed bones on Clive's plate, it looked as though the meal was well in progress. Seeing me, both men cheered. Finestone rose to give me his seat, which was closest to the fire, and Clive lifted his glass in a toast. He had already had quite a bit to drink.

"Daphne where did you disappear to? One second Finestone said you were there right behind him and the next moment," he snapped his fingers—"Poof! You were gone! Vanished like a ghost!" and he laughed, strangely, I thought, with a glitter in his eyes I did not like.

"I took a wrong turn," I said and began to devour the bread and fruit the boy's mother brought to me on a chipped earthenware plate. The boy seemed particularly pleased to see me again, and rushed back and forth to fill up my glass and bring me slabs of toasted bread rubbed with garlic and dribbled with bitter olive oil. I daresay his parents would have faced serious consequences with the tourist authorities if I had disappeared definitively into the tombs. That is, if my disappearance had been reported by anyone.

The meal of cheese, meat, and red wine revived me, and as we made the long drive home to Bomarzo, I dozed in the backseat, crowded in between Finestone and Clive with my head propped on the most readily available shoulder, which was Finestone's. The professor stroked my forehead with unexpected tenderness and bid me sleep. And if I dreamed of tombs and winged beings that night I do not remember.

CHAPTER EIGHT

I thought it was very likely that the handful of tiny feathers I had gathered from the floor of the tomb had come from the same species of bird as the large plume Amelia had found in my room while dusting on the morning I had fallen ill. They were brown with a purplish sheen, tipped with a zigzag of white speckles. The next morning, when I opened the bottom drawer of my desk to take out the box of signatures where I had put the feather, I saw that the objects in my drawer had been disarranged. I am an extremely orderly person, almost obsessive in the way I keep things. The folders full of my letter paper and envelopes, my bag of pens and pencils and sheets of blotting paper were not in the way I had left them. Alarmed, I checked the bottom of the drawer where I kept the drawing of the Sacred Wood carefully wrapped in newspaper. It was still in its place, but the papers piled on top of it appeared slightly out of order and I had no doubt other hands had touched them. But something *was* missing, I immediately noted, as I opened the box of signatures: the doll's head had vanished. I searched carefully through the box and then through all the drawers again, but it was gone. Was this another of Amelia's acts of petty thievery? And why would she have stolen the doll's head? That in itself seemed a singularly ominous gesture, a sort of warning. Then I noticed that the packet with the feather had also disappeared.

Whoever had taken these things from my drawer could very easily have found my map of the Sacred Wood. Removing the sketch from its newspaper wrapping, I puzzled over it a moment, then noticed a single long blond hair glistening smack in the middle. That was proof enough, I thought, as I inspected the hair, then burned it in the flame of a match. That girl seemed to have made a regular habit of going through my things.

I sat down to scrutinize the parchment again, and remarked on how precisely the dotted lines seemed to retrace Finestone's recent discoveries of the statues, or at least of the major ones he had shown me. A line of dots led first to the sphinx, then to the battling giants from where little arrows pointed straight to the Hell Mouth. An itinerary was becoming apparent, a sort of lop-sided spiral, a pilgrim's progress, leading from one statue to the other, which Finestone obviously was familiar with. This confirmed to me that he too possessed a copy of this very drawing or at least of the information or the instructions it summarized. Random dots led away from the Hell Mouth toward the bare-breasted statue in the center, which, I somehow sensed, held the key to the mystery, representing the X spot where the treasure, in whatever form, would finally be found. It was a point of arrival, for no other trails were marked beyond this statue.

I spilled the objects out of the box and scattered them across the map of the Sacred Wood. Here outside the gate I had found the doll's head, now missing. There by the wrestling giants, I had found the pearl button. Not far from the fountain, I had come across a slew of cigarette ends and a swatch of cloth from a man's trouser leg or jacket sleeve. Here was Amelia's poison garden. Nearby I had found a rusted pick left under a hedge and some threads of purple silk. And in a fountain ten years ago, a child had been drowned. What were the links among these disjointed signs?

Signatures are like unopened letters slipped under the door, or if you will, like unpaid bills accumulating unpleasantly when you have ignored them too long. Sooner or later your creditor comes calling and you find yourself in a mess. What event was in preparation? Surely it regarded me directly and was no doubt connected to the attacks I had already experienced, or so I had believed till now, at the hands of our maid, Amelia.

Yet thinking back on my adventure in Tarquinia, I felt confused, ill-at-ease with myself and with my own interpretation of the facts. For example, I could not say exactly what had happened to me down in the tomb. It was impossible for me to explain how I had managed to wander so far underground as to come out many hours later in a completely different place from where I had entered, when I had hardly been aware of time passing at all. Had I been sleep-walking, or was I in some altered state of consciousness? Had I had been ensnared by a hallucination? Was the experience an aftermath of Danilo's deadly smoke, which I hadn't touched for days? It's true that at times I felt a peculiar craving which made my head spin and gave me nausea, but I tried to ignore it. Could the whole bizarre experience have been a mental symptom of withdrawal as Nigel had suggested? Who or what had touched my shoulder in the tomb? That owl I had seen? Or a bat? A flake of earth falling from the ceiling? Or were all these eerie sensations simply the product of an overwrought imagination?

Since that incident in the bath, I had suspected that Amelia wished to harm me or give me a very bad fright, but the girl obviously had nothing to do with this last adventure in the tombs. Need I revise my interpretation of the signs leading to this moment? What of Nigel and the others? Why had they not turned back immediately when they had discovered I was not with them? Had that been a conscious decision? Clive's perhaps? Or Nigel's? Had one of them meant to lose me on purpose? To give me, perhaps, a scare? They *had* come to fetch me in end, I reminded myself. But I was not convinced of their innocence, and this made me consider both Clive and Nigel in a new light. And what of my winged companion? I shuddered as I remembered the yellow glint in the owl's eyes, so much like the incandescent gaze of that creature in my dream. Was he the epitome of a delusional state to which all these other events were related?

These questions would have to remain unanswered for the moment, but one thing was clear to me now. The sketch was no longer safe in my desk drawer. It was necessary to conceal it from Amelia, for she was still in the habit of rifling through my belongings and continued to pose a threat to my possessions, if not to my person. I looked about the room, searching for a suitable hiding place; then realized what better place than where I had originally found it? I moved the dresser away from the wall, and wrapping the sketch up again tightly in a sheaf of newspaper, slipped it into the crevice in behind the backboards of the dresser.

The gong sounded for lunch and I went to join the others, although the atmosphere at table was strained. At the conclusion of the meal I did not stay for coffee or cognac, which was to be served on the lawn, and came straight back upstairs, but as I was about to open my door, a noise caught my attention. I turned round and saw that curtains to the icon angel were open and that the painting itself hung askew in its niche down at the end of the hall. It looked almost as though someone had removed the painting from its place then had hurriedly hung it back up again without bothering to straighten it. I approached the icon and studied the haggard face. The dull browns and grays yet naturalistic detail of the snake's scales and of the angel's feathers created a connection between the two figures, I thought, as though the angel were a further phase in the evolution of the former, like a moth broken forth from a cocoon. Musing on this, I reached out to straighten it, and was startled by a voice behind me: *"Cosa fate?" What are you doing*? Whirling round, I found Amelia staring sternly at me with hands on hips. It was the first time in days we had spoken face to face. I was so taken back I felt intimidated.

"Nothing," I said, and retreated toward my room. Before opening my door, I glanced back at the icon. Amelia had disappeared and the painting now hung straight.

Later that afternoon while my companions indulged in their inviolable siesta, and for once neither Clive's restless pacing in the attic or Finestone's manic typing next door could be heard, I slipped out of the villa and proceeded toward the park where the workmen had not yet resumed their labors after pausing for lunch. It was a strange sunny day with cumulus clouds sweeping across the sky, covering the sun for a moment and casting flickering shadows on the ground, only to be swept onwards again leaving a stretch of cloudless blue.

I had not been back to the Sacred Wood since I had recovered from my illness, and I was curious to see what work had been done on the statues in the meantime, to see how new discoveries tallied with the map. No boons did I expect to collect out of the mouth of beasts; however, Danilo's hallucinatory treats were something I would have to forego if I desired to keep my sanity. I had told the boy not to bring me anymore, explaining that as I was still suffering from a cough, I found it unpleasant to smoke. To his credit, he did not press me to change my mind.

I rambled through the Wood, seeking fresh inspiration. After all, I reasoned to myself, opium, hashish, or absinthe merely stimulate a process in the mind which exists in potential without them: the propensity for remote viewing, the ability to perceive the invisible. Surely other non-chemical forms of stimulus exist. The statues in the Sacred Wood, I felt, had sprung from the fertile kingdom of imagination, from some seedbed of universal truth or vision with which I must enter more deeply in contact if I were to succeed in decoding the signatures breaking upon me with increased impetus like waves upon a shore.

Pushing through the gate, crawling my way through the weeds and bushes, I caught sight of a lithe figure stealing through the shrubs up ahead of me. Amelia again, this time in inexplicable haste. In addition to the basket she always carried with her while wandering in the Sacred Wood, today, slung across her shoulder, she also carried a hoe. Behind her trailed the cat.

Keeping well out of sight, I followed her to the predictable destination: the poison garden she tended in the center of the wood, shielded by a tall hedge. Here I hid behind the bushes and watched as the girl quickly set to unburying something from the ground from in between the many apples. As she brushed the dirt away from a baby-sized bundle she had extracted from the earth, I had to bite my lip to restrain a cry of horror. Here was evidence of what I had feared! The girl had murderous inclinations. She laid the bundle gently in her basket and hurried out again along a path which ended at an exit giving out into the woods beyond the estate walls.

I recognized the place, for the spot was marked on the drawing, and from Finestone's descriptions of the surrounding countryside, I surmised that this was where the trail began leading up a ridge to the Etruscan ruins above the park which he had visited with Clive. Unlike the imposing gate of stone and iron of the main entrance, this discreet exit was simply an opening in the wall, closed off with a bit of fencing nailed to a post, with no padlock or other closure to keep it locked, all half hidden by tendrils of Virginia creeper. Anyone at any time might sneak in and out unobserved. Was it wise to follow? I had never ventured into the forest of ilex and oak trees outlying the walls of the Sacred Wood, partly discouraged, I suppose, by Finestone's stories of snakes, of which I had seen living confirmation. The less-frequented trails were sure to be invested with vipers and perhaps wild boars. As I stood pondering what I should do, Amelia was hurtling up the steep slope at breakneck speed, with her little cat scuttling along, sometimes ahead, sometimes behind, tale bobbing in the air, as if the animal shared her haste and her intention. When she was midway up, I decided I was game, and stepped through the opening in pursuit.

The way was steep and slippery with acorns, pebbles, and slick mud, but spring was not absent here. Anemones, periwinkles, cyclamen flickered amid the dead leaves. Here and there in sunnier spots wild apple trees were decked out in pink. I managed to keep pace with Amelia until I reached the top of a ridge behind which rose the wall of the gorge. I found myself in a place whose magic was not created by art, but by recondite forces of nature. Here were giant boulders thickly furred in moss, scaly with orange lichen, where violets, dandelions, ferns, and anemones burst forth in profusion from every crevice. The boulders half concealed a series of small caves where inside I saw roughhewn sarcophagi and rectangular troughs carved in the rock, now filled with stagnant rainwater and dead leaves. The boulders and cave walls were covered with the well-worn traces of ancient inscriptions, now illegible. Given the size of the troughs and sarcophagi, I surmised that the place must have been at one time a children's cemetery, and remembering the words on the map—The Mothers in Mourning—I now understood their meaning.

Amelia strode on ahead of me, her long skirt snagging in the brush. Abruptly she sat down on a stone, removed her bundle from her basket, unwrapped it, and exposed its contents to the fading light. Pressing it to her bosom, she cried out and her cat yowled in unison. I peered closer, bracing myself for the hideous vision of a murdered infant or aborted fetus, destroyed no doubt by the poisons she grew in her garden—I was astonished to see that the form she held so lovingly to lips and breast was none other than a doll. I recognized the head at once. It was the one I had found in the grass outside the park, and which she had taken from my desk. Somehow she had glued it back onto its ragged body of sawdust and muslin.

Loosely fastened on, the china head nodded back and forth as Amelia rocked and fondled her surrogate child, murmuring a lullaby. The shattered blue glass eye stared out toward my hiding place.

Who would not feel pity for such a display? But the girl was obviously raving mad. If I had previously suspected it, now I had proof. It was not wise to remain there, spying upon her, for her reaction might be violent. Since she had pilfered the doll's head from my drawer, it was likely that she still might have some resentment against me for having found it in the first place. I slunk away as cautiously as I could, back down the hill, where I ran smack into Finestone who was sauntering up the ridge, decked out in his walking gear.

He greeted me with a wave of his white linen fedora. "Nice to see you about, Daphne. I take it you must be feeling better now?"

The perturbing effects of the acts I had just witnessed must have left a trace in my face. I am sure I looked as ghastly as I felt. For he added, "You are looking pale. Is there something wrong?"

"No just a bit out of breath, you know."

He offered me a sip of water from his flask, which I gladly took.

Finestone appeared to be in no hurry, nor did his finding me there seem to disturb him in the least, still it occurred to me that he too might have been following Amelia for the purpose of spying on her. Just as that thought crossed my mind, the sound of a raucous quarrel burst in upon us from the top of the ridge where I had just left the girl and her doll.

I recognized those voices at once. It was Amelia and her mysterious suitor, though this time the man's voice seemed deeper in tone and more menacing than on past episodes I had overheard. In the midst of their altercation came the sharp cracking of a blow, punctuated by an acute cry of pain. Amelia darted out from behind some bushes and ran down the ridge straight toward us, nearly colliding with me as she brushed right past me and trundled on in the direction of the Sacred Wood. Her face was partly covered by a shawl tossed over her head, but that could not disguise her or hide the bright red blood spurting from her nose and dribbling down the front of her dress. The little white cat galloped at her heels in a frenzy, caterwauling like a demon from hell.

As girl and cat streaked past us, Finestone gasped, called her name in undisguised anguish, and broke from me to rush after her; but a shout stopped him in his tracks: "Let her be!"

Finestone wheeled around with an astonished look on his face, and there high on the ridge from whence Amelia had come stood Manu framed by the sheer wall of the gorge behind him, which by some optical illusion made him appear enormously tall. He held a staff in one hand and beat it against the palm of his other hand, as though threatening a vicious dog.

"Let her alone, Professor! She is unharmed."

I was incensed that Manu would use such brutality on the girl. It was quite possible that he had broken her nose. The man was a villain and a tyrant. I had begun to like him less than I liked his daughter, for she, at least, was no hypocrite, and was perhaps even justified, I now thought, by mental infirmity, while Manu pretended to be civil. Approaching us, he composed his broad face behind a hideous smile, displaying his ruined, yellowed teeth, nodded politely, and bent over to uproot a stone from the path with the tip of his staff and toss it to the side, then proceeded back toward the villa.

Finestone made no reply. His lips, bloodless, trembled above his ruddy tuft of beard. The knuckles of the fist clutching his cane had turned sickly white, and I saw he had had to restrain himself from attacking Manu outright. I thought of the blade hidden in his cane and wondered if he might have used it to protect the girl. He brought his right hand to his chest as if to calm his heart. The features of his face crumpled together in an alarming grimace—I feared the man was about to have a heart attack.

"Jacob," I said, terrified, not knowing what to do, addressing him for the first time by his first name, "calm yourself. Let me undo the buttons of your shirt."

He shook his head and waved me away. "It's nothing. A touch of indigestion."

I tried to persuade him to return to the villa and lie down, but he refused. We rested awhile, sitting on the stones, then Finestone rose to continue his walk and I felt I must accompany him, even though I too felt tired. He insisted on heading up the ridge to the place where I had seen Amelia cuddling the doll, and I had the feeling he was looking for something. Once again I examined the strange niches and figures carved in the rock face, and pondered the fragments of Latin inscriptions eroded beneath the moss.

"What is this place?"

"The local people call in *Le Madonelle.* These niches may have been used as shrines to the Virgin."

"And yet," I said, pointing out the tiny rectangular troughs carved in the rock, "it would seem to be a children's cemetery."

"Perhaps in Roman times. Earlier, in Etruscan times, it was probably a place of animal or human sacrifice. Later, in the Middle Ages, this spot was sacred to Mary. Maybe they thought she watched over the children's graves." He sat down on a stone again, leaned his chin on the handle of his cane, and looked around with a sigh. "I don't know why, but this place gives me a feeling of complete peace. Perhaps it was a place of healing."

Indeed, perhaps that is why Amelia came here to fondle her doll—to heal a tormented conscience or allay unbearable grief. I noted she had plucked a bouquet of anemones and had set them in one of the niches. I gathered a bouquet of periwinkles and dandelions, and stuck it in another niche, in honor of all mourning mothers.

Finestone's eyes were grave, his manner overly subdued. I wondered if he had also witnessed the scene I had watched of Amelia and her doll, but I dared not ask. Evening was falling and I suggested we head back to the villa.

As we entered the gate again, Finestone pointed to an area nearby with his stick, saying, "You must see what the workmen have recently uncovered while it is still light."

At the edge of the Sacred Wood, not far from the rear exit, stood a squat, leaning tower which looked as though it might tumble over with the slightest shove. Finestone smiled when I told him my impression, saying it was as solid and immobile as the rock beneath our feet. It only *looked* askew.

"Not unlike yourself," he added, "you are far more sure-footed than you like to appear."

I supposed this was meant as a compliment. Ruin, then, was only apparent not substantial.

A clever piece of work it was, I thought, as I walked round the base and gazed up at this tilted, tipsy tower. Nerval's poem sprang to mind: "*Le Prince d'Aquitaine* à *la tour abolie. . . .*" But unlike the struck tower of the tarot pack, this oblique structure didn't speak to me of catastrophe. Rather, I felt it was connected to the titans in combat near the main gate. It evoked a rude disruption of common sense, being thrown off balance, having one's stable, four-cornered sense of reality shaken off-center.

I mentioned this to Finestone as we climbed the staircase to the entrance of the tower and stepped into a large empty room where the floor slanted sharply upwards, but he replied only, "It's the *window* then that's important here." As he went toward it, leaning heavily on his cane up the steep gradient, he nearly tripped and stumbled forward but quickly steadied himself. I advanced with mincing steps and was amazed to feel my strength giving out as my knees began to wobble. An elastic force was pulling me back toward the entrance and had set my head whirling. I flung out an arm, hoping to brace myself by touching the wall, but it was too far away for me to reach.

"Good heavens," I cried, "I think I'm going to faint!" As I uttered those words, Finestone turned and lunged at me, nearly toppling over, but caught himself in time. God knows how he managed to break my fall, but he seized me by the waist with one arm, and kept us both propped up with the help of his cane. In an instant, I, too, regained my balance, and tried to ease out of his grasp, but the good professor just held on so tightly I could hardly breathe. His face was so close I could taste the brandy and onions on his breath, as the goat-like wisps of his red beard tickled my neck. I was somewhat alarmed when I realized he was about to kiss me, for he was staring at me with a peculiar gleam in his bloodshot eye.

"It's all right now, Jacob," I gasped. "You may let go!" and I turned my face away. Quite unintentionally, I focused my eyes on the window, then on a patch of sky beyond where crows flapped in the treetops.

He disengaged himself and we recomposed ourselves, gradually adjusting to the distorted perspective the room had spun around us. I realized that I might soon have a new admirer, and, despite the onions, I examined him from this new point of view. The impression was not entirely unfavorable. In a way, a liaison between the older scholar and the mature British writer who shared so much in common made much more sense than my affair with Clive, or Finestone's with Amelia; but the heart is immune to common sense, and such is our misfortune. I dispelled the thought immediately.

"But how does it manage to alter one's perceptions?" I asked when my nerves had steadied again and we were both able to move easily about the room without losing our balance. This required a simple physical adaptation, an odd sort of effort, like learning to ride a bicycle, or walking undisturbed across the deck of sailboat pitching on the waves.

"You notice, of course, that the floor is built on a steep slope. If you were outside in an open space, or even enclosed by trees, walking up such an incline, you would feel that you were going uphill, but this would not disturb your balance and cause you to fall. But here the fact of being boxed in tightly by four walls and a roof undermines your equilibrium. It's an architect's trick of perspective, that's all, nothing supernatural about it. All psychology, my dear."

"Aha! A trick. *Inganno o arte?*"

"Of course, you have guessed there is indeed a deeper meaning. That's why the window is important," he suggested. "A new perspective is required to keep oneself from falling."

It was true, focusing on the square of sky in the window had helped me recover from my dizzy spell.

Coming down the stairs again as I followed Finestone out of the leaning tower, my foot crunched something on the bottom step and I bent down to retrieve it—a familiar-looking round object made of blue glass, cracked but not shattered, by the heel of my shoe. It was the lid of my lip rouge pot with the name of my favorite Parisian apothecary emblazoned in gold letters across it, along with the name of that particular shade which I reserve for glamorous evening wear. The pot must have been stolen from my drawer, and since it was a shade I only wore on elegant occasions, I had not noticed it was gone as I had had no opportunities to use it in weeks. It might conceivably have been missing from my drawer for several days. This could only mean that Amelia had been pocketing my things again, and I felt disgusted at the thought of her poking her rough little finger with her yellow bitten nail into my expensive Parisian rouge pot. Not far off on the dirty pavement something tiny and silver gleamed in a narrow crevice between the paving stones. It was a little steel screw—probably from Clive's folding easel. I put both objects in my pocket. So I had discovered that the leaning tower was probably their clandestine meeting place—but why would they need such a place for their trysts, considering the fact that she spent every night, it seemed, up in the attic with Clive?

Finestone, who had preceded me, was now several yards down the trail, from where he called out to me, urging me to follow.

There in the twilight, dominating the center of the Sacred Wood rose a monumental fountain composed of several huge forms sprung from the earth, thickly tufted with ferns. Atop the basin, filling with water, lay a corpulent, stern-faced god with weedy beard. The iconography of recumbent pose and tangled beard identified him as Neptune, but the ponderous bulk and the blank eyes suggested Pluto, the merciless king of the underworld, truly a fitting ruling spirit for this ungardenlike-garden. Straight within the line of his blind gaze sprawled a giantess with small breasts, smiling serenely into his face. On her head was a platter of fruit and flowers. They formed a pair, I thought. I next noticed that she was chained and I *knew* then exactly who she was.

"Persephone, Pluto's bride, prisoner in Hades six months out of the year," I announced.

Finestone was delighted that I had guessed correctly. "Perhaps Vicino's visitors to the Sacred Wood reenacted a search through hell to rescue her so that springtime could return."

"Are you suggesting that they were adepts of the Eleusinian mysteries?" I asked.

The myth of Cybele's search for her missing daughter, Persephone, the goddess of spring, was the core of Greek religion in antiquity. Aspiring initiates, often blindfolded and guided by priests, would carry out the ritual search through a wood at night. Finding the goddess and releasing her meant recovering innocence, being reborn. I had read somewhere that this ancient ritual had secretly been revived in the times of the Renaissance by Neoplatonic pagans who rebelled against the church. I thought of the words scribbled in the center of the map: "Innocence," "Sophia," and "Heart's Desire"—all things that might be symbolized by the goddess of spring. Was the purpose of the drawing I had found to guide seekers on such a search? And was it guiding me?

Finestone had not answered my question, which I now reformulated. "Have you found evidence that Vicino and his friends carried out such rites in this place?"

"Why else do you think he called it his Sacred Wood?"

He pointed out an inscription nearby recently cleaned of debris and moss: *"Che ognuno v'incontri ciò che più gli sta a cuore, e che tutti vi si smarriscono."*

I translated as best I could: "May each seeker find what he most desires and may everyone lose their way."

I contemplated the gray stone goddess, with her mild features and her head full of fruit, signifying abundance, joy, summer, waiting for her mother to liberate her from the king of the dead and from his shadowy realm of changeless ferns. Tears bathed my eyes. I touched the sculpture's mossy, decaying toes.

"It is such a strange coincidence. The child I lost so long ago . . . ," I murmured. "I named her Persephone." Then a somber thought struck me: It might have been here that the Orsini child had drowned, but knowing how reluctant Finestone was to speak of that event, I did not ask.

I tried to envision what the place might have looked like in the times of Vicino Orsini, lit by torches under the full moon. I imagined the huge shadows of the boulders and the statues flitting across a lush, restless curtain of summer leaves as the seekers tread a blindfold path on their way to rescue Persephone.

"Do you think, Jacob, that the artist, the genius as you call him, who designed the Sacred Wood, was devoted to Persephone?"

He frowned and stroked his beard. "Perhaps not to her as a pagan goddess, but to the salvation and immortal spring she represented."

"And do you think he found that immortal spring?"

I was keenly interested to hear his answer to this question, but before Finestone could speak, we were interrupted by a hearty hello shouted from a few yards away, and looking up we saw Danilo making his way toward us through the trees and brambles, his coattails all aflap. He waved at us and slowed his pace, and, upon reaching us, stopped to catch his breath and mop the sweat from his brow with a handkerchief, spotted, I noted, with fresh blood. He must have been thrashing about in the woods awhile, for burrs, leaves, and mud clung to his trouser legs, and the cuff of his shirtsleeve was torn. He was too flustered with overexertion to string two English words together and seemed somewhat surprised, even annoyed, to find us there. Yet he quickly masked his reaction like an expert gambler who has been dealt a rotten hand, and burst out in jolly, inviting tone, "Ah Professor, Signora Daphne. All afternoon I look for you here in the Monster Park. Where have you been? But never mind. We must hurry. It is getting dark. I take Signor Nigel to sulfur bath for his rheumatism. And I know you enjoy them too, Professor. You must come. And you also Signora. It is wonderful to cure a cold."

I had heard of course of the miraculous powers of these sulfurous vapors, but had not yet tried the spas and watering holes where the local people flocked for cures. I saw no reason to decline the invitation. Danilo's claim that he had been searching for us was obviously a lie, and I wondered what he might have been up to, wandering around in the Sacred Wood alone and scratching himself on brambles so badly as to have soiled a handkerchief with blood. Still I replied that a long soak in a hot bath at sunset sounded quite pleasant, and I agreed to come along. We hurried back to the villa so I could fetch my bathing things. Finestone went to look for Amelia to see how she was, but the kitchen was dark and the pantry locked up. The girl was nowhere to be found. I thought she was probably weeping in a corner somewhere, nursing her wounds, or maybe had run away, which, considering the circumstances, was probably the best thing she could have done. Manu, usually so ubiquitous, had also disappeared. Their absence seemed to bother Finestone, who perhaps, was concerned the man might do further harm to her. He must have felt powerless to intervene, however, for in the end, he decided to join us for our visit to the baths, despite whatever misgivings he might have had about leaving the girl alone with Manu while we were away.

Up in my bedroom, assembling a towel and robe to take to the sulfur baths, I paused a moment before the mirror to tidy my hair and apply a bit of lip rouge. Of the several pots I kept neatly lined up in the top drawer of my dresser, one was missing, and I knew of course who had taken it. Looking round the room, checking for other signs of intrusion, I noticed that the pillow and coverlet on my bed were slightly wrinkled. Inspecting closer, I found a scattering of white cat hair on all the pillows, which I brushed energetically away. Tidying the bed, I was disgusted to find the mangled body of a dead lizard with its tail chewed off, curled up underneath a pillow where the cat must have left it. I plucked the shriveled cadaver from the bed with the fire tongs and flung it onto the smoldering coals in the hearth where it produced a pungent stink. Furious, I pulled away all the bedding and threw it on the floor. As for that impudent little cat, it was time something was done about it.

CHAPTER NINE

It was exactly like I had always pictured Hell after reading *Paradise Lost* at school. A pool of murky, stinking, sulfurous water bubbling up through thick yellow ooze at a boiling fount. Naked bodies of indeterminate sex, plastered with mud, lay writhing in the waters, the clay masks of their faces hidden by the dense, putrid vapors. Only the faintest illumination strayed from the intermittent moonlight piercing the low-lying clouds and from the flames of a bonfire crackling near the pool's edge. In the fitful firelight, I saw mud-smeared figures rise from the water, climb over the high rim of the pool and plunge out of sight with a splash into another unseen body of water where their shrieks echoed in the night. All that was missing to complete the scene was a Signorelli devil with a fork in hand.

Something was crawling through the steamy shallows toward where I stood on the lunar-like mound of encrustations which had formed at the pool's edge. A hand reached up from the water to grab my ankle and I screamed.

"Signora Daphne," said Danilo's voice from the steam, "Do not scream. It's only me. Why you still stand there? The water's fine. First hot, then cold." And he pointed to the spot where the other bathers had disappeared, a pool formed by an icy spring, and from whence they were now returning with groans and sighs of satisfaction, jumping with another resounding splash back into the steaming pool.

Not far off, I noted Nigel sitting cross-legged in the shallows, smoking. Clive, who had joined our party at the last moment, was floating belly-up in a crucified position in the middle of the pool. Beyond the swirling vapors, Finestone, clad in his dressing gown, crouched near the fount, with a long tube in his mouth, sucking in steam from a crack in the ground. With that tube in his mouth, he resembled a small elephant. He waved to me, removed the tube, and called, "It is most salubrious for the throat and sinuses. You must try!"

Danilo frowned, "Don't stay too long, Dottore," he called. "Too much sulfur is poison. It put you to sleep and give you bad dreams."

"Nonsense!"

Danilo repeated his invitation then slunk off on all fours like a crocodile to join Nigel and Clive.

Pinning up my hair, I timidly stuck in a toe. The temperature was delightfully hot, over a hundred degrees. I pulled off my kimono and in I stepped. It was a magnificent sensation to be immersed in that heavenly hot water, with a cold wind ruffling my hair. But after lolling a few moments near where the water gushed in from the fount, I found it much too warm, so I paddled off to the far end where it was considerably cooler. Beyond this edge of the pool lay an olive grove, where sheep were grazing in the new grass. I could hear their bells tinkling.

The vapors drifting up from the water clotted then dispersed above the pool, creating a cocoon around me, obscuring the view totally at moments and making it quite impossible for me to recognize my fellow bathers in the darkness at the other end. The steam cleared unevenly in the crisp air, revealing patches of cobalt sky with a sprinkling of stars which then vanished again into a milky cloud. I lay gazing up at this shifting vision with my back resting against the high rim built by the deposit of sulfur crystals along the water's edge. Perhaps it was the heat, or the slightly narcotic effect of the sulfur steam which Danilo had warned us about, but soon my eyelids began to feel heavy and I decided I needed a dip in the cold spring in order to revive my spirits.

Getting out of the pool was like trying to scramble back into a rowboat after being dunked out into deep waters for the sides of the pool were high and slippery as glass. Twice I grabbed the edge and tried to heave myself up, but all to no avail, I just slid back down again. On my third attempt, I was seized from behind, twirled around, and tossed face down into the water, and then my head was pushed under. But this time my hands were free to claw at my assailant's stout, hairy leg, which I could not see in the turbid white water, but which I could certainly *feel* and into which I sunk my teeth. As my mouth filled with the tang of blood mingled with the rotten taste of sulfur, the hands let go. I bobbed up for air, but was seized again and sent flying on my stomach across the water. A cold gust of air parted the thick curtains of steam, and I saw a large, presumably male shape clamber out of the pool and head for the olive trees, scattering the frightened sheep as it vanished into the darkness.

Shaken, chest-heaving, I treaded water, then sloshed back to the edge where I clung to the rim and tried to catch my breath. When the spasms had quelled, I looked about for the others. A breeze dissipated the wisps of sulfury vapors and I could just make them out sitting around a fire on the far side of the pool. This time I managed to hoist my body up and out of the water. I found my kimono and slippers and put them on, and, teetering on the pale, slick mud of the bank, made my way over to join them.

The men were all in their dressing gowns now, sitting on campstools, drying themselves at the fire, while Danilo grilled us sausages and slabs of cheese which he had brought along packed in a basket. He knew how to make himself indispensable on occasions like these.

"Daphne," said Nigel with a touch of concern as I approached the men, "You're just over a cold and your hair is soaking. Put a towel around it or you'll catch your death. Remember how Edmund . . ."

"I don't feel cold at all," I interrupted, needing no reminding as to how Edmund had died. And it was true, I felt neither hot nor cold, but I was still in a vague state of shock.

"But you're shivering!" and he handed me a towel which I wrapped around my head.

"And your lips are so white," said Clive. "You look as though you've seen a ghost."

"I feel fine," I said, rubbing my hair with the towel.

Tonight Nigel was solicitousness personified. "Come sit here by the fire. Danilo, please give Daphne a glass of wine."

Danilo flashed me a smile, and quick to obey, held up the flask of red Montepulciano wine and poured me a generous glass as I took my place near the fire. He leered at me as he handed me the wine, which I sipped greedily, grateful for the comfort it brought. When the hem of Danilo's dressing gown swished aside for a moment as he poked and turned the sausages on the fire, I glanced down at his slim, brown legs, but saw no telltale tooth marks or dribbling blood. His lean calves were covered by the faintest fuzz, rather like a girl's. I drew my campstool closer to the fire, and pretending to stare into the flames in reverie, I observed Danilo, Clive, Finestone, and Nigel from the corner of my eye, wondering if it was one of these four gentlemen who wanted me dead.

Nigel? I considered the years of affectionate friendship that bound him to my family which he surely would not betray. But did those years hold long-repressed rancor or jealousy that might spur a gentleman to murder? Certainly our youthful liaison had left no trace on *his* heart, nor on his pocketbook, considering how things had worked out for me. Would my brief affair with Clive be sufficient motive for murder? He was well aware that it had ended. I reflected on the practical side: The sums produced by my works were already in his hands. Moreover, it was hardly likely that he would harm the goose that lays the golden egg, at least not until I had produced a new source of income for him, i.e., a new novel. It didn't make sense at the moment for him to desire my demise.

Was he physically capable? In his youth, he had gone in for boxing and cricket but in recent years had run to fat. A patch of wooly paunch protruded from his silk dressing gown as he gobbled his sausages with gusto. He was a big man of robust build. Regretfully, I could not eliminate him from the roster of suspects. Was he agile enough to go running off through the olive trees at such a pace, as my assailant had done? This I doubted, but I knew he could easily pay someone who was—with my own money, I might add.

Clive. I knew so little of him, of course. The name came to my lips and died like a sigh. Our intimacy had surged and waned in so short a time. To all effects, he was now a stranger to me; but I had seen glimpses of a complex, passionate nature that may not know the limits of its strength. I remembered the physical force with which he had taken me, though admittedly, by no means against my will, on our last night. Clive was one of those newfangled American types who had suffered from a lonely and deprived childhood, engendering in him an insatiable craving for approval and a compulsive need to seduce anyone on his path.

Could such a high-strung and sensuous nature be inclined to murder? I thought it could indeed, but I also thought that Clive was, physically speaking, a lazy person when it came to anything aside from painting or sex. Only in the heat of jealous passion would he be able to summon enough energy to strangle or drown another human being. There would be no planning to the act, but simple impetus, seizing a propitious moment that should unexpectedly present itself when he might find himself alone with his chosen victim. With no planning, of course, clues would doubtless have been left, and I had no real clues to speak of. Besides, such an act would also require a passionate motive, now utterly lacking between us.

This considered, Clive did not seem to be a likely suspect, but perhaps I was a poor judge of his character. Could he be one of those monsters who first seduce and then kill for the sexual thrill? If that were so, why had Nigel not fallen prey long before? There must have been plenty of occasions. Or did I perhaps remind him of his mother? That was a classic murder motive for the psychologically frail and the sexually ambiguous. My blood ran cold when I thought of how our love-making could have concluded.

And what to make of Finestone? He was the one most difficult to fathom. The mild manners, the gentle humor, and the bashful, distracted air were a mask concealing a far more ruthless and sexually driven nature which was likely to emerge if given an opportunity. I remembered the penetrating glance of complicity he had exchanged with Amelia when I first met the man. Yet Finestone was of an analytical temperament and would never act without having sufficiently pondered the advantages, disadvantages and consequences of his actions. If murder were consonant with his aims, he might not shirk at the thought. He was extremely intelligent, and he would plot his course of action with admirable foresight and studied deceit to make sure he would never be caught.

His attraction for the Sacred Wood revealed a perverse streak in his character, and his doting fondness for Amelia, probably a rotten weak spot. I had no doubt as to who had dominated whom in the bedroom. She could probably turn him in and out like a worn-out sock. Was he capable of performing murder to win back her favor? Perhaps, I thought. But what had that to do with me? He was the least physically suited to athletic escapes or actions requiring brute force, being the least agile of the four. Looking down at his bare feet in the grass, I saw that the toes of his right foot were deformed, as might have been the result of the accident he claimed to have had in childhood, when his foot was mangled beneath the wheel of a cart.

Lastly there was Danilo, who, smiling quizzically at me, filled my glass again and said, "So silent tonight, Signora Daphne."

I merely smiled back and raised my glass to him in a mute toast. It was excellent wine, with the warm, astringent taste of old leather and oaken barrels. In some ways, Danilo was the most likely candidate, an outsider with a far-from-spotless background. He would be the obvious first choice as suspect for any police commissioner enquiring into the episode, and I could envision him dressed in black, padding on soundless feet, performing dozens of crimes from burglary to blackmail, extortion to forgery; but I balked before the idea of physical violence. Danilo was not the type to raise his hand to a woman, except perhaps in a fit of jealous anger. My raw instinct told me he *was not the man*, but was I still in a position to trust my instincts? True, the hashish he had been providing for me might very well have been lethal, but if poisoning me had been his intention, he might have done so before quite easily, with the first or second batch.

As for the plump, muscular calf covered with bristly hairs that I had seized in my teeth underwater—the only real clue I had, and which I had only *felt,* and, as it were*, tasted*, but not seen—it clearly did not belong to Danilo whose slender legs looked almost hairless. It might possibly belong to Nigel, Clive, or Finestone—all of whom possessed thick calves and an abundant quantity of body hair, with Finestone being the most hirsute. Conceivably it could also belong to the paid accomplice of any one of my friends.

Returning after midnight from our picnic supper by the sulfur baths, we found the villa dark, not a candle, lamp or fire burning, not even a coal aglow in the stove, and still no sign of Amelia or Manu. Danilo led the way in for us with a cigarette lighter held up like a torch, all the while deprecating the maid for being so unreliable, and lit the great candelabras in the hall. The men, still hungry, invaded the kitchen in search of bread and prosciutto. I didn't join them, but took a flask of wine from the kitchen shelf—intending to drink a glass or two, just perfect for a nightcap—lit a candle for myself and went upstairs, wondering somewhat anxiously how I would weather out the night after having been attacked at the pool. I was determined to stay up till dawn if necessary to keep guard. To that end, coffee would perhaps have been more advisable than wine, but the stove was out, so none could be had. Besides I needed a little something to settle my nerves.

Coming up the stairs, I stopped short when I saw the door to my room ajar, for I always locked it when I went out. A faint glimmer of candles came from within, laced with moving shadows. My heart knocked against my chest as I approached the door and peeked in.

In the half-dark, I saw Amelia standing by the mirror opposite the bed which had been freshly remade, although the bedding I had stripped away earlier was still piled on the floor. Holding my plum evening gown up to her body, she turned her head from side to side, making little admiring *moues* at herself in the mirror, puckering and smacking her lips. Her face was pitifully blotched and blue where Manu must have struck her repeatedly. She tossed the dress on the armchair, reached into her apron pocket and drew out a small blue object. I watched, incensed, as she dipped her finger into my rouge pot, daubed some rouge inexpertly on her lips and returned it to her pocket.

I lost control then, banged the door all the way open and stormed inside.

"Ora basta!" That's enough! I shouted.

The girl twirled round to face me with a hideous leer on her swollen mouth, grotesquely smeared with lip rouge.

"L'avevo stirato." I ironed it, she said simply, pointing to the dress, losing none of her sullen composure. She made the motion of passing an iron through the air.

I strode across the room, set my wine flask and candle down on the dresser, and gathered my dress from the armchair. The silk was still warm and the heat of the iron had released the fragrance of my own perfume captured in the fabric. But I also smelled a slight taint of sulfur, or was that from my own skin? Amelia scooped up the bedding and skipped out the door before I had time to reply or dismiss her.

"You don't fool me one bit!" I cried from the doorway, adding in English under my breath, "You little bitch."

A door slammed down the hall. I was quite sure she had understood me perfectly.

Grumbling, I hung the dress up in the wardrobe and poured myself a glass of wine to soothe my irritation. It tasted sour—as though it had gone off slightly—but I drank it anyway, thinking that it must have been left uncorked, or perhaps the sulfury scent still clinging to my skin and hair had altered my sense of smell and hence my sense of taste. It was only the very first sip that had an odd aftertaste, the next sip tasted fine.

I began undressing for bed. I had just put my topaz ring away in the little black velvet box in the top drawer of my dresser when I heard an impudent mewing sound from below. My God, that damn cat again! I knelt down, reached under the dresser and grabbed the beast by the scruff of the neck. It yielded docilely and made no protest as I set it down firmly outside the door. As light-footed as its mistress, it scampered down the corridor in the direction where Amelia had gone and I bolted my door for the night.

CHAPTER TEN

By morning, the cat had got back into my room and was playing with my hair, tugging at the tangled strands on my pillow, swatting my cheek with needle-like claws. It pounced to my chest and pumped its paws against my breast, tearing the lace bodice of my negligee and snagging into my flesh. I cried out in pain, and reached up to remove the offending creature, but my hand touched only air. The phantom cat had vanished—or was this a dream? An icy gust of wind jarred me fully awake. I must have left the door to the terrace unlatched and the wind had blown it open in the night.

Before I even opened my eyes, I was aware of two other unpleasant sensations: a dull headache, as if an iron band were being fastened tightly around my skull with increasing pressure, while along my spine, I felt something damp and cold. I reached out to pull the blanket into place for it had slipped off, leaving my body exposed to the chilly air. I was astonished when my fingers felt something wet, cold, and sticky.

My eyes shot open then, and instead of the high wooden beams of my bedroom ceiling, I saw the statue of Persephone staring down at me. The great plate of sculpted fruit on her head teetered in the air like the dish of a scale swinging from a chain, then slowly steadied itself as my eyes focused.

A crow squawked overhead in a terse blue sky crisscrossed by lush branches and vines. Its raw cry almost seemed intelligible to my ears. "Careful! Careful!" it croaked, and I thought I was still dreaming. I saw now that I was lying in the Sacred Wood, not far from the Pluto fountain. That great bearded fellow was frowning at me from the top of the basin, and I thought I saw his lips move as if to speak, to admonish me for my intrusion.

With great effort, I sat up, and felt my spine pull away from the clinging, cold mud on which I was sprawled. The hallucination was slowly subsiding, but not my headache; and I understood that the circumstances in which I found myself were really happening to me, although they were inexplicable.

It was early morning. My negligee was soaked in dew and mud. I had no dressing gown. My head throbbed. I rubbed the painful spot on the back of my skull where I had been struck, or where perhaps I had hit my head against a stone after slipping in the mud. I touched my mud-caked hair and picked a few tiny leaves and twigs out of it. My toes felt numb. I wiggled them to warm them a bit and then realized I was barefooted. I looked about for my slippers, but they were nowhere in sight.

What I was doing lying out here in the mud in my emerald green negligee, I hadn't a clue. All I remembered of the previous evening was climbing the stairs on my way up to bed while the others were having a midnight snack in the kitchen, and finding Amelia in my room. We had had an altercation, and she had run off. Then I had put that cat out the door.

As my mind grew sharper and able to observe and reason, I studied the ground around me. There were no tracks but my own, and an obvious streak in the mud where my foot had slid, causing me to fall and hit my head. A fine line of paw prints traversed the mud and disappeared into the bushes.

A rooster crowed somewhere, not far off. The sun couldn't have been up for long. My body was stiff from lying on the cold earth, but I stretched myself and managed to stand up. I noted then that my forearms were covered in scratches where, perhaps, I had gone poking through the brambles—or perhaps where Amelia's cat had scratched me. I began to limp down the trail, but every step was excruciatingly painful, for my feet were cut and bleeding.

When I got to the gate, it was locked, and of course I did not have my key. There was no question of climbing over it to get out. The gate was over twelve feet high, and spiked with very sharp iron spearheads. I reflected that it might be awhile before anyone found me. I looked up toward the villa, where I saw all the shutters still closed. Shouting would do no good. There was no one around to hear me. There was still the back exit in the woods, but to return to the villa from there, I'd need to hike down into the gorge and back up again, impossible to do without shoes. I was stuck here until Manu or Finestone came to unlock the gate for the workmen.

I sat down on a mossy stone near the sphinx. My nerves snapped and I began to weep. Long pent-up emotions suddenly broke forth from some trapped spring. I wept for myself and for Persephone, for Peter and Edmund, for my mother and my father, dead so long ago, and for Clive, for Hawthorne Lodge, and for my own foolishness. I had to blow my nose on a grape leaf, since there was nothing else at hand, and when I had finished, I felt much better and even my headache began to abate.

Now feeling more awake, I scanned the closed row of blue gray shutters again, hoping to see one pop open, and to my great surprise, discovered something I had never noticed before. One pair of shutters on the upper floor was only painted on the façade of the house in a perfect *trompe l'oeil*. Only now, as the sun came up over the crest of the gorge behind me, illuminating that side of the villa with full force, was the trick apparent. The imaginary shutters corresponded to the hall leading to the library. It occurred to me that there behind the fake window a secret room might be hidden.

Now I thought I might like to bathe my face, hands, and feet in the fountain, so I hobbled back to Pluto, where I washed my hands and refreshed my face. I climbed up and sat on the edge of the basin and stuck my feet in the water to rinse off the mud and examine my wounds, which did not turn out to be terribly serious. Splashing my toes in the cold water was soothing. The sensation evoked a memory from childhood, of wading along the banks of a brook in the soft mud, and I began to laugh, doubtless because I was partially in a state of shock. Then I heard heavy footsteps behind me, crunching down the gravel path. I looked around, frightened, to see Manu standing before me, stripped to the waist, holding a bloody bludgeon in one hand and a basket in the other. Too paralyzed to scream, I only sat there staring, while he, in turn, stared at me.

"What are you doing here at this hour of the day? Have you been out here all night—alone?" he asked calmly, approaching me with the club. He set down the basket and dipped the bludgeon in the fountain and the blood dissolved instantly in a cloud of red.

I glanced at his basket. It was full of dead rabbits, which I supposed explained the bludgeon, and a bundle of wild asparagus spears. Still I was afraid.

"Do you need help? You must be cold, half-naked as you are," he added.

I didn't like the way he had emphasized the words "alone" and "naked," and his manner seemed inappropriately familiar and surly. To say nothing of his improved knowledge of English. I pulled my negligee across my breast, but he was right, of course: I was more than half-naked for the wet silk covering my breasts was torn and quite transparent.

"I am perfectly all right. Please open the gate," I tried to sound authoritative, but my voice quavered. I jumped down from the fountain and nervously looked toward the gate, hoping to catch sight of someone passing by, a workman or peasant, but we were alone.

"Can you walk by yourself? Are you hurt?" Then *"Ma siete scalza, signora!"* *"You're barefooted!"*

I ignored this and shook my head. "I'm fine," I insisted,

determined to show that I was perfectly capable of returning to the villa on my own two feet, but I stepped on a sharp rock which jabbed straight into my heel. As I winced in pain, my knee gave out. I stumbled forward and collapsed in the mud. Manu came over to help me up, then pulled me tightly to his chest. His breath stunk of old wine and his skin was damp and cold as though he had just been bathing in an icy stream.

"Mi lasci!" I cried, *Let me go!* and I pummeled his bare back with my fists.

"Calmatevi Signora! Calm down. I am not going to hurt you."

But the arms did not let go, and his chafed fingers rough as sandpaper groped through the thin silk for my breasts.

A shrill voice cut the air, *"Buon Giorno!"* and the palpating hand fell away.

Amelia appeared from behind a laurel bush, looking much better than she had the night before. Her lip was no longer so swollen and the bruises on her neck were not quite as purple. She looked refreshed, actually, as if from a good night's sleep or a lover's embrace. Behind her trailed the cat waving its tail in excitement.

Manu still kept me clutched to his chest. Turning to Amelia he said, *"La Signora ha bisogno di aiuto. Portiamola su in casa. Ha perso le scarpe."*

It took my brain a little longer than usual to translate what he was saying to Amelia. *The lady needs help. Let us accompany her back to the house. She has lost her shoes.*

"No," I protested, "please leave me be. I am all right now."

I managed to wrench myself free and to remain on my feet unassisted. The girl eyed me from head to toe. I knew I must look perfectly dreadful, since for once she did not snidely smile, but only regarded me with solemn amazement.

"Ci sono serpenti in giro. Dalle le tue scarpe, ho detto!" *There are snakes about. Give her your shoes, I said!*

At this suggestion, she clenched her jaw. I could see the idea revolted her as much as it did me, but Manu would not take no for answer. He repeated his command and she obeyed, slipping off her wooden sabots and placing them before me on the wet grass. I looked at her feet, small white, delicate, finely veined in blue, the nails perfectly trimmed and buffed. They were the feet of a Madonna, certainly not of a peasant, unlike her hands which were red, rough, with jagged nails yellowed by housework.

"Put them on, otherwise how will you manage to walk?" Manu said. It was not a suggestion but an order.

Protesting was of no use. I put the sabots on my feet and allowed myself to be accompanied back to the villa, propped up between the two. I hated to admit it, but I *did* need their help and would never have made it back without them. My head had begun to throb again, my knees felt weak, and the soles of my feet were bruised and bleeding. Amelia balanced Manu's basket on her head as we hobbled along. Blood from the dead rabbits dripped through the basket, trickling down the side of her face and neck, staining the collar of her dress. It dribbled on the ground as we proceeded and the cat promptly licked it up again.

The house was silent as we came in. I presumed that the others were all still fast asleep. I heard the library clock strike seven as they helped me laboriously up the stairs and into my bedroom where they settled me into an armchair.

"Give her a good hot bath!" Manu ordered.

I cringed at the thought of another attack in the water, but craved nothing more than a good hot soak. My head and bones were sore, and I was filthy with mud. Given the circumstances I could hardly refuse and had no strength to resist.

Amelia retrieved her sabots from my feet and went downstairs to put the cauldron on to boil for my bath. In half an hour the tub was filled. This time Manu helped carry up the pails of hot water, while I lounged in the chair, bewildered, watching them coming and going with canisters and pails, pouring water into the tub and stirring in the oils. I was wracking my brains for an explanation as to how I had got in this state.

When the bath was ready, they left me alone, and I got into the tub. The water was deliciously hot and my aches and pains soon subsided, but my mind clouded over when I tried to recall the events of the evening before. At last I gave up the effort and let myself doze, and when the water had begun to cool again, I heard that whispering voice in my ear. Not a voice exactly, more like a soft movement of the air, a slight tickling buzz gradually assuming a rhythm, then almost taking on the intelligible form of words. My head dropped to one side, but a thought, an image—my daughter Persephone as I imagined her—popped into my head, and I snapped awake again with the full realization that yes *that was the last thing I remembered before falling asleep the previous evening!* That droning in my ears. The water in the bath was very cold now and I was surprised to find myself shivering. Deep wrinkles etched the skin of my toes and fingertips, now as white and bloodless as wax. They looked as though I had been soaking for hours. On a stool near the tub, Amelia had left a bell for me to ring in case I required her help in getting out again, but I managed to climb out myself, and to dry myself with the fresh linen towel hanging on the hook by the tub.

My emerald green negligee lay in a heap on the floor. I shook it out to inspect it, for I knew it must be ruined, and so it was. The hem was torn, wet, and streaked with mud, and the exquisite lace on the bodice was ripped. God knows where I'd find the money to replace it, if I managed to make it back to Paris alive. A white bundle had been placed for me on the bed. It proved to be a nightgown of fine white muslin, freshly starched and perfumed with lavender, as plain as a nun's with a bit of tatting around the collar, and the letter O embroidered on the bodice. I slipped it on and crawled into bed. A strange thought crossed my mind before I fell asleep: *This is the third bath. Il terzo bagno.* But what did that mean? The last thing I was conscious of was the sound of the clock in the library striking eleven a.m. and the tap-tapping of Finestone's typewriter through the wall.

It was late in the afternoon when I woke again, propped up on plump down pillows with the covers pulled over my breast. I think it was the sound of my own snoring that jarred me awake. The light streamed in through the door to the terrace, filling the room with a golden glow, for someone must have opened the shutters. A dark form hovered to the side of the bed. I gasped, thinking that my winged creature had returned, but it was only Nigel, I saw, as my eyes gradually focused. He was sitting in a chair drawn to the bedside with a grim expression on his face and a book in his lap. He reached out to squeeze my hand. His fingers felt cold and clammy and he did not smile.

"You'll be wanting your tea. I'll have it brought immediately." He rang the bell on the bedside table and Amelia served the tea with unusual promptness. This time it did not taste as though a broom had been dipped in it. Was it possible she had finally learned how to make a proper cup of tea?

Nigel observed me sternly as I sipped. I still felt dizzy. The room swirled around me and the portrait of Giuilia Farnese reflected in the mirror appeared distorted as if glimpsed at the bottom of a well, but the tea soon helped to settle my head and stomach.

After a long silence, Nigel finally said, "This is the third time, Daphne, if not the fourth, if we count Paris, that you have lost control."

Good heavens! I was in for another lecture and I was hardly in the mood.

"What did Manu tell you?" I asked warily, thinking over how I would phrase my explanation, since I myself had no idea what had happened.

"That you were prowling half-naked in the park before dawn, and bathing in the fountain. He said you were . . . in a state of inebriation."

Inebriation! I thought, he's the one who stank of wine, and I recalled with some disgust the sensation of being pressed against that hard, smelly body, and the nauseous fear that he might try to kiss me. I could still feel that rough hand on my breast. How far would he have gone had Amelia not emerged out of the bushes at the crucial moment? Strange to think that she would have been the one to rescue me from an attempted rape by her father.

"Well, were you?"

"Was I what?"

"In a state of inebriation."

Given the situation, perhaps truth *was* the best tactic, though I have rarely found that to be case. I took a deep breath and replied.

"I know it sounds absurd, but I have no idea what happened. I can't remember much about last night, after we came back so late from the baths. All I recall is coming up the stairs and finding Amelia in my room. Then she ran off. Yes, maybe I had a glass of wine for a nightcap. . . . Maybe it was the effect of the sulfur? Danilo did say it can give you bad dreams."

Nigel sniffed in irritation.

"Maybe . . . I was . . . sleepwalking? I had an aunt who sleepwalked and they had to put a basin of cold water by the bed, so she'd step into it and wake up if she got up in the night. . . . Though I don't know . . ."

"Daphne," he squawked hysterically, "Don't lie to me!"

I was shocked by his violence.

"How dare you speak to me in such a tone, Nigel? I am not lying, I honestly don't . . ."

The words died in my throat as he flung out his hand and stuck something under my nose. It was my hashish pipe which I kept hidden in my desk drawer. While I had been lying there asleep, he had been poking about my things! I snatched at it, but he held it out of my reach.

"It's not what you think," I began, immediately realizing I couldn't have chosen a worse way to begin. He would never believe what I had to say, but I went on to say it anyway. "Yes, I admit it, I have smoked a few times since our arrival, but my supply ran out some time ago and I haven't . . ."

"I don't know what to do with you, Daphne. You can't be left to your own devices without going to hell. Where have you been getting the stuff? You know you could go to jail? You know you could cause me to go to jail?"

"I confess I brought a small stash with me from Paris but it's all gone now," I sobbed.

Nigel shook his head in disbelief.

"Who has been furnishing you with this? Clive? Finestone? "

"No. No one!" I shouted. I was determined Danilo should not be punished as well. "I told you, I brought it along with me from Paris."

He broke the pipe in two and stuffed the pieces in his pocket.

"Go ahead," I cried, "I don't mind. Take it! I have given it up anyway. I really don't need it. I haven't used any in literally ages. Believe me!" That was *true* and tears streamed down my face as I spoke.

"Like all addicts, you're pathetic!" he snarled, then rose and left the room.

I cried for while till my tears ran out, then sat up straight on the pillows. The pot was still warm, so I poured another cup of tea, which by this time was very strong, and knocked it back, trying to stop my mind from spinning. I was humiliated, I was ashamed, but more importantly, I had been unjustly accused, and there is no greater source of fury. My fury demanded action, but I had no idea of what I should do. I tried to quell my agitation and to make myself for once *think.*

There came a scratching noise from the door to the terrace. I looked up and saw the pink driveling nose of Amelia's albino cat pushed up against the glass. It mewed again insistently, wanting to come in, I suppose.

"Go away," I said, knocking on the window to chase it away.

"Go back to your mistress." As I watched it slink away, I suddenly remembered: The cat! I had found it under the dresser and then put it out, but before that I indeed had drunk one or maybe two glasses of wine from a flask I had brought up from the kitchen. Surely no more than that, certainly not enough to make me lose consciousness. I looked around the room for the straw-bottomed flask, but Amelia must have been in to do the room while I was asleep, for both the flask and the glass with its dregs had been taken away. The tub too had been emptied and the alcove put in order, and my ragged negligee had been removed.

Then I understood. There was a very logical, clinical explanation for my bout of sleepwalking in the Sacred Wood. The wine had been drugged. And I thought of the little herb patch Amelia tended in the Wood with its rows of rue, valerian, datura, and wormwood.

CHAPTER ELEVEN

I must have still been under the effect of the drugged wine, for despite all that strong tea I had drunk, I slept all afternoon, all through the night, and woke the next morning a bit earlier than usual, feeling famished for I hadn't eaten anything in over twenty-four hours. Slipping on my dressing gown and stepping out to the corridor on my way down to the kitchen, I noted that the villa seemed unusually quiet. No sounds came from the other rooms or from outside. The typewriter in the library was silent. Clive and Finestone were either still asleep, or already up and about. I went to Nigel's room at the end of the hall, but he didn't answer my knock, and the door was locked, which meant he was out. The stillness in the villa that morning made me uneasy. I didn't want to be alone there with Manu lurking about. Thinking back on it all, I had concluded he might have been the mysterious assailant who had attacked me in the sulfur baths, though I had no idea why he should have done so or how he had followed us there.

Amelia was not to be found downstairs in the kitchen. I remembered it was market day. She had probably set off to do the shopping. I didn't mind having to get my own breakfast, for I had decided that from now on it would be best if I procured my own food and not trust any food or drink prepared by others. But the stove had gone out and the pantry was locked. Rummaging in the cupboards, I found nothing but stale bread and a rind of bacon, all yellow and shriveled. Two unwashed coffee cups in the sink and a scattering of breadcrumbs on the table indicated someone had already been down for breakfast. I had no idea where the others could have gone, but since it was a lovely day at the beginning of May, I thought perhaps they had all gone out for a walk. In any case, it looked like I would have to starve till lunchtime, unless I managed to break into the pantry. I poked at the keyhole with a butter knife, but to no avail.

Returning upstairs as the clock in the library chimed half past ten, I heard the sound of a door shutting softly but could not tell which door: the one to my own room, to Nigel's, or to the library. I went along the hall first to Nigel's room, which was still locked, and then peeked into the library. It was quite deserted, but stepping out again, I noted that the curtains covering the angel icon had been left open and the winged creature seemed to be regarding me with a look of stern disapproval. Remembering the false set of shutters I had seen from inside the Sacred Wood, I suspected the icon might conceal the entry to a hidden room, but as I was reaching out to try to remove the huge painting from its niche, I heard a crash downstairs.

I went to the top of the landing. "Who's there?"

An anguished voice cried out. "No worry! Nothing broken!" It was Danilo, and I hurried downstairs where I found him in the great entrance hall where a bronze statue of a cherub lay on its side on the floor. It had been knocked from its niche in the wall. My Roman friend appeared to be in great agitation.

"The cat. I trip, and this happen, but luckily not damaged. I was looking for my gloves. My driving gloves, I cannot find them." He picked up the sculpture, dusted it with his hand, and put it back on its marble stand. "Thank goodness, not damaged!"

Danilo was the smooth sort of fellow whose face never belies his real feelings. I could not believe he could be in such a state simply for a lost pair of gloves or for a statue knocked over, no matter how valuable. Besides, his yellow suede gloves were clearly in sight on the little shelf of the hat stand near the door, where he always tossed them upon entering the villa. When I pointed this out to him, his mouth twitched in annoyance, and he strode over to the hat stand, snapped up the gloves and stuffed them into the pocket of his tweed jacket.

Then through the window, I saw Nigel's car parked right outside the villa, at the bottom of the stairs, as if ready for a speedy departure.

"Were you going for a drive?" I asked, "with Nigel?"

He seemed perplexed or, perhaps, put out. "No, I return from driving Mr. Nigel to the train station in Viterbo," which was the largest town nearby.

"Oh?" Nigel had said nothing about taking a trip.

"He is gone to Rome for the morning, and I must come back and get him on the five o'clock train."

"A trip to Rome? Funny he didn't mention it."

I was piqued of course. If I had known he was going all the way to Rome, I would have asked him kindly to do a few errands for me as well, for I had run out of stockings and needed some new ones; but remembering how we had parted the day before, it was no surprise if he had neglected to inform me of his plans. I was puzzled, though, that he had chosen to take the train rather than drive. Nigel adored his car and hated traveling by train. The train from Viterbo to Rome was particularly dirty, full of soot, and as slow as an inebriated snail.

Danilo still seemed edgy even though he had found his gloves. I had the impression he was waiting for something to happen, or perhaps for someone to appear, for he kept glancing behind me at the windows looking out over the grounds. Every slight sound had him on the alert. I remarked to myself that this was the second time I had seen the fellow, generally so unruffled and suave, in such a nervous state. The first time had been just the other evening when Finestone and I had run into him in the Sacred Wood. How long had he been wandering about the rooms before I had come down? What was he doing there all alone? The villa was full of small objects of great value, which would be very easy to pocket, as Clive had repeatedly affirmed. And then of course, we would be blamed if anything went missing.

Whatever he might have been doing downstairs alone, I thought it was a good idea to interrupt him and keep him from doing any more of it. And seeing that he had the car ready, I thought why not turn the situation to my advantage? The most pressing thought on my mind at the moment was getting some food in my stomach.

"Everyone seems to have gone," I said. "I haven't had anything for breakfast. I'm starving and I don't know when the maid will be back with the shopping. Why don't you take me somewhere to a café where I can get something to eat? Besides, it's a beautiful day for a drive."

Seeing him hesitate at my suggestion, I asked, "That is, unless you have something better to do?"

He shrugged his shoulders to signal consent. "Nothing better. Only pick up Mr. Nigel at five."

I ran up to my room to throw on some clothes, tidy my hair, and dash back down again.

Amelia's cat had taken refuge under the car. Danilo had to stamp his foot several times in order to dislodge it. The animal crawled out from under the car, staring up at us with its baleful pink eyes. The creature looked hungry and somewhat neglected, I thought, but what could I do? There was no food in the kitchen. "You'll just have to wait till your mistress gets back," I said to the cat. "I can't help you." The cat mewed in protest and scuttled away.

"Aren't you going to ask how I am?" I asked Danilo, lighting a cigarette as we rolled down the drive. We started up the treacherous curves.

"How are you, Mrs. Daphne?" he asked so obediently that I had to laugh at his earnestness.

He shot me a puzzled glance. "Why you laugh?" His tone

sounded offended.

"Didn't Nigel tell you that I was *indisposed* yesterday? *Malata.*"

"You were ill, Mrs. Daphne? I am very sorry," he said, sounding truly concerned. "Are you all right now? Do you want that I call a doctor?"

I shook my head. Did he really know nothing about my little adventure . . . or was he only pretending not to know?

"It was nothing, I had too much wine and it went to my head."

I was braced to catch his reaction to this—and there was, yes, a faint twitching of the mouth again and tweaking on an eyebrow. Only an expert could have detected such subtle facial movements, which clearly indicated that he was *guilty.* Guilty of what I could not say, but most certainly guilty of something, and it was now my task to find out what.

As I reached into my handbag again for a handkerchief, I realized I wasn't wearing my ring. I had gone out in such a rush, I had forgotten to put it on. Damnation! Amelia would have plenty of time to go through my things while I was out on this jaunt with Danilo.

On we drove through the quiet countryside where spring was fully upon us. Tall hedges of yellow gorse grew thick along the hillsides where pink anemones and a few timid scarlet poppies peppered the long grass. Clusters of dark red fruit dotted the wild cherry trees lining the road. We stopped to pick handfuls and gobble them down. Not quite ripe, they were exquisitely tart. The dark red juice stained our fingers and a spot soiled my white voile blouse.

The road twisted through a chestnut grove stretching along the flanks of a mountain and finally led us to a hamlet carved of gray stone perched along a cliff overhanging a verdant gorge. The solemn gray gothic archways and towers of the village displayed a ponderous grace, like lacework hewn in stone. Pink and white azaleas growing in pots on every balcony added a cheery touch to the stern gray walls, and pretty pieces of cloth and lace-work had been hung from the windows like banners in honor of some festivity.

To my great delight, as we drove up to the main piazza, we encountered a procession pouring from a church and heading our way, preceded by the strident brass notes of a marching band playing a somber tune. Danilo explained that in the month of May many local villages celebrated their patron saints, and today, May 8th, this hamlet was celebrating Michael the Archangel.

The villagers in tattered clothes turned to stare at us as we tumbled out of the car. A carpet of petals, pink, yellow, mauve, had been strewn on the streets in fanciful arabesques which we could not avoid stepping on as we looked for a place to stand out of the way. The air was fragrant with rose petals, broom, and rosemary all crushed beneath our heel, mixed with pungent smoke from the chimneys.

At a stall on the piazza kept by old crippled woman with a tuft of gray beard, we bought anise cakes still warm from a wood oven. I greedily devoured mine and the old crone, watching me, nodded in approval at my appetite. We found our way to a bel-vedere overlooking the gorge from where we could observe the proceedings without being a hindrance. From where we stood, looking across the gorge, we could see a small chapel had been built nestled in a fissure of the cliff, engulfed by ferns and hazel-nut trees.

The cortege snaked by us through the cobbled streets. At the head strode four bearers in white robes carrying a crudely carved wooden statue of their angelic protector bedecked with flowers, ribbons, and snippets of lace. Its great brownish purple wings were unfurled and in one hand the angel held a scale high; in the other he seized a spear aimed at the earth. At the end of his spear writhed a weird creature—part bird, part serpent; part demon, part human.

Behind followed the marching band, and behind them

thronged the village folk—old and young, crippled and infirm—singing hymns, ringing bells, chattering gaily as they walked. A few munched the same anise seed cakes I had just tasted. Mangy dogs straggled after them to lick the crumbs from the ground. At the rear, stern and authoritative, marched a dozen booted policemen in uniform, flanked by several notables in black shirts. We watched from a balcony above as the cortege wended down through the gorge and up a steep trail toward the chapel lodged in the bosom of the cliff. Overhead in the cloudless sky, hawks swooped down in the vortex of a draft as the village clock struck one.

I remarked to Danilo how charming it was, but in reply he scowled, spit on the ground, and grumbled, "Michael's the patron saint of policemen and soldiers and always carries a spear. I like the Madonna better." And he made the sign of the cross.

From his tone, I gathered he held neither policemen nor soldiers in high regard, a typical reaction of someone who had perhaps spent some time behind bars.

"In the old days, if you loved another man's wife or stole a loaf of bread, they put you in the stocks at St. Michael's feet and everyone spat on you. Ones like me they hanged. But the Madonna, she forgive all if your heart is good."

The cortege had reached its destination, a small square outside the rustic chapel where the worshipers stood packed along the edge of the gorge. The doors of the chapel were opened and the angel was carried inside. The priest's chant wafted across the gorge as the mass began. I watched fascinated as the congregation knelt in unison on the rocky ground bordering the precipice and echoed their response. How simple was this pious act of humility and acceptance. If only I could join them and wash my heart free of the past.

The spectacle did not interest Danilo, who drew out his cigarette case, took a smoke for himself and offered me one. I instantly recognized the case. It was the one Nigel had bought for

Clive!

"A pretty case," I said admiringly.

"A present from a friend," he said, snapping it shut and returning it to his vest pocket.

I speculated as to how the cigarette case might have come into Danilo's possession. Was *he* the one pilfering things from our drawers, then, and not Amelia? Was that what he had been doing this morning when he had knocked the statue over? But would he show me stolen goods with such nonchalance? This I doubted.

Danilo had turned away from the gorge. Leaning on the crumbling parapet of the belvedere, he faced the street, his thin lips sucking at his cigarette. He had a handsome, wolfish leanness about him, enhanced by the very well-cut suits he wore made by an expert tailor. From the first, my instinct had told me that, Nigel aside, Danilo preferred women to men. He would have looked distinguished in Renaissance garb, with tight leather leggings and a flounce around his neck. He was not an evil man, a hardened one, or even an opportunist, I thought, but one who had to make do with what he had in order to get on in life. Was I so different from him? I was not surprised that he might have been stealing things from us. I could quite imagine he had an ageing mother in Rome who needed medicines and care.

Danilo frowned again and thrust out his pointy chin to call my attention to something. There straight across the street stood a little girl in a ragged red dress and a filthy apron, gawking at us. The last of the stragglers had reached the chapel on the other side of the gorge, leaving this child behind. From the way she was staring at me, I could not tell if it were my bright red hair and lipstick or my cigarette that had attracted her interest. She was about the same age as the shepherdess who sometimes brought her sheep to the lawn. I fancied she might even be the same girl.

She came over to us and sat down on a step along the

parapet. She was a pretty little thing despite her smudged face and patched dress, with an Etruscan cut to those dark eyes. She made me think of my dear dead Persephone, but all little girls with sparkling eyes reminded me of Persephone. She clung to the handle of a red basket which she held out to me.

"Take one," she said.

"Che cos' è?" What is it? I asked peering at the contents, which proved to be pictures of human figures with numbers printed on the back. I could not always understand her dialect, so I glanced at Danilo for assistance.

"Lottery tickets with pictures of saints," he said.

I have never been lucky at gambling. Still I said, "How much is a ticket?"

The child quoted an outrageous price, but I was feeling generous. Probably her family would use the money for food or some other necessity, if she was lucky enough to have a family.

I reached out to choose a ticket from the basket, but she pulled it away.

"First the money," she demanded, so I opened my purse, counted out the coins, and handed them to her. She scrutinized them with an expert eye and slipped them into her apron pocket. Then with grave expression, she shook the basket, stirred its contents with her hand, and held it out again. I closed my eyes, reached in and plucked out a ticket.

"Buona fortuna," said the girl. "You got a good saint, that's a good sign. The lottery is Thursday." That was three days away.

She held out her basket now to Danilo. He shook his head, spoke sharply to her, threw her a coin, and shooed her away.

"What is your name?" I called as she ran off.

"Sophia," she shouted and scampered down the road leading into the gorge, presumably to join the others.

"I wonder what will become of Sophia when she grows up?"

Danilo grunted. "Whore or drudge. A poor girl cannot choose. Either way, a slave."

Indeed, I thought, aren't we all, one way or another.

Only one word was printed on the ticket, the name of the village Vitorchiano. I remembered that name. It was where Finestone had taken Clive on a walk, up along the wild paths beyond Bomarzo and Le Madonelle, and I asked if that was where we were.

"Yes," explained Danilo. "We have come along the new road, but there are trails through the woods connecting all these hill towns and villages."

The number on my ticket read 5, which I have always regarded as my lucky number for I was born on December 5th. Did that mean my luck was going to change? The saint was St. Michael himself. I stared at the beast at the end of his lance, and indeed, he looked familiar.

The petals at our feet were all scattered now, the patterns undone, the flowers trampled. The compact cortege had broken into groups. We could see them sitting on the ground, enjoying a picnic beneath the hazelnut trees growing along the ledge of the gorge. Some of the worshipers had taken notice of us and were staring at us, or perhaps at our car, from across the yawning gap of the gorge. The clock struck quarter to two and I reminded Danilo that I was still hungry. He suggested we go have lunch at a tavern near the lake. That sounded like a good idea, but I had only a few coins in my purse. I hoped he didn't expect me to pay. As we turned to leave, we both noticed that there across the gorge, two men in black shirts were pointing us out to one of the policemen. It looked like the right time to leave.

We lunched near Lake Vico, at a tavern under a canopy of beech trees—the fare was simple but wholesome served on bare plank tables set near the shore. As we ate, Danilo told me a bit of about his life. It was a story of poverty, violence, and loss, of earnest striving and bitter disappointments; but he shrugged it off with melancholy irony—the way some Italians will do. At last I asked if there were someone "special" in his life—a partner, a companion, a friend. He smiled at me quizzically and said, "You mean a woman, and of course there is." He sighed, smiled ruefully and said, "She is beautiful, she is wise, and rich, of course, and she *is taken.*"

He consulted his watch again and frowned. "We must hurry now Signora Daphne. Signor Nigel"—why he persisted with this "Signor Nigel" business was beyond me; he knew we knew about his relationship with Nigel—"arrive soon at the station."

Driving along the curving road through the woods, we got stuck behind a flock of sheep being led somewhere, which slowed us down considerably, and by the time we reached the station of Viterbo, we were nearly a half hour late to meet Nigel's train. The platform was deserted, the waiting room empty. The stationmaster scratched his head when Danilo asked if he had noted an English gentleman hanging about. No, he was afraid he had not noticed anyone. Neither had the drivers of the horse-drawn cabs waiting outside the station, nor the waiter from the café set under the yellow-striped awning across the street. The next train from Rome wasn't due in for another two hours. We surmised that Nigel would either be arriving on the later train, or perhaps had hired a cab to return to the villa on his own, though none of the cabmen had noticed him. I kept an eye out as we drove back to Bomarzo, but we encountered no cabs along the way.

Returning to the villa, we were surprised to find Nigel safely ensconced in the library, drinking whiskey, musing over a volume of Keats. He smiled brightly as we entered the room, snapped his book shut, and came to meet us. His shoes left a smudge of dark, black earth on the worn red carpet.

"There you are! I was wondering what had happened. Seeing you were late, I had a cabbie bring me back. Have some whiskey." And he went to the cabinet to pour us some.

Danilo declined the drink and stepped out for a moment, saying he had to check the motor of the car which he claimed had been making strange noises, although I had not noticed anything amiss while driving home.

I was more in a mood for tea than whiskey so I rang the bell for Amelia.

"The girl's gone off again," said Nigel gruffly, pouring himself another glass after my ringing had brought no response. "She must be having a holiday."

"It is a holiday," I said. "We watched a very pretty procession in honor of St. Michael. Does that mean I won't have my tea?"

"It probably does, Dear, nor your dinner."

"Oh!"

"Unless she returns. The cupboard is barer than old Mother Hubbard's. I suggest we have Danilo drive us to a trattoria in town. Shall we leave, say at half past eight? Otherwise we risk going hungry till tomorrow."

I went up to rest and get ready for dinner. Finestone was in the library; I could hear the tap-tapping of his typewriter. I thought I should tell him that we would have to dine out, but I didn't want to disturb him while he was working. He'd find out soon enough. Finestone was methodical. He ceased work every night at eight o'clock, dressed for dinner, and came down to the dining room several minutes just before the gong summoned us to table at half past eight. It was still early, so there was no need to disturb him just yet.

I took off my shoes and lay down on the bed for a while then went to the wardrobe to decide what to wear for the evening. I saw at once my purple dress was gone. I strode to the dresser and opened the drawer. My necklace and ring were gone, too. Amelia had bolted, *that* was clear. Now had she bolted with Clive? Or was she upstairs in the studio with him at that very moment?

I banged on the trapdoor leading up to Clive's studio.

If the two of them were in bed together, I could care less. I wanted an explanation.

"Clive! Is that girl in there with you?! Damn it! Open up, I say!"

I was beside myself with fury.

The hatch opened, the little stairway folded out, and I bounded up into the penumbra of the studio where Clive stood glaring at me beside the open hatch. A rumpled cocoon of blankets lay in disarray on the narrow leather sofa where he had been napping alone.

He yawned and rubbed his face. "What the hell is the matter with you? You're hysterical these days!"

"Where is that girl? This time she has stolen my dress and my ring!"

Dusk was falling and it was quite dim in the attic, but the faint gleams of light filtering in through the western skylight offered sufficient illumination for me to notice a rather large canvas perched on an easel in a corner where the ceiling sloped down. The whole room was filled with canvases and paintings, I should add, lined up along the floor, propped against the wall. They were ugly paintings, several of which I had already seen, displaying not an ounce of taste or skill. But this portrait, which I had never seen before, now illuminated by the last light of day, stood out from the rest, and I gazed at it intently.

Seeing that I had noticed it, Clive dashed in front of the easel and threw over it the first thing that came to hand, which was a pair of boxer shorts snatched from the floor, in a futile effort to conceal the picture.

I don't know what arrested my attention most: the extreme skill showed by the painter who had chosen a Flemish style, the content of the portrait, or simply Clive's feeble attempt to hide his handiwork with his underwear. Each option was pregnant with meaning which would inexorably come to bear on what was to happen next: an event which rudely and definitively altered the course of our lives.

I confess that though I marveled at the immense progress he had made with his painting in order to produce such exquisite work, the thing that most overwhelmed me at that moment was the subject of the portrait, which showed Amelia riding on the elephant statue in the Sacred Wood, clad in what was unmistakably my plum silk evening gown, with my mother's moonstone necklace glowing on her bosom and my own cherished topaz ring flashing on her finger.

"So it is you who have taught her to become not just a whore but a thief!"

He said nothing and just stared, wistfully, I thought, at the portrait.

"Beauty deserves beautiful things," he said, "and it was only a loan."

I smacked him across his smug face.

"There was no need for that," he said. "She promised she would give them back."

"She'll rue the day she was born. I shall report this theft to the police at once. Your pretty bird will be put in jail, if she hasn't already flown the coop."

I thundered out of the attic, down the stairway and out into the corridor, where I intended to find Danilo and command him to drive me to the nearest police station. Instead in the darkened hallway, I found Nigel and Finestone, both looking grave, listening to one of the workmen who stood apologetically with hat in hand, begging them to follow him into the Sacred Wood at once as something dreadful had happened.

CHAPTER TWELVE

Evening had fallen in the Sacred Wood which was always in perpetual shadow. We trooped there along the trail toward the Pluto fountain, where we immediately spotted the corpse.

I have described a dozen murdered bodies in my books, but my personal experience of cadavers was really quite limited to a few family members and a couple of specimens at the Royal College of Surgery where Nigel had taken me to study one afternoon early on in my writing career, so that my descriptions of corpses would be realistic.

Still I could tell she had been dead for several hours. Clad in my plum silk gown, illuminated by torches held high in trembling arms by two of Manu's workmen, Amelia resembled nothing more precisely than a mangled stork of dark plumage. She lay on the grass and mud beside the fountain from which the workmen had fished her out—on the very spot where I had awoken just the day before from my somnambulistic nightmare. My moonstone necklace glinted on her breast.

Her head was bent at a strange angle, cruelly revealing the mottled blue and red marks on her neck, where it looked as though she had been strangled with a rubber hose or by someone with huge hands. But strangling did not appear to be the only cause of death. Her head had been bashed in on one side and blood was smeared on the ground and along the rim of the fountain. The bloodstains had already begun to take on a tainted smell, and attracted swarms of flies. Her bloated face was the color of pale cheese rind soaked in oil; her blue eyes were open in horrid surprise; the bodice of her, that is *my,* dress was ripped and stained with mud and algae from the bottom of the fountain. It looked as though she had first been beaten and struck on the head and then put in the fountain where she had lain face down for several hours.

Clive now came running along the path, bellowing her name. Upon reaching us he stopped in his tracks, and after a chilling pause, fell to his knees beside the body and gave an anguished cry. Cradling the dead girl in his arms, he rocked her back and forth, shedding copious tears and howling at the top of his lungs.

I was moved by this tragic display. Stumbling forward, I gently touched his sleeve, "Clive dearest, come away"—but his only response was a snarl and a flashing of teeth. "You!" he hissed. "You killed her!"

The accusation hit me like a blow in the face. My jaw dropped open, my eyes stared. The fellow was raving. I knew not what to reply. He turned now to Finestone who had crept forward to kneel beside him while tears rolled down his chubby cheeks and dripped down his beard.

"I swear to God the English bitch killed her," growled Clive.

Nigel reached down to lay his hand on Clive's shoulder. "Steady, man, you don't know what you're saying."

"And you helped her, you bugger."

Nigel was so shocked he could only reply, "Oh," and remove his hand.

We both shrank back, helpless and horrified, among the ferns and flickering shadows of the torchlight.

Manu arrived, alerted by one of the workmen who were huddled in a small group at a respectable distance among the statues. He stared at the dead girl, and though the bovine composure of his face remained unaltered, his complexion rapidly changed hue and consistency till it resembled dark, soft clay. His eyes clouded, his immense body shook, and he collapsed against a mossy boulder with a single, colossal sob.

Finestone had seized the girl's hand and was slowly caressing the fingers locked by *rigor mortis*. A flare of the torches illuminated an object that tumbled to the grass, released from her clutch. It was my topaz ring.

"There's your proof! She pulled it off your finger as you were strangling her," shouted Clive, and began blubbering again as he clasped the body to his breast.

"The man is out of his mind with grief," I murmured to no one in particular.

Finestone plucked the ring from the grass, turned it around examining it, and held it out to me in a trembling hand. "I believe it's yours."

After a brief hesitation, I took it and put it on, lest it be lost or pocketed by one of the workmen, though I felt uncomfortable at the idea that my ring had just been on the finger of a corpse.

"I swear to God you are my witnesses!" yelled Clive after I had reclaimed my ring.

The workmen had come forward to attend Manu who still stood shaking against the boulder while Finestone attempted to calm the overwrought Clive. He finally managed to disentangle him from Amelia's body, though he refused to be led from the spot. He sat in a heap beside her with his head in his hands.

Nigel, recovered from the shock, took control of the situation. "We had better inform the authorities," he said, and then with special emphasis and a sidelong glance at me, added, "none of us should leave the villa, of course."

"Go ahead inform them! I know who's to blame!" screamed Clive. He looked on the verge of apoplexy.

There was nothing I could do for Clive or for Amelia or anybody else at that point and I had no wish to stay there with the body, waiting for the police to arrive. "I shall be in my room," I said. "Call me when my presence is required."

"I'll make you pay!" Clive shouted as I turned toward the

villa, now illuminated with torches the men had lit all along the path. My knees began shaking before I had gone five paces, so I sat down on the rim of the fountain and watched as Clive and Finestone cleaned the mud from her face. My own face was on fire, and I felt myself perspiring. I scooped up a handful of water to bathe my face, and as I did, I noted something white gleaming under the water, half buried in leaves lying at the bottom of the basin. It was that damned doll's head again, this time sightless for its other eye was missing. The doll's mangled body lay farther out of reach, tangled in the long tendrils of water weeds spiraling up from the depths. I winced with pity remembering Amelia as she had clutched that doll to her breast and sung a lullaby. The doll's head had returned to me like a ball on the rebound. This was a signature I knew I must not disregard—and reaching into the fountain, I plucked it from the bottom, shook off a few drops of water, and wrapped it in my handkerchief. Now more calm and composed, I rose and returned to the villa.

I craved a cup of boiling tea, but I did not know how to light the stove. If tea was out of the question, whiskey or gin would do as well. I went straight to the library and poured myself a stiff shot with a jittery hand. The neck of the bottle clinked against the glass. I must keep myself under control, I reminded myself, checking the amount I poured for a second round. It would not do to meet the police investigators in a tipsy state with my breath perfumed with spirits.

I took the bottle and went to my room, sat down at the desk, and stared at the walls. Clive was raving mad to accuse me. They wouldn't dare do that, I thought. They couldn't, they wouldn't; but they might and I thought uneasily of Danilo's warning, "*Ones like me they hang.*" I opened my desk drawer and took out my box of signatures, and dropped the damp doll's head back in. Staring at those odds and ends, I felt exasperated with myself for not having read the signs correctly before to see that Amelia would be the victim and not I. I picked them up now, each in turn—the cigarette ends, the doll's head, the swatch of cloth, the pearl button. But they said nothing to me. I closed the box and stuck it back in the drawer. For a moment, my eyes were drawn to the portrait of Giulia Farnese above the bed. How mournful she looked and how stern. I must have a smoke, I thought, so I opened my purse, fumbling for a cigarette and out fluttered my lottery ticket stub.

I picked it up and studied the saint. How often in my life had I felt like that poor devil writhing at the end of his spear. But roles are always changing. "St Michael the Angel," I whispered and held the image to my lips, "help me." Then I pressed the ticket in between the pages of a Baedeker on my desk.

It was nearly ten o'clock at night when Nigel returned with the commissioner and the coroner who had come all the way from Viterbo. The coroner was a plump jolly-looking fellow who might have been a baker or a pastry cook. The commissioner was a small, slim, intense-looking man in his early fifties, slightly wall-eyed and balding, and he wore a diamond on his pinky. He must have been at dinner or perhaps at the theater when they called him out on duty, for he was nattily dressed in formal evening wear. I was astonished to discover that he spoke excellent English with an incongruous, slightly Irish accent. I guessed we were of the same age, though he might have been a year or two older than I.

While a small group of bully underlings went about the villa, rifling in our drawers and wardrobes and inspecting the grounds, Nigel, Clive, Finestone, and I were asked to remain in the dining room where we sat stiffly around the table avoiding each other's eyes, like skeptics at a séance. Clive had fallen into a near catatonic state. Finestone's body looked withered and deflated as though the last puff had been stamped out of him. Manu and the workmen were detained in the kitchen. I half-wondered where Danilo had gone, but I thought he might have been separated from us because we were foreigners and he was

Italian. One by one, we were called into the library to be interrogated. Nigel went first and was in there for over an hour, then Clive was called in. I was next, but it wasn't until after midnight that my turn finally came.

Normally at night the villa was lit only by a handful of candles, but now the chandelier and candelabras in the library were all ablaze making the room almost as bright as the day so that the place looked even more tawdry and run down. The commissioner, seated in an armchair, rose and beckoned me to sit down in the adjacent chair and my interrogation began. While we spoke, he took notes on a pad bound in leather.

"Your profession?"

"Writer."

This piqued his curiosity.

"A woman writer! Writer of what? For the newspapers? For *ladies'* magazines?" From his tone, it was clear what he thought of women writers.

"I write novels. Mysteries."

"Mysteries! Then, should I know your name?" He read from his pad: "Daphne . . ." He peered more closely at me. A lady novelist is a rarity in these parts.

"My *nom de plume* is Marilyn Mosley."

I crossed my legs and took out a cigarette. Gallantly he leaned forward to light it.

"Ah, *Signatures*! Of course, I know of your book, Signora. The whole world was speaking of it last summer. An intriguing book for a man in my profession. The mysterious crime is solved thanks to the detective's ability to read the signs left on the scene of the crime not by either criminal or victim, but by destiny itself."

This summed it up very well. "So you have read the book?"

"Sadly, no. My wife read it and explained the theory to me. Most ingenious and fanciful, though, of course, no self-respecting investigator could take such ideas seriously, charming as they are in a work of fiction. We must rely on forensic science, psychology, hard facts and logic. Alas, I have no time for pleasure reading."

"A pity."

"But now that I have made your acquaintance, perhaps I shall find the time."

I made a little half bow in my chair. "I would be honored."

"I shall get it from the American lending library in Rome. I'm sure it would help me improve my English, though I confess, I rarely have the opportunity to converse with lady writers."

I stared at him, wondering if he hoped he might learn something more about one of his potential suspects by reading her novel, but all I said was, "I am flattered by your interest in my work, but I assure you, your English is impeccable."

He beamed at that, saying, "I studied at an Irish school in Rome. The Irish fathers were exacting masters. I have read your poets and your philosophers, and your greatest novelists. And now I have the pleasure of meeting an English novelist in the flesh!"

He looked now at the topaz ring and asked to examine it. I slipped it off and he scrutinized it in the candlelight.

"An item of value?" He asked returning it to me.

"Sentimental more than monetary."

"Yet it was found on the victim's finger. Or so says Signor Brentwood. Have you any explanation for that? When did you discover the ring was missing?"

"Just shortly before the men found—the body—in the fountain."

"*The body. The body*, you say, just like an English writer of mysteries. You realize of course that you should have left it just where it was, and that you were tampering with evidence?" There was a touch of hysteria in his voice.

"I did not want it to be lost. You know servants. . . ."

He sighed and made a dismissive gesture with his hand. He did not want to hear my opinion of servants.

"Was anything else missing?"

"A moderately valuable moonstone necklace in a gold setting, of great personal significance to me, and one of my evening gowns."

He checked his notes again. "The items worn by the victim."

"Yes. I do hope my necklace will be returned to me at your earliest convenience." The dress, of course, was ruined.

"Never fear, we are not jewel thieves, *Signora* or *Signorina* Daphne?"

"I am the widow of Colonel Peter Reynard-Simms," I said sharply.

He thumbed through his notepad, perused a few lines and said, "Mr. Brentwood claims

that you gave your permission for the victim to model these items for a portrait he was painting."

I laughed out loud at that. A sharp, dry single laugh, rather like a cough. "Then Mr Brentwood is a liar. I must say," I added, "that she had a habit of helping herself to my things."

He shot me an inquisitive look.

"On a few occasions I have found inconsequential things missing from my drawers."

"Could you specify?"

"A pot of lip rouge, cigarettes, a doll's head, a feather."

"A feather?"

"A turkey feather" I affirmed.

"A feather from Turkey?" He was puzzled.

"No, a feather from a turkey." Since I did not know the Italian word, I racked my brains for the French, which he would surely know, *"Un dinde!"* I cried in triumph.

"Oh! *Un tacchino!*" He raised an eyebrow and peered at me as though I were out of my mind.

"I said inconsequential things that had value for no one other than myself."

"And you suspect the victim in particular of carrying out

these thefts?"

"She was the one. Of course."

"On what do you base this certainty?" He read the list of objects from his notes: "cigarettes, a pot of rouge . . ."

"*Lip* rouge," I corrected.

"A turkey feather, a doll's head . . ."

"She had free access to my room and on more than one occasion I found her spying in my closets and drawers. I saw her help herself freely to my cosmetics."

"But what would have been the point of stealing such objects?"

"Spite." I said, then pressed my lips tight as I extinguished my cigarette. I knew I mustn't say a word more, but now that I had let this one word out, I had left myself open for attack.

"Tell me something about your relationship with the victim."

"I had no relationship with the victim. I rarely saw her."

How could I confess I *loathed* her?

"Yet you exchanged, on more than one occasion, strong words, or so Mr. Brentwood tells me, and you made threats against her in his presence as recently as the day of the murder."

"I was displeased when she handled my things without my permission, that is all. Perhaps I lost my temper once or twice."

I lit another cigarette and exhaled a plume of smoke, but I knew that coquettishness would get me nowhere with this enigmatic individual. I could feel his gaze, palpable as an annoying fly, traveling from my wrist up along my arm encased in a white voile sleeve which could disguise but not completely conceal the scratches on my arm. I realized that I had made a bad mistake in not changing my blouse before my interrogation began, and in fact, he said, "Those nasty scratches on your wrist . . . I beg your pardon, would you please push your sleeve up a few inches so that I may have a look."

I could feel my face go red. "No need," I said, " they reach up as far as my elbow."

"Most unpleasant, for a lady of such delicate skin as yourself.

How did you come to be so badly scratched?"

How could I say I did not know . . . , for I had discovered them when I awoke in the wood. "Trying to capture a wild kitten."

"A wild kitten! A panther, I should say." He paused, closed his eyes and seemed to reflect. "When was the last time you saw the victim alive?"

"Yesterday evening, on return from the sulfur spring. I found her in my room. On the pretext of ironing some of my garments, she was going through my wardrobe and using my cosmetics."

"You were not pleased."

I shook my head.

"Tell me now your whereabouts this morning and your movements during the day."

I complied with his request.

He asked me to tell him the name of the lake tavern where we had had lunch, but I drew a blank. "But I have a lottery ticket I bought in Vitorchiano at one o'clock."

He smiled wryly at the mention of the lottery.

"Are you a gambler, then?"

I shook my head. "That is one vice I am free of."

"Tell me something about the nature of your relationship with Mr. Nigel Havelon."

"He is my publisher. And a family friend of long-standing."

"Mr. Brentwood?"

"A friend."

"An intimate friend?"

I bristled. What *had* Clive told him. "Briefly."

"You were aware of course that Mr. Brentwood was intimate with the victim?"

"I suspected it."

"Only suspected?"

"Yes, I knew."

"And you were hurt, angry when he ended his affair with you?"

"It couldn't last forever."

He looked me over now, the way some men will do, as though trying to determine whether they may afford you an ounce of civility or must treat you like a whore—and asked in an oily, insinuating voice, "Were you also the lover of this Danilo?"

"That is none of your business, but the answer is no."

"Is this the man in question?" He showed me a police photograph of Danilo, very unflattering, with a huge nose. I had guessed rightly then, concerning his far-from-spotless past.

"Are you aware that he has a history of petty crimes and that his real name is Franco Sammartino?"

My eyes opened wide at that! The name Danilo was much more fitting and refined, but I only said, "I am not surprised, but he is not a bad person."

"Have you anything else to say?"

"I should like it down on record that I was twice the victim of an aggression. I was nearly drowned twice by an unknown assailant."

He knit his brows as I told him the story, not in an entirely coherent manner, and when I had concluded, he removed something from his pocket and held it before my eyes. It was a piece of the pipe Nigel had stolen from my drawer and broken. From his pocket, he took a small tin box, opened the lid, and stuck it beneath my nose. The smell of hashish paste set my mind awhirl and I had to look away.

"You know what this is?"

I nodded woodenly, concerned about how he had come by the paste. I had ordered no more from Danilo in a while, and I certainly had none left. For one wild moment, I feared someone had left it in my room so the police would find it, but instead he said, "This was discovered in the park tucked away in the mouth of a stone beast. Mr Havelon tells me it belongs to you."

I said nothing and just stared, anticipating his next question, and I was not off mark, for he then asked, "Are you in a habit of consuming this or other similar substances?"

"I have been, I *was*, briefly. In England," I hastily underlined, "only for medicinal purposes." But I was never really an addict, and I never forced it on anyone else, I wanted to say, to shout, but I kept mum, knowing that it would be useless to add more at this point. He had made up his mind about me and I was likely to end up in jail if I said anything else.

The conversation then took a downward plunge as he pressed on, "Had you consumed it when these moments of aggression occurred? This theft?"

I flashed "NO!"

"Mr. Havelon has informed us that you have had more than one episode of memory loss, mental instability . . ."

God help me, I felt so enraged that my whole body began to shake. My head bobbed and I couldn't keep it still. I thought my brain might explode. I could very well imagine what Nigel had told the Commissioner of my latest romp in the park, how I had been rescued half-naked and totally amnesiac, in the very spot where Amelia would later be found dead.

"And that he brought you to Italy because you needed rest."

A shriek rent the air—I was astonished to realize that it had issued from my own lips, rudely startling the commissioner and myself even more.

"Signora, are you ill? You are quivering like a leaf. Shall we call a doctor?"

I was trembling again, quite out of control. Was I so far gone?

"Water," I croaked, and pointed to a carafe on a sideboard. "Please, just a drop."

He fetched me a glass of water and I took a long quaff. He watched me as I drank, leaning forward in his chair, as if ready to pounce, expecting, I suppose, a tearful confession.

"This whole experience is very trying for me," I said, making an enormous effort to stifle my nervousness and summon some self-composure as I put down the glass. "Could we please interrupt our conversation and continue at a later time, tomorrow morning perhaps? It must be nearly two a.m."

"I would have thought you were inured to homicides and the like."

"The difference being that mine are imaginary, not real."

"Indeed. That's all, Signora. You will please understand if I ask you not to leave the premises within the next twenty-four hours without first advising us of your destination. At our next conversation, I would be grateful if you would produce your lottery ticket. Thank you for your cooperation."

I rose to leave, finally in command of myself. The shaking had stopped of its accord, almost surreptitiously.

"One last thing," he said, as he accompanied me toward the double doors of the library, "You must have formed yourself some suspicions, some hunch regarding the murderer's identity?"

I stopped in my tracks, wondering if this were a trap. I certainly had not yet had time to apply Marilyn Moseley's analytical skills to this case, in which I had found myself so unwittingly entangled.

"Alas, my dear Commissioner, I must say, in this instance, I haven't a clue. For the present, I bid you good evening."

"If you have any further thoughts," he said taking the hand I proffered, yet without the customary Italian hand-kissing, "please do not hesitate to share them with me. I trust in your collaboration."

"Of course." I murmured. What an amazing character this man was. Utterly unfathomable.

As I was shown out, Finestone was shown in for his questioning. He cast me a desperate glance as we crossed on the threshold. He looked exhausted by the wait. I saw that his typewriter had been confiscated along with reams and reams of his mysterious manuscript all piled in the corridor, waiting for a policeman to cart it away.

The clock struck half past two as the library doors closed

behind me and Finestone's interrogation began. I breathed a sigh of relief, glad not to have to answer any more questions. It was obvious that I was at the top of the suspect list. An older woman's jealousy is always a valid motive. Make her a seductress of younger men—and a drug addict, a and writer of mysteries—and you have the perfect murderer.

I was so worn out I could hardly stand and my head had been whirling ever since I sniffed the hashish paste. My stomach was in knots and I had eaten nothing for hours, still I wanted nothing more than to collapse on my bed, shut my eyes and blot all this out. When I opened the door to my bedroom, I found Nigel sitting at my desk, smoking. The air in the room was so dense with smoke that he must have smoked over twenty cigarettes to produce such a cloud. I could see that the night was not over yet. I waved the smoke out of my face and coughed.

"Hello, Darling, finished so soon?"

Soon! That was a laugh. My interrogation had lasted a good two hours, at least.

I wondered if he had been there all along, listening through the wall, so I said, "Why are you sitting at my desk, Nigel?"

"I was waiting for you to finish, dear. They have turned my own room topsy-turvy and there's no place to sit down. Besides, I thought you might like to have a little chat."

I suspected he had been looking for my new manuscript, so I said, "If you're looking for my manuscript, you are wasting your time. I confess. I have been a bad girl and I haven't yet produced a complete chapter. It's all been stops and starts. You'll just have to wait till we are back in Paris. After what has just happened you can hardly expect me to concentrate properly."

In order to let him know it was time he left, I began getting ready for bed. I removed my earrings and set them on the bedside table, poured some cold fresh water from the jug into the basin on the dresser, rinsed my face and patted it dry. He watched faintly amused as I daubed cream on my face, and I thought to myself, here we are just like an old married couple.

"That's all right, Darling, I suspected as much. The police have already carried everything of use away, including your more than precious pages. But I suppose you'll have lots of time on your hands in the future for your writing."

"What is that supposed to mean?" I sat down on the bed and took off my shoes.

"Getting it off your chest will make your feel better. You owe it to the memory of your brother."

Then I understood what he was driving at. "You must be out of your mind!" The two of them, Clive and Nigel, were going to have Amelia's murder pinned on me. "It's true. I did not like her, but that doesn't make me a murderer!"

"Until a postmortem establishes a more precise time of death, we'll be having to account for all our movements in the last twenty-four hours. The coroner did mention to me that roughly guessing she died in the morning. Have you an alibi?"

The words brought a shiver to my spine, I confess, but I did not want to show Nigel my uneasiness, which I knew he would take advantage of.

"Of course, Darling. As I told the commissioner—I was touring the countryside with Danilo. And I have evidence to prove it. Do you mind leaving me alone now," I yawned, "I must get my beauty sleep. In any case I think Manu is a very likely suspect. That man has always been so beastly to his daughter"

Nigel snickered at this. "Daphne you're so naïve for a woman of the world. Manu was her *husband*, not her *father*."

This came as such a shock, I thought I might be sick, though the news seemed to make a perverse sort of sense.

Something was beginning to click in my brain. "Then he is indeed the most likely candidate."

"Except that the poor man seems truly broken up by this event."

"It's not hard to counterfeit grief," I said sharply.

"I must inform you, Daphne, that the commissioner has quite

other suspicions. He thinks Danilo may have been involved."

I drew in a deep breath. How did he manage to be so well informed?

"That's preposterous! Danilo was with me the whole morning and afternoon until our return to Bomarzo in the late afternoon."

"He might have performed the deed before you set off."

It's true, I thought, the villa had seemed deserted that morning, and Amelia was nowhere to be found when I came down to the kitchen, hoping for a cup of tea and a piece of toast for breakfast. For all I knew she may have gone missing the night before. I had not noticed that my dress and ring had been taken from my room until just a few hours ago, when I returned from my excursion with Danilo, minutes before the body was found.

"Or he might have had time to drive back to the villa, leaving you there, watching your procession, do his dirty business and then come and fetch you."

"In that case, he would need me to furnish him with an alibi."

"Quite so. Or perhaps you helped him. After all you despised her."

I fought to restrain my anger.

"You are an evil man for saying this Nigel. I never would have thought."

"Reason with me. It's all quite a logical sequence. How else can you explain Danilo's disappearance? The boy has run away, and that certainly looks bad in the eyes of the police."

He left me alone and I went to my desk and tore open the drawer where I kept my manuscript and notebooks. All had been taken, even my pens, and the box of signatures. Luckily the book where I had pressed the lottery ticket was still there. I shook it out vigorously, but the ticket had vanished. It was already in the hands of the police; or worse, I thought, perhaps Nigel had taken it. Then I remembered the drawing of the Sacred Wood. Next to my jewelry it was the most valuable thing I owned, though of course, I didn't actually own it. I was only safe keeping it for the time being. Recent events had occurred so precipitously that I had not had a chance to examine the drawing again after my last tour in the Sacred Wood with Finestone. In fact, in the back of my mind, I had decided that it was time I shared it with the professor, as he was the only one among us able to interpret it and benefit from its real meaning. That seemed even more urgent now that the police were confiscating our belongings. I went over to the dresser, discreetly moved it away from the wall, trying to be as stealthy as possible, so that the policemen downstairs might not overhear me and think I was up to something. Reaching into the crevice in the back of the dresser, I found only a stocking wadded up there. The drawing was gone.

Two restless days passed with the villa under siege. Armed guards watched the entrance, the gateway and the drive. Since there was no one to prepare our meals or see regularly to the household chores, baskets of lasagna and roast lamb and wild salad were brought for us from a tavern in the town, but none of us were hungry. A village girl came in the mornings to light the stove to provide jugs of hot water and an occasional pot of tea or coffee. Only Nigel kept a regular mealtime schedule, dressing impeccably at half past eight to dine alone on a tray in the library and sip his wine before an extinguished hearth. The kitchen had turned into a bivouac for Manu and the workmen, while one of the large halls downstairs near the entrance was taken over by the coroner and then by the undertakers. In the hustle and bustle Amelia's cat seemed to have disappeared, or at least during these three days it had ceased from annoying me. It was strange to think it might have been witness to Amelia's murder. And I thought what a pity it could not speak.

We were not exactly prisoners, yet we were not free to leave and all our movements were closely watched. We had no contact at all with Manu or any of the workmen under his charge, and we avoided each other's company. On the few occasions that the four of us did meet, a great tension crackled in the air. None of us had been accused, and yet it was clear we suspected each other, and all of us were suspected by the commissioner's men. None of us had been interrogated a second time, and we had received no further news of the autopsy, if one had been performed, or of Danilo's disappearance. The commissioner had not asked me for the lottery ticket, nor did I know if it had already been confiscated by his men, whom I assumed had taken the box of signatures from my desk. And as for the drawing of the Sacred Wood . . . it might be anywhere. I speculated on who else might have known of its existence? Amelia, of course, had seen where I kept it and might have told Clive about it. Or he might have glimpsed it on my desk the night he had come down the trapdoor. The next morning he would have had plenty of time to ferret it out and study it at leisure while I was in the Wood with Finestone. Nigel might have found it, or maybe Danilo, who also may have had time to poke about my room while I was out on any number of occasions. Or perhaps the police had taken it. But who besides Finestone might understand its meaning or estimate its value? It was unwise to ask questions, which would arouse further suspicion, especially should it turn out to be valuable. I waited out the events and spent most of my time brooding in my room, but I slept fitfully and had no appetite. I was quite frankly terrorized as to what would happen next.

The funeral took place on the third day after Amelia's murder. A mass was to be held at the town cathedral, which seemed rather grandiose for a serving girl's last rites. Nigel thought we should attend for the sake of appearances and the commissioner let us go, accompanied always by his guards. That morning, I dressed in black, defiantly slipped on the topaz ring, threw a black lace scarf over my head, and went downstairs to have breakfast before heading to the town with the others.

Stepping into the dining room, I was amazed, if not shocked

to see Manu, now cleaned up, shaved, and clad in stiffly fitting ceremonial clothes, with a black ribbon around his sleeve, sitting at the huge oak table with a gold pen in his hand, signing a pile of papers with the ease and dash of a Paris banker. A gold ring flashed on his callused hand. As I came in, he glanced up at me in with a baleful eye, which he then blotted with a handkerchief, nodded to acknowledge my greeting, and returned to his task, ignoring the astonished look on my face.

A tray with coffee and rolls lay on a side table. Manu waved at it distractedly and told me to help myself, so I did.

I poured a cup of coffee and drank it while staring out the window. Why ever had I agreed to come to this place? I surveyed the god-forsaken landscape, the infernal gash of the gorge in which the villa was set. Heavy gray clouds were massing over it, veiling the transparent disc of the sun. Then a bright ray burst through as I heard a car coming up the drive. Shortly afterward, the commissioner joined us in the dining room.

"*Buon giorno*, Signora Daphne," he said, then turning to Manu, he gave a rather half-hearted Fascist salute, and said, "*Signor Conte, Buon Giorno*."

Signor Conte? Manu was a *count*!

But there was no time for explanations for this bizarre revelation. The commissioner had come to fetch us for the funeral.

Enormous beeswax tapers illumined the gloomy interior of the cathedral, where before the altar stood the bier, draped in silks and satins of black, gold, and purple, heaped with calla lilies and white roses. It was, all in all, a fitting funeral for the countess Amelia whose coffin was closed to conceal her brutal disfigurement. Michael the Archangel stared down from a stained-glass window above the altar, holding in one hand a scale and in the other a sword, striking down evil and weighing souls. How would he weigh Amelia's, I thought? And how would mine be weighed by more mortal judges?

Tattered villagers crowded the back pews, where we were

lucky to find a place to sit. Other mourners stood in back by the great bronze doors, or along the sides, half leaning on the columns. In the front next to Manu sat a row of dignitaries in black shirts. The priest's voice boomed through the church in a solemn monotone for nearly two hours while a chorus of white-clad boys with ruddy lips interpolated from time to time, "Ave Maria" or "Amen," in angelic tones. To the right of the bier knelt a row of Franciscan friars with their cowls hiding their faces, droning their prayers, while to the left, a row of nuns hummed on like plaintive bees.

Grief and mourning are contagious, such strong emotions travel like a wave through a crowd. Before the mass was over I was nearly in tears, though I had no fondness for the woman. Finestone too was weeping silently, while Clive wailed openly like a bereft child, attracting far too much attention to himself. Only Nigel seemed untouched, and after the last prayer had concluded, he gave me a nasty look and handed me a handkerchief, whispering, "You are a dreadful actress, you know."

After the service was over, Manu, or rather the count, stood at the door next to an archbishop who'd come directly from Rome for the occasion, receiving condolences from the humble and the proud. Of the three or four hundred people who had attended the mass, only a tiny crowd remained to accompany the countess from the square outside the cathedral to her final resting place, beneath the dome of the chapel in the Sacred Wood.

As we filed along down the hill from the town and into the gorge, I felt a sprinkling of rain on my face. The sun had disappeared again, engulfed in a mass of black and gray. Manu followed the hearse heaped high with calla lilies, drawn by high-stepping black horses, while a band in blue uniforms played a somber march. It was odd to think that I had witnessed a cortege of joy and celebration just three days earlier, and now here I was among the mourners.

Clive, Finestone, Nigel, and I wended our way several paces

behind Manu, who was directly followed by a group of relatives and friends. Finestone seemed to have taken Clive under a protective wing. Since the evening of the murder, they had been inseparable. He had kept vigil in Clive's room for the whole dreadful night of the murder and now he stuck close to the weeping boy's side, murmuring words of comfort. I felt deeply sorry for Clive who, however, now regarded me as a living personification of evil, and refused to even look my way. Finestone was so deeply grieved, he had aged ten years overnight. Talking with him would have brought me some relief, I think, and he gave me a friendly glance now and then as we all marched on, perhaps to say that he took no stock in Clive's absurd accusations. Nigel had assumed the proper, distant, pinched look required by the occasion, completely absorbed within himself, head bent, eyes fixed on the toes of his exquisitely polished shoes, face shielded by his American fedora. I kept my distance from *him* after our last encounter alone the night of my interrogation. I had no desire to speak to him. I fell back a few paces and strode on alone, wondering which one of our crew might be the murderer. Behind us walked two of the commissioner's men, keeping us in check. As for the commissioner himself, I had lost sight of him in the crowd.

Before we reached the villa, something furry touched my ankles, I looked down to see Amelia's cat, rubbing itself on my leg. Its white fur was dirty and matted, its pink nose had turned yellow, and its eyes were encrusted with mucus. The poor creature looked as though it hadn't eaten in days. With a crazed yowl, it darted up to the head of the cortege, where Manu strode behind the bier. I winced as I watched him kick the animal aside, and it slunk off through the bushes. That man was a beast.

When we entered the great gates of the Sacred Wood, a heavy rain began to fall. The fine lace scarf covering my hair was soaked through in an instant and I cursed. Quick steps sounded behind me on the gravel, someone grabbed my arm and a large black umbrella promptly snapped open above my head.

The commissioner had come to my rescue.

"Thank you, Commissioner, and very good timing."

"Signora Daphne, you are welcome."

"I did not notice you in the church," I said.

"I do not set foot in churches unless necessary when I am investigating a case. I am still a free thinker."

I knew not what to reply to this, so I was silent. Rain drummed upon the umbrella as we walked side by side in between the looming statues which observed us through blank stone eyes.

"How is the case proceeding?"

"It will be solved very, very soon, I hope, Signora."

I opened my mouth to ask another question, but the lugubrious blaring of the horns made a normal tone of voice impossible. The commissioner dismissed my attempt to speak with a flick of his sallow fingers, and in a pause between the strident notes of brass, seized my hand. "Dear Lady, whatever you wish to tell me, it can wait. We shall see you all shortly, tomorrow afternoon." He underscored his words with a firm pressure on my wrist, which made me think the word *handcuffs* and my heart skipped a beat.

"One thing, I ask you," he said before releasing his grip as the music ended. "If you have any news of your young friend Danilo, please tell one of my men immediately. He is wanted for urgent questioning." With that, he thrust the handle of his umbrella into my hand and was gone.

We crowded into the tiny chapel where the coffin was interred in its sepulcher of stone, and after a last farewell and posing of wreathes and roses, the mourners dispersed, leaving only the count, kneeling in tears at the head of the sepulcher, while at its foot, crouched a particularly devoted Franciscan monk, face hidden by his cowl, murmuring an endless Ave Maria as the tapers burnt down. Gazing round at the vaults crowding the chapel, I noted another sepulcher which had also been occupied within recent years, belonging to an eight-year-old child. I surmised it was the tomb of the daughter Amelia had lost to the Sacred Wood. The deranged scene I had witnessed of the poor woman with her doll must have been connected to this tragic event.

Returning to the villa, we all went our separate ways. No one had any desire to speak to anyone else, except Clive and Finestone, who retired to the library together for a shot of whiskey or two. Nigel retired to his room, and I to mine. Sitting on the bed, I tried to collect my thoughts. Manu had the best motive for murder—revenge for his wife's outrageous adultery. But Clive might have reacted violently upon discovering her with another man—the man she met while wandering in the Sacred Wood, or perhaps even with Manu. I shuddered to think that Clive and, before him, Finestone had been so bold as to seduce her in her husband's own house. If Clive were the murderer, that would explain why he seemed so determined to arouse suspicions against me. Nigel too seemed convinced of my guilt, or was that only a pose? And Danilo? His escape cast a lurid light on my own alibi for the morning of the murder—and even the lottery ticket, the only proof that I was not to be found at the villa that morning, had disappeared. Presumably if I could trace the child who had sold it to me, I could provide evidence that both Danilo and I had been very far from the scene of the crime on the morning of her death. However, Amelia might have been murdered much earlier before we set off. And Danilo's behavior that morning had been suspicious, to say the least, when I had found him wandering distraught in the villa.

I retread in memory my many walks in the Sacred Wood, picking up the clues scattered there over time—the bashed-in doll's head, the purple thread, the gold-tipped cigarettes, the quarreling voices, the swatch of cloth, the pearl button, the bloody bludgeon. Yet one detail escaped me: the identity of her secret lover. What would Marilyn Moseley and Edna Rutherford have made of it all? I had no idea. Some vital signature had escaped me. And then there was the drawing. Its disappearance coincided with Amelia's murder and Danilo's flight—and that was surely more than just a coincidence.

By this point I was exhausted. The villa seemed unusually silent. I missed the tapping of Finestone's typewriter next door, and of Clive's pacing in the attic studio overhead, making all the floorboards creak. I knew the hours to come would be some of the worst in my life, so I thought I had better get some sleep. I closed the shutters to the terrace, tossed off my shoes, and climbed under the covers fully clothed.

When I woke it was pitch dark. The clock in the library was striking twelve. I heard a strange scratching or stirring noise from the alcove and was instantly alarmed, thinking that enormous rats had got into my clothes in the wardrobe. I lit the candle on my bedside table, threw off the covers and advanced slowly toward the alcove. There on the desk crouched the winged creature, clasping his knees to his mighty chest, his beautiful bare feet planted firmly on a pile of books I had borrowed from the library, wings folded, his crinkly hair and broad, pearly toenails phosphorescent in the dark. He smiled and a yellow ray beamed from his eyes, but this time I shielded my gaze with my hand.

"You!" I said, "Who the hell are you anyway?"

"You might think of me as the Power. The power of freedom, the power of bondage, the power of desire, the power of art, the power of illusion! Call me by whatever name you choose." He held out his hand to me. *"Ogni pensiero vola."*

"No," I said, "I've done with you. Renounced you for good this time! You certainly have gotten me into enough trouble."

He laughed, "Easier said than done, dear Daphne. Your release or captivity are up to me to decide." Vaguely part of me knew this was a dream. His voice sounded familiar to me, someone I knew. . . . But who?

"I take many, many forms."

"You are evil."

"Not at all. I simply guard the door."

"What door?"

"The door of revelation."

My nerves were crackling again, and I could hardly withstand the intensity of this encounter. I did not want to be swept up again by the passions he could stir. I thought a smoke would calm my nerves, and in answer to my unvoiced desire, the creature flung out his arm to offer me a cigarette from an exquisite silver case. I took one and he lit it with a snap of his fingers. I recognized the case as he closed it and put it on my desk: it was the one Nigel had bought for Clive which I had last seen in Danilo's hands, engraved with the word *Desire*.

"My work is nearly done. After your redemption, I won't come again. Remember, Dearie, the worst of all evils is willful ignorance, the refusal to see what's right in front of your nose."

With those words he began to hum and then to chant a litany. I recognized the lilting rhythm that had punctuated my dreams for weeks as a low singsong murmur, but now at last the words were clear:

> *The Barefoot sister wends her way through the mouth of hell*
> *in search of one she loved and lost before from grace she fell.*
> *In gloom and fear she carries on through lust and wrath and*
> *lies until by unexpected grace she at last obtains the prize.*

The great wings rustled then unfurled with the sound of paper crumpling, touching the walls from tip to tip. Somber brown with a purplish tint, they filled the room with a heavenly scent, a mix of musk and myrrh. The door to the terrace banged open and out he flew into the night. The candle blew out in the gust of his wings and there came a stink of singed chicken flesh.

A loud thump woke me, and I sat bolt upright in bed and saw that the shutter and door to the terrace were ajar. A sweet smell lingered in the air mingled with acrid cigarette smoke. As the clock struck twelve, I recalled my dream with sudden force. Lighting a candle, I rushed out to the terrace. It had been raining, for the terrace floor was wet, but had stopped. Strange clouds billowed in the northern sky. Nothing else was amiss. I stepped back inside and inspected my desk in the alcove; nothing was out of place, but beside the brimming ashtray was Clive's silver cigarette case and a single brown plume.

But there was no time to puzzle on this. I had work to do if I were to save myself—and Danilo, to boot—from an unjust accusation.

Sophia

CHAPTER THIRTEEN

The commissioner had deployed three men to guard the villa—one downstairs, one just outside to patrol the yard, and make the rounds of the side exits, and one at the main gate to the road, fearing, I suppose, that we might try to escape by car. He had not considered the terrace as a possible route of escape, for somehow in their investigation of the premises, they had overlooked my hidden staircase, for no guards were posted there. Shortly after midnight, I went out into the corridor where all the lights had been put out and all the doors were shut. Downstairs from the dining room came a sonorous snoring—the downstairs guard must have fallen asleep in an armchair—a stroke of unexpected luck. I returned to my room, donned my black cape, and sneaked out to the terrace where I lit a lantern and hurried down the staircase, feeling very much like Edna Rutherford must have felt while venturing out on one of her nocturnal adventures. When I reached the bottom, I was surprised to see that the iron door leading out to the space behind the hedge had been left unbolted from the inside. I had not used this exit since before Amelia's murder, and the last time I had used it, I had bolted it securely behind me when I had returned upstairs. Whoever had last entered here had also left a very recent trace. Fresh mud was thickly smeared on the bottom step, although the outline of the footprint was too blurred for me to make much out of. It was large enough to be the print of an adult male foot; that was all I could tell. Stepping outside, I blew out the lantern, for until I reached the park, I would have to move in utter secrecy.

Shielded by the tall hedge, I skirted the wall of the villa in order to check on the whereabouts of the man who guarded the exterior, and I saw him sitting on a stone bench near the wall, warming himself at a small brazier. I watched as he reached down to remove a packet from a basket beside him and unwrap it impatiently. It proved to contain a chicken leg which he gnawed greedily. Next he pulled out a flask and put it to his lips. Another stroke of luck for me: I had chosen an excellent moment for my escape. He would be too busy with his midnight supper to take notice of me. I crept back through the topiary, then shot out of the hedge and ran for all I was worth through the tall, wet grass toward the gate of the Sacred Wood. Fortunately, my key to the gate, which I kept in a pocket of my jacket, had not been discovered and confiscated by the commissioner's men. I unlocked the gate and slipped inside. Safely concealed by the mass of foliage, I lit my lantern again, turning down the flame.

Never had the Sacred Wood seemed so eerie as it did that moonless night, illuminated by my lantern. Swaddled in dense vegetation, dripping with rain, smelling of moss and mushrooms, those rough-hewn statues took on a more vivid and disturbing aspect, half sunk in darkness, like unformed images in a dream. In the flickering lamplight, they did almost seem to move.

My path led me to Persephone and Pluto. It was sobering to think that this pagan pair had been perhaps the last vision to fill Amelia's eyes, after she had focused them on her murderer's face. A patch of blood still stained the ground where the girl had been found, which was the very spot where I too had fallen and hit my head. An inexplicable remorse mixed with pity and repulsion rose up in me, as the image of her mangled form lying there flashed before my eyes, superimposed upon the image of her cradling a broken doll. The thought that she had died in the same place where her daughter had drowned was almost too much to bear. A revelation pierced my consciousness: She and I were alike in many ways.

Something strange happened at that instant. The poisoned antipathy I had felt for her ebbed from my body in a single convulsed sob. I dropped to my knees and asked forgiveness, though for what exactly I did not know, forgiveness for being me, perhaps, and as the tears bathed my face I also felt with inexorable clarity I could not be any other than I was, and such was my fate.

As I was rising to me my feet again, resolved to carry on my nighttime flight, I noticed something floating in the fountain, a small white scrap of paper. I scooped it from the water with a branch, then examined it in the light of my lantern. It was a railway ticket and, though the ink had run, I could clearly make out a date stamped on one side: the date of the murder, May 8th. Could this have been Amelia's ticket? Had she been planning a trip? Or could it have been dropped by the murderer? More than a signature, this was also what the commissioner might have called a scientific clue.

But I had no time for speculations, so I put it in my pocket and hurried on. Exiting through the rear exit, I headed up in among the trees, up toward Le Madonelle, where I had seen Amelia with her doll and where I had returned shortly afterwards with Finestone. I supposed it might take four or five hours to reach the village of Vitorchiano and I planned to get there by sunrise, before the priest rang the matins.

Crossing the woods at night was a scary proposal. I tried not to think of the foxes, wolves, or deadly vipers that made their home in among those crags and boulders. The trail was thickly layered with leaves and strewn with acorns as slippery as marbles in the mud. As I picked my way across potholes and jagged rocks, thorns and brambles impeded my passage; branches thrashed my face. My shoes were ruined within the first half hour, my face scratched, my cape irreparably torn.

I said a prayer as I passed the niche in the boulder where Amelia had left the bouquet of anemones. The flowers were still there, all wilted and brown. Le Madonelle, which had seemed so charming to me by day when I had first seen the place, seemed downright sinister at night. My flesh crept as I passed over the spot where Finestone and I had stood just a few days before. I felt an overwhelming sense of oppression and loss.

Someone or something had been digging in the earth here. The stratified carpet of dead leaves had been disturbed. Had Amelia buried or unburied her doll again? Perhaps boars had been digging for truffles or grubs. I fancied I could hear them breathing in the underbrush, peering out at me from their dens. The nocturnal sounds of the forest set me on edge as I proceeded: night birds shrieking in the treetops, branches creaking and snapping as weasels or foxes observed my progress, or perhaps guided me on. From time to time, I noted movement in the underbrush. A porcupine peeked out at me from a ferny nest, and once my lantern caught a broad shape crouched in the bushes. At first glance I froze in terror, convinced I had met a wild boar or a wolf, but whatever it was shied from my light and scuttled away.

I found my way out of the woods as the morning star preceded sunrise. Crossing a meadow, I followed a road to Vitorchiano. Just before I reached the village, I met eye to eye with an owl perched on a post outside the rear city gate. With a squawk, he flapped away as I hurried past. A few souls were up that morning before dawn, peasants on their way to the fields with wooden hoes over their shoulders and hunks of bread or cheese or bacon bundled in rags dangling from their belts. They must have been startled by the sight of a disheveled outlander popping out of nowhere, but no one spoke to me. With my torn clothes and scratched face, I knew I looked a fright. I stopped to bathe my face in the village fountain, then cupped my hands to drink from the stone trough as the sun rose over the lip of the gorge.

From the main piazza, a road snaked down through an arched gateway into the gorge and up the other side. This was the road the procession had followed to Saint Michael's hermitage, and I continued in that direction. At the bottom of the gorge, the rubble-strewn road petered out into a track through the nettles, crossed a putrid stream choked with dead leaves, and rose steeply again. The last hundred feet were a vertical ascension up the cliff wall through a fissure carved by an absent stream. The door to the hermitage stood open. A few narrow pews were lined up before the altar where the wooden effigy of Archangel Michael with scale and sword was illuminated by a hundred candles and oil lamps guttering at his feet. I was not surprised to discover that Michael was the spitting image of my winged nocturnal visitor—*sans* tail, however. I had already guessed that these two characters were somehow connected, though one was the alter ego of the other. Behind the altar, the grotto extended deep into the cliff, and there at the back where a giant taper was burning, knelt a hooded friar. His murmuring litany filled the cavern with a reverberation like the buzzing of a hornet. I was loath to disturb his morning ministrations, but when after ten minutes or so he had failed to note my presence, I came forward, and tapping him lightly on his shoulder, spoke out in my awkward Italian: "Father, I beg to disturb you. I need your urgent help. I must find the little girl who sold me a ticket to the lottery here during a procession three days ago."

At my touch, the priest gave a shout and as, he jerked his head round, his hood slipped back on his head. Framed in its sackcloth folds was Danilo's gaunt face set in a grimace of horrified surprise, as though he had been bitten by a venomous reptile.

"Danilo!" I gasped, astonished. "What on earth are you doing here? Why have you run away? You must come back and let them question you. The innocent have nothing to fear!"

"Signora Daphne, I have been to you a friend," he whined. "Why you betray me?"

Heavy steps resounded behind me and a voice rang out in the rocky chamber: "*Signora. dovete venire con me.*" *You must come with me*—and a hand was laid none too delicately on my shoulder. Spinning round, I found myself face to face with one of the commissioner's lackeys. In the entrance to the grotto stood the commissioner himself. Pensively he observed the scene, chewing an unlit cigar. At his feet crouched Amelia's cat that had somehow managed to follow us here. The animal looked half dead with exhaustion.

"She led us to him, she did. Just as you said she would," said an officer as he pounced on Danilo and clapped a pair of handcuffs on the boy's swarthy, hairless wrists.

The noises I had heard—the creaking branches, the crunch of gravel and rustling of leaves had been produced by the commissioner's men as they followed my trail. How stupid of me to have mistaken them for a party of wild boars. Weeping and cowering, Danilo was led away. I held my wrists out to the commissioner, expecting to be braceleted with handcuffs myself, but he impatiently pushed my hands away to show that this would not be necessary.

"Then I am not under arrest?" I asked incredulously.

"I will accompany you back to the villa where you will be kindly asked to stay put for another few hours so that we may come to the end of this matter."

"What about the cat?" I said, pointing to the animal, feebly lapping rainwater from a puddle outside the grotto. "We cannot abandon it here. That cat belonged to the countess."

The commissioner instructed one of the men to take the cat back to the villa and see that it was fed.

We picked our way down the gorge and up again; the commissioner helped me along the more treacherous spots. Danilo, handcuffed, preceded us along the trail, occasionally tripping on sharp rocks protruding from the ground, while the guard behind him jabbed him in the back with a club whenever he stumbled or paused. In half an hour or so, we were back in the village. A small crowd of peasants and black-shirted notables had gathered around the commissioner's car parked in the main square under the towering statue of the angel. The mob rushed at us as we headed toward the car, jeering and gesticulating, shouting, "Assassini! Assassini!"—Murderers! Murderers!—while the guards struggled to restrain them. In the fray, the terrorized cat leaped from the arms of the guard who was holding it and bounded away. Though Danilo was the prime target of their wrath, a woman managed to spit on me before a guard pulled her away. Danilo and I were rudely pushed into the backseat, and the commissioner climbed into the passenger seat up front.

Turning to hand me a handkerchief so I could wipe my face, he apologized for the people's behavior.

"Your nation is not popular with us these days," he said.

Danilo, still in handcuffs, hid his head against my shoulder, trying to shield his face from the view of the crowd pressing close to the vehicle. I could feel his body trembling as his lips silently formed what I imagined was a prayer. I patted his cheek to comfort him, as I scanned the snarling faces pushed flat against the windows, searching for the little girl who had sold me my lottery ticket; but I did not spot her. As we drove off, I looked out the rear window up at Michael's grim expression, remembering Danilo's remark: *They put you in the stocks and spit on you—ones like me they hanged.*

There was a hubbub in the villa when we arrived. An entire squad of policemen were at work inspecting the premises. A guard accompanied me to the library where Manu sat at a desk, still dressed in his seedy mourning attire. He looked as though he had been up all night—with a stubble of heavy beard on a wan face, and dark pouches under his eyes. In the morning light, his shirt looked gray and the cuffs were stained with soil and grass. The room was in great disorder, with books tossed from their shelves and all the drawers of cupboards and desks pulled open spilling out their contents. Many paintings and prints had vanished, leaving rectangular patches on the walls where they had once hung. Empty frames and broken glass were strewn about the floor. The commissioner was in a furious mood, for all this had happened while the place was supposedly under guard. What's worse, Clive and Finestone were reported to be missing, and the guard who had been posted in the dining room had just awoken from his armchair, with a dreadful headache and a sizable lump on his noggin.

"What has happened?" I asked—though it seemed obvious: Clive and Finestone had escaped taking with them as many valuable objects as they could possibly carry away between the two of them, after knocking the guard on the head.

We went first to Clive's room, where the bedclothes had been drawn back to reveal a bolster and pillows placed there to mock his sleeping form. A similar scenario awaited us in Finestone's bedroom, where the good scholar's paunch and bulk had been cleverly simulated by Amelia's overturned washtub bundled in rags. But when I saw his white fedora, white linen jacket, and silver-tipped cane neatly posed on the stand behind the bedroom door, I suspected foul play. Finestone would never have gone anywhere without these things. His gold-rimmed bifocals were still on the bedside table.

When I pointed this out, the commissioner replied, "In the heat of escape, things get left behind."

"But could he walk very far without his cane? Though he rarely used it indoors, he always took it with him outdoors. And he was almost blind without those spectacles."

"They make up a convincing disguise and most useful the moment one decides to discard it."

"I disagree," I said, for at the sulfur pool I had glimpsed his misshapen foot. Beside, this cane concealed his secret blade.

Would he have run off in the night without it? I had also seen how nearsighted he was. He would never have left his bifocals behind, But then, I mused, he might have owned a spare pair of spectacles.

We next inspected the studio upstairs where the air reeked of turpentine, oil, cigarettes, and dust. Though Clive was not a very tidy person, never had I seen the studio in such disarray. Every surface was strewn with half-dried tubes of paint, sketches, pencils, charcoal, books, cigar stubs, dirty socks, and other clutter. This room too had been ransacked, but why? Glancing around, I soon noted what I was searching for perhaps only half-consciously—the sign that Clive could not be far off: his foldable easel—and there it was, in a corner by the window. I picked it up to examine it. One of its joints was missing a screw—perhaps the one I had found on the floor of the leaning tower—which had been substituted by a tiny twist of wire. Then something else struck me: many of Clive's paintings had vanished, but who could have taken such worthless pictures?

A shout from the hallway summoned us downstairs where we saw that the commissioner's men had pulled the angel icon from its niche at the very end of the hall, revealing a small door behind it. I took a deep breath as I watched them pry the door open. I had always suspected that icon concealed a secret or two. The door swung open into what appeared to be a storage room and I followed the men inside. The room was lit by a series of vents in the wall through which a golden light filtered swarming with dust motes. It was crowded with cumbersome pieces of furniture draped in sheets, but along the shelves, were dozens of tea sets and other toys for a daughter. A narrow cot was pushed against the back wall, and on the floor by the bed were three pairs of wooden sabots, of the sort Amelia wore. A crib and a high chair were tucked in a corner, and on one shelf was a row of a child's shoes progressing from infancy. There were eight pairs in all and on the last pair a pearl button was missing. This was, then, the key to Amelia's madness—the sorrow of a lost child. Above the bed a row of dolls smiled down with painted pink lips. The atmosphere in this mausoleum was so eerie that I began to weep.

The commissioner paced about this shrine, visibly struck by its peculiar atmosphere. Then with an abrupt gesture, like a torero flapping his cape at a bull, he grabbed an edge of the sheet covering one of the furnishings in the center of the room, revealing to my astonished eyes a pile of boxes and trunks where two or three dozen paintings were stacked. He picked up a couple of canvases and examined them on both sides: They appeared to be copies of the portraits hanging in the library and along the corridors, created by the hand of an exquisitely skilled forger. One or two were still quite fresh and had smudged the sheet with spots of pink, the very color Clive had mixed with such patience and expertise copied from a Turner landscape.

"This one will interest you," said the commissioner, holding one before my eyes. It was one of Clive's perfectly awful paintings of an owl and the moon which he had painted at the beginning of our stay. I shrugged and said I did not understand why he thought it might interest me. With a smirk of triumph, the commissioner turned it around, and there on the back was painted a copy of the portrait of Giulia Farnese that hung above the bed in my room. In fact, all the forgeries we had found in the storeroom had been painted on the reverse side of Clive's crude and amateurish pictures.

Examining the portrait closer, I saw that it was almost the perfect likeness of Amelia. Only now did the resemblance come through so clearly and startlingly. I would never have been able to distinguish this copy from the original portrait, except for one detail which immediately leapt to my attention: the jewels she was wearing in the portrait. Gleaming on her finger was my own topaz ring.

"But in the original, the lady was wearing a ruby, not a topaz. That is *my* ring,"

"Exactly."

"But why has he changed the ring?"

"This sort of purposefully wrong detail can be interpreted as the forger's signature, or perhaps as a provocation. Of course, the catalogue and documents could always be altered with a description of the forgery instead of the original. Or it could also be described as a newly discovered painting by the school of Lotto. Of the sort you read about in newspapers: *Florentine chambermaid discovers priceless painting in old trunk in the cellar.*"

"But these horrible pictures, obviously not antique, are painted on the other side."

"That's easily solved," the Commissioner said, as he took a knife and ripped off the canvas on which Clive had painted his picture, revealing the wooden frame on which the canvas of the forgery was stretched.

"So Clive . . . and Finestone . . . are professional art thieves and forgers. And to think I believed Finestone was a scholar researching the Sacred Wood."

"And so he is. But a fly-by-night variety. He probably needed a reliable source of income to support his studies, the aim of which may not necessarily be purely academic. Hence his liaison with Mr. Brentwood. I'm sure they are miles away by now. I have alerted the border authorities. We may catch them yet."

"No," I said, "my guess is that they haven't gone far, and perhaps, I dearly hope, they will return to offer us an explanation. . . . But what has all this to do with Amelia's, I mean, the countess's, murder?"

Moving a rug by the bed, one of the men found a trapdoor and climbed down to see where it led. *"Porta alla cucina,"* he called up from the hole. It led to the pantry room where we had always supposed Amelia slept at night. That explained how she always slipped in and out so stealthily.

"It is obvious what this all has to do with the murder, I think," announced Nigel from the doorway, intruding upon us. "Perhaps she discovered their plan and tried to stop them."

"I admit there is some logic to your supposition," said the commissioner, casting Nigel a canny look.

"Well, of course there is. Their disappearance is an obvious admission of guilt."

"I disagree." I objected, "Both men were fond of the victim and I don't think either one of them could have harmed her."

"But money overcomes all emotions," said Nigel, "even heartfelt devotion, and those paintings were worth a fortune, I say! They made off with a Lorenzo Lotto and two Turners!"

"You are well informed," said the commissioner.

"I recognized them the moment I stepped into this place. The paintings, I mean."

"Then you are an expert."

"Of sorts."

The commissioner stared at Nigel without reply, as though deep in thought, and this annoyed him.

"It's solved then," Nigel said sharply, with a clap of his hands as if to divert the commissioner's attention. "You have your murder suspect, and now we should be allowed to leave. Daphne, I suppose you still wish to travel with me back to Paris. I suggest you pack your bags, for with the commissioner's permission, I intend to return tomorrow, or as soon as we are free to go, of course."

"Pack your bags, Mr. Havelon, pack your bags. But before I can let you go, I beg you all to meet with me in the library." He checked his pocket watch. "I assure you, this whole affair will be concluded within a very short time."

"Very well," said Nigel coolly, and left us. The commissioner's enigmatic air had ruffled him.

The policemen had begun to disassemble Amelia's shrine-room, and so the commissioner and I adjourned to the library.

"But the crime has not been solved." I objected. "Who killed the countess?"

"Aha! Dear lady detective, what do your signatures tell you?"

Was this, perhaps, another trap? Was I still under suspicion?

I sat down on the leather sofa by the window. The commissioner offered me a cigar, which I declined. I pondered a few moments and then pronounced from somewhere deep in my diaphragm a name. It was wholly logical and no surprise. Manu.

"Exactly!" he said, "Any idiot would have come to the same conclusion. No supernatural intervention needed. But we have no proof, only a valid motive. A confession will be the only solution."

I had almost forgotten the train ticket I had found. I took it from my pocket and handed it to him, saying, "This is the last detail, or signature, if you will. It was floating in the fountain where the body was found."

The commissioner studied it, then nodded. "My dear Signora Daphne," he said with a slight bow, "against all expectation, you may have helped solve the murder; with the help of facts, however, not ghosts."

I said nothing to this. He would never understand about Persephone.

He pulled something from his pocket and flashed it before my eyes. "I take it this is yours? It was found in Mr. Havelon's trouser pocket."

I was surprised and relieved to see my lottery ticket, but before I could pluck it from his hand, he returned it to his vest pocket. "You may have it back when all this is over. In the meantime, this too is yours," and he placed a bundle wrapped in chamois skin into my hand. Unwrapping it, I found my moonstone necklace.

"Grateful thanks," I said and slipped it around my neck.

There came a scratching from the window. Amelia's cat pushed its nose against the glass, begging to be let in with an almost human-sounding wail. The commissioner opened the window and the cat leapt inside and scuttled straight for me, where it crouched at my feet with a mournful meow. I supposed it hadn't eaten since before Amelia's murder. It certainly looked as though it had been through hell, like me. On a nearby table was a tea tray with the remains of what must have been Nigel's breakfast. Noting there was still a bit of cream in the pitcher, I poured it into the saucer and gave it to the cat, along with a scrap of bacon and a piece of egg-sopped toast left on the plate. The cat gobbled the food greedily, and when it had finished, it jumped onto the sofa beside me, and began scratching at the cushions, purring in nervous excitation and waving its tail. Fearing it might scratch me, I tried to push the animal away, then noticed a bit of green wedged in between the cushions that the cat began to pluck with its claws. What on earth was my negligee doing here, I thought, recognizing the color, and, taking hold of the green strip, I tugged out a rag which had once been a prized item in my wardrobe and which now looked as though Clive had been using it to clean his paint brushes. The fine silk was blotted with turpentine and paint, but also spotted with fresh stains that looked like blood. I unfurled it before the commissioner's eyes as the cat climbed into my lap and pawed at the fabric.

Tearing the cushions from the couch, we found more rags wadded up, stuffed deep inside the empty spaces of the wooden frame. Recognizing one of Finestone's striped shirts, I pulled it out only to find that it too was stained with blood. Still damp, it was too fresh to be Amelia's.

"I'm afraid this story is not over yet," I said. "I fear my friends are dead."

CHAPTER FOURTEEN

Upon the stroke of noon, the gong sounded and we were summoned to the library, our little party reduced to a quartet: Nigel, Danilo, Manu, and myself. I winced to see poor Danilo still in handcuffs, trembling like a sensitive hound in a cold wind, slumped in a chair across from his antagonist, Count Emanuele Orsini, who had taken a seat at his inlaid desk, like a magistrate sitting in judgment. I had not yet had time to get used to his abrupt switch of identity from rough handyman to aristocrat, nor to the improved linguistic skills that had accompanied it. The count, it seemed, enjoyed playing the part of a simple workman.

The room was still in shambles. The walls denuded of their precious paintings and fine prints revealed scabby patches of flaking plaster where green mold had seeped to the surface from deep within the walls. Books tossed from the sagging shelves were piled on chairs, with torn-out pages strewn all over the floor. The crystal cabinets were empty of their silver and Etruscan artifacts save but a few pitiful shards. The place had been ransacked for every item of value and then re-ransacked by the police for clues.

The commissioner stood in the middle of this disarray, still chewing his cigar. He examined us each in turn with a prodding gaze so forceful I felt nailed to the spot. At last his eyes came to rest upon Manu. "Are you sure you wish to be present during this interrogation?" he asked the count who nodded with grave dignity.

There on one of the writing tables by the window was my box of signatures. The commissioner lifted it before our eyes and, with an impulsive gesture, almost of disgust or perhaps provocation, dumped the contents across the table. The little doll's head rolled off and smashed onto the floor in two pieces, which he hastily retrieved and put back with the other things. I noted with some surprise that my lottery stub, Clive's cigarette case, and the train ticket I had found in the fountain had been added to the objects I had collected over the weeks.

"Signora Daphne, I invite you to read your *signatures* to us."

"I should have been forewarned," I said icily. I did not relish being made fun of. It seemed hardly the proper place or time.

"I insist," he said sternly, nodding toward the writing table, which I approached like a reluctant pupil to a piano for a school recital.

I gathered up the fragments of the doll's head in my hand and at that moment was flooded by an inner light of perfect clarity. How was it I had not known, not understood before? The signatures unveiled themselves and spoke to me directly. I saw myself transported to a vast open plain. The ground was not solid, but soft as a sponge, and I felt quite giddy as I stepped across it, moving, it would seem, with no effort of physical motion, guided by something—or someone, a being of small stature—who held me by the hand, but remained just outside my peripheral vision. Pictures and feelings unrolled before my eyes, sensations from dreams, the flicker of amber eyes, the smell in the tomb, the sensation of water filling my lungs. My own experiences blended into Amelia's, my own being was her being, and my eyes were hers; but they were not the eyes of the flesh. As I held the shattered doll's head in the palm of my hand, I knew exactly what had happened to her and why, though the images expressed themselves as emblems rather than photographic images. That is to say they did not bear the likeness of real, known things. There were dark patches too where the pictures were obscured by a sort of fog or smoke.

Touching in turn the objects scattered on the writing table, my hands read and understood. Like words of a foreign language now mastered, the signatures strung themselves into a meaningful sequence. Unhesitatingly I began to explain: The doll's head was the first signature, the omen of the countess's death, caused not by strangling, but by an injury to the head. The splitting in two pieces which had just occurred, indicated her double nature, and the choice she had been forced to make which destroyed her. The purple silk thread torn from my own gown was what bound her to me, my own entanglement in this tragic affair, the inexplicable twist of destiny through which she would die wearing a dress and jewelry that belonged to me. The pearl button was the seed of her sorrow, sign of her daughter's death. The cigarettes stained with lip rouge indicated her many secret meetings with many lovers. Like the cracked blue glass lid of my rouge pot I had found in the tower, these things connecting us spoke of our rivalry, our unsuspected affinities, and of my own unwitting role in her death: for my coming to this place had set in motion the events through which she would be destroyed. The screw, from Clive's easel, found with the red-stained cigarettes, linked her to Clive and to Clive's forgeries. It also suggested that things between them would become unscrewed, unhinged, and fall apart. The name *Desire*, engraved on the cigarette case, suggested that unfulfilled wishes and desires, jealousy and silver—i.e. *l'argent*—were the underlying motives of this tragedy. The lottery ticket gave us the day of the murder May 8th, and the unpunched train ticket suggested an aborted flight. It also clearly indicated that the murderer had not left Bomarzo. A dark fog now enveloped the last mental picture: a face lost in a swirl of smoke—I could not identify it—but it was *not* Manu and that gave me pause. I fell silent. Depleted of strength, I dropped with wobbling knees into the nearest armchair. Someone brought me a glass of water which I gulped down. Glancing around at the others, I noted then that Nigel was smirking at me with snide amusement. The commissioner, who had taken a seat on the sofa while I spoke, instead appeared preoccupied, gazing out the window. It struck me that he had not heard a word of what I had said, and I wondered why on earth he had obliged me to go through with my little performance. Then as if interrupting his train of thought, he turned to me abruptly.

"Fanciful indeed. Even admirable. Intuition may sometimes play a minor role in solving crimes. For you are correct, the countess died of a blow to the head before her body was put in the fountain. Now, for science and psychology." Taking out a notebook, he sighed, turned to Danilo, and said, "Tell them your real name."

Danilo screwed his eyes up as if in pain and looked down at his elegant shoes scuffed and covered with mud. "Franco Sammartino," he mumbled.

"How did you make the acquaintance of Mr. Havelon? "

"At a café, near the Pincio. He wanted a guide and driver."

"Mr. Havelon, are you in the habit of taking unknown individuals into your services, without references?"

"He seemed perfectly respectable," said Nigel. "He spoke decent English and was familiar with this out–of-the-way corner of the countryside, and he had references. He showed me a letter written by the wife of the secretary to the British Consul in Rome."

The commissioner raised his eyebrow.

"Could you tell us why you came to this, as you say, out-of-the-way corner of the countryside, in the first place?"

"I have already answered that question in our previous interrogation. I will repeat it now. I came to help Daphne, a dear friend of my family, to recover from a serious illness caused by addiction."

Liar! I thought.

"But my well-meaning efforts were undone by this blackguard

who has betrayed my trust!"

"False! False!" cried the overwrought Danilo. "He gave me a powder to mix in the hashish. It was only to calm her nerves, he said, because she was nervous and had been ill. But I used only a little. I wanted to be sure it not hurt her."

I was astonished. "So it was you who drugged my wine that night as well," I said to Danilo. I next confronted Nigel. "That was on your orders, too, I presume?"

"How can you believe such a half-baked story? The man's a proven thief as well as an impostor and, from the looks of it, a murderer, too."

"I am sorry the wine made you sick," said Danilo. "It was only supposed to make you sleep, but you drank too much."

"And woke up half naked with a hangover in the park where I was almost raped by *him!*"

"Yes," the commissioner cried, rising to his feet, and beginning to pace up and down before the empty shelves. "A nice peaceful sleep, so that you would not overhear what was happening in the villa. But something went wrong, did it not? The wine was intended to be doled out to the whole company over the next few days, to assure sounder sleep than usual while the original paintings were replaced with forgeries. But it was drunk by Signora Daphne all by herself, for a nightcap, and it had a rather unpredictable effect on her."

I glared at Nigel. "You beast! How could you?"

"I have nothing to do with any of this ridiculous story!"

"By and by, Mr. Havelon, we will get to that. All questions will be answered to our satisfaction."

The commissioner went to the writing table and picked up an object. Clive's cigarette case flashed in his hand.

"Who is the legitimate owner of this case?"

"It belongs to Clive Brentwood. I bought it for him as a gift. Daphne can confirm," said Nigel.

"Can you confirm Mr. Brentwood's ownership of this

cigarette case?"

"Nigel did buy it for Mr. Brentwood," I added, "though then I saw that Danilo had it, and I confess, I wondered if he had been rifling in our drawers . . . and yesterday it inexplicably turned up on my desk, after you," I turned to Nigel, "had been sitting there."

"All lies," said Danilo vehemently, snatching for the case, which the commissioner held out of reach.

"*That is mine, She* gave it to me! And then it was stolen from my pocket."

She—it now dawned on me—could only have been Amelia, who had probably pinched or received the case at one point from Clive. Then *Amelia*, or the Countess, or however we were supposed to refer to her, was Danilo's "taken" mistress, and he her mysterious interlocutor in the Sacred Wood. I do not know how I could have been so blind as to have missed it before. Perhaps Danilo did murder her out of jealousy, or spite? I looked at him with fresh eyes now.

"Sammartino, when did you . . . excuse me, Count, we must address this question . . . first become intimate with the countess?"

"Right after I came to this house. The same night. She was . . . desperate . . . for love."

The count pounded his fist on the desk, rattling the ink well. "You cur!"

"You are an animal. You beat her always without mercy. She deserve better than you."

The two men proceeded to insult each other in Italian, until the commissioner intervened.

"Silence! Otherwise I put you both in jail." Turning to Danilo, he resumed his interrogation. "Your meetings took place in the park, that is to say the Sacred Wood?"

"Sometimes there, sometimes in Mr. Clive's studio."

"Then the countess decided to include you in her plan."

He nodded.

"Plan?" I asked.

The commissioner now addressed me. "From our inspection of the count's papers, it has emerged that all the objects of value in this house are to be sold to foreign collectors through an auction to take place in New York. Is that correct, Count? To pay back debts. Dr. Finestone, an expert from New York was invited to Bomarzo so that he could appraise the items and prepare a detailed catalogue."

That explained the long hours Finestone had spent typing and scribbling alone in the library. He was writing no scholarly tome; rather he was compiling a precisely annotated catalogue of artworks and valuables in the villa's collection. But what then of his research in the Sacred Wood? Had that only been a lie? A way of deviating our attention from his true purpose in Bomarzo? And yet, I could hardly believe it, remembering how his eyes glowed whenever he discussed his theory.

The commissioner removed a piece of paper from the vest pocket of his jacket and flapped it before Manu's nose. "I have a letter here written by you to Finestone, arranging his visit to Bomarzo. Shall I read it?"

The count dismissed it with a wave of his hand. "The war destroyed us. We were forced to make this decision. *Gli inglesi*"—The English—here he broke off and spit into his grimy handkerchief, "have made our money worthless and are driving us from our ancient homes."

"I must add that some of the paintings were to be ceded to honor a gambling debt."

Manu threw up his hands and said nothing.

" Dr. Finestone, a very practical man, proposed that copies of the paintings should be made and remain in the villa's collection as a testimony to its past glory, to keep its walls from looking so bare and, of course, so that no one would suspect that the originals had been taken out of the country for auction. My guess is that he suggested this to the countess alone, with whom he had, it seems, a special relationship, and Mr. Brentwood, one of Dr. Finestone's close associates, was called in for this purpose. But since he was without funds, he convinced his new friend Mr. Havelon, whom he had met in New York, to take him along on a trip to Italy, and in order to avoid arousing suspicion concerning his presence in Bomarzo, he pretended that he had never met Dr, Finestone before.

Once the countess had discovered Mr. Brentwood's extraordinary talents, she realized that his copies, or rather, forgeries, could profitably be sold to collectors elsewhere in America, and that her American friends would be able to assist her in such a project. She most likely kept this secret from her husband, being relatively estranged from him. But he too had probably come to a similar conclusion, and had made his own offer to Finestone concerning the forgeries. What do you say, Count?"

Manu sat glowering at his desk and mumbled a low assent.

"Then when Mr. Sammartino, alias Danilo, came into the picture, the countess changed her mind. She decided to keep all the originals and perhaps some of the forgeries for herself and escape with Mr. Sammartino before the others discovered what she had done. And the day you were to elope was the evening of the May 8th—or at the latest the 9th. Signora Daphne, confirm the date on the ticket."

He picked up the ticket from the pile of signatures and handed it to me.

"The ticket is indeed stamped with the date, May 8th." I reflected a moment. "Of course," I said, "that's why you were wandering about the villa on the morning of the murder, you were looking for Amelia—I mean the countess—for your last-minute preparations. Doubtless she intended to escape while wearing my dress and taking my valuables as well!"

"Perhaps she decided not to go with him, so that is why he killed her," said Nigel.

"I am innocent," Danilo blubbered.

The commissioner glared at us for having interrupted.

"Perhaps what Mr Sammartino, alias Danilo, was doing when Signora Daphne found him downstairs that morning was checking to see if the countess had already substituted the paintings with the forgeries, but the most important ones were not yet in their places."

"The paint was not dry!" sobbed Danilo. "But we could not wait any more." Turning to me, he whined, "I promise we would repay you for your dress and jewelry. She had to escape in clothes in which she not be recognized. But we were not going to take a train. We were going to take Mr. Nigel's car. . . ."

"I hope you noted that confession of intended theft of my motorcar," Nigel interjected.

"Indeed you couldn't wait longer, for you had been discovered by . . . by someone who could not bear to part with one of you, by someone who is in this room now at this very moment."

Throughout Danilo's interrogation, Manu had sat brooding at the desk, head bowed, eyes closed as he listened; but at this he looked up with penetrating gaze and said calmly, "You cannot think I would murder my wife? The whole town knows she was no longer faithful to me. This would not be the first time she ran off with a young man. And she always returned a few days later, begging me to take her back. And I always did. These lovers were part of her strangeness. After we lost our daughter"—here his face grew fierce.—"she went a little mad. I try always to watch out for her. I hide all traces of our dead child, for I could not give her another one. She find them all and put them back in that room. She was obsessed," his lips quivered, and he pointed an accusatory finger at the writing table where the signatures were piled, "with that doll. Putting it in the fountain. Taking it out again. Burying it in the Sacred Wood. Unburying it again. Every year we must go through this charade. Always I take and hide. Always she find."

"A ritual," I whispered, "the ritual of the Mothers in Mourning."

The commissioner's eyes swept the room and came to rest on Nigel, who said, "This is preposterous. I demand to see a solicitor."

"All in due time, Havelon."

The probing eyes now moved to my face. "Describe to me your morning of May 8th, Signora Daphne."

"I woke earlier than usual. Ten o'clock, I suppose. Amelia . . . the countess . . . was nowhere about. It was she who usually prepared my breakfast. I went down to the kitchen to see if I could find something to eat, and I ran into Danilo . . . who said he was looking for his gloves. And that he had just accompanied Nigel to the station."

"Yes, on May 8th, I went to Rome early," said Nigel, "and I can attest that the victim was still alive when we departed for the station, for she served the two of us coffee."

"It is true," said Danilo. "That was the last time I saw her alive."

"Murderer!" shouted Manu. "I will see that you are hanged."

"Calm yourself, Count," said the commissioner. "Mr. Havelon," he began, "tell me your day on May 8th."

"Well, I rose early, had breakfast, served to me—by the countess—for I wanted to run some errands in Rome."

"Do you not usually go by car to Rome? Why did you decide to take the train, so much more inconvenient and uncomfortable?"

"I had decided to leave my car and driver at Daphne's disposal. I thought a drive in the open air, considering how ill she had been the day before, would do her good. So I agreed with Danilo, or Mr. Sammartino, that he would accompany me in the morning to the station, and then return to the villa and suggest to Daphne that they go for a drive!"

"How kind and thoughtful. The perfect friend!"

"Can you confirm that those were your instructions?"

"Yes. I took Mr. Nigel to the station. I waited in the queue to buy a ticket for him. I gave him his ticket, accompanied him to the platform. He got on the train and, after it go, I drive back to the villa; but he did not tell me to take Miss Daphne for a drive. Only that I must return at five o'clock to the station."

"*I* suggested we go because I was starving, and I wanted to go somewhere where I could get something to eat." I said.

"Of course, you never intended to return to the station to fetch Mr. Havelon. By five o'clock that evening you had hoped that the countess and yourself would be far from Bomarzo. But when you returned to the villa to look for her after driving Mr. Havelon to the station, you could not find her."

"Yes," Danilo sobbed. "I thought she change her mind. In the last few days, she was nervous; we argue. That dog of her husband the night before almost broke her nose. After that I say, tomorrow, no matter what, tomorrow morning, we must go away from here forever. Then when Mr. Nigel say he leave the car with me and go to Rome by train, I tell her to be ready to leave when I come back from the station."

"But she would not go without the paintings."

"I did not care about the paintings. I wanted to go weeks before. She insisted on taking the paintings. We needed money to live, she said, money to go to America. That morning, I saw the paintings had not been changed."

"You mean to say that the originals had not yet been removed from their frames and substituted with copies."

Danilo nodded. "That meant she not ready to go. Must wait. I look for her everywhere in the villa. . . ."

"But she was not in the place you agreed to meet her, or in any of her usual places, as Signora Daphne has informed us . . . because she was already dead, savagely murdered in what our dear count insists on calling *the Sacred Wood.*"

Manu now let out a roar of grief.

"Perhaps you invited the Signora to go for a drive in order to create an alibi!"

"I am innocent!" cried Danilo again and began to weep like

an inconsolable child and I could but pity him.

"Tell me, Mr. Havelon, at what time did your train depart?"

"I took the eight o'clock train departing from the Viterbo station. I arrived in Rome shortly after ten o'clock.

"What did you do then?"

"I bought a newspaper and sat reading it in a café, then went to Thomas Cooks but it had closed earlier that day, before noon, so I had a lunch near the Via Veneto, walked about the town, and took the three o'clock train home."

"Do you know the name of the place you stopped for lunch or the name of the street?"

"We have already been through this," growled Nigel through his teeth.

"It is for the benefit of the others that I ask you to repeat your story."

"As I said before, I'd have to take you there to show you. I don't know. I saw a place, I liked it, and I sat down."

"And then?"

"I had arranged for Danilo to fetch me at five. There was no sign of Danilo when I reached the station, so I got in a cab and drove home. An hour or so later, Danilo and Daphne appeared. And then we received the news that the countess had been found dead in the park."

A knock at the door interrupted Nigel's report. It opened to admit a policeman accompanying a tawdry-looking man in a gray railway uniform. The commissioner took the man aside, spoke with him a few minutes, pointed at Nigel, and then Danilo. The man nodded.

The commissioner introduced him as the stationmaster of the station in Tre Croci, the first stop down along the Viterbo-Rome line. The stationmaster confirmed that the "the gentleman in question," here he indicated Nigel, had been noted getting off the train at ten minutes past eight o'clock at the station in Tre Croci before the controller had had time to punch his ticket.

From there he had been seen proceeding alone on foot for parts unknown, climbing over the tracks and up the wooded embankment above from the station.

As for Danilo, he had never seen him before.

"So Mr. Havelon, you never went to Rome on May 8th. You got off the train and somehow found your way back to Bomarzo."

Nigel folded his elegantly manicured hands and rested them in his lap with a priestly gesture. "I wish to telephone to the British consulate."

"Then," I said, picking up the train ticket again and examining it once more, "this was *you*r ticket, which you must have dropped on your way returning through the Sacred Wood."

"Then you! You are the murderer!" shouted Manu, jumping up from the desk and throwing himself on Nigel who covered his head with his hands to protect himself. It took two policemen to pull the count away from Nigel, who seemed, despite all, quite unperturbed.

"Spare me your theatrics, Count," he said, smoothing his hair back down. "You, of all people in this room, know I am innocent."

"Not quite, not quite," said the commissioner. "Returning through the park, your Sacred Wood, you came across the countess and the count, having, perhaps, a vivid argument about Mr. Sammartino, or perhaps, about the paintings, for the count had discovered her plan. It was a violent quarrel, much more violent than usual, wasn't it, Count? But her death was not intentional."

Manu wrestled free from the guards and shot up from the sofa where he had been restrained.

"How dare you!"

"Havelon here witnessed the event from the beginning to the tragic end, and threatened to blackmail you when you realized the countess was dead. But seeing as though you had no money, the two of you had to agree upon a method of payment. All you

264 • SIGNATURES IN STONE

had were the paintings—of great value—of this Havelon was well aware, and the forgeries which had been made. They now all had to be secured in the count's possession. To this end, Mr. Brentwood and Dr. Finestone would have to be eliminated. And this was accomplished, most conveniently, upon returning from the countess's funeral. Mr. Havelon, free to move about the villa without arousing suspicion of the guard downstairs, simulated their escape; then the two of you dragged the bodies down into the wood by means of the hidden staircase."

"The mud on the staircase," I murmured as I began to put the pieces together. "Now I understand. That was your footprint."

"That's absurd," cried Nigel. His face had lost its usual ruddy hue and taken on the bilious tinge of suffocated rage.

"And before dawn this morning, after disposing of Mr. Brentwood and Dr. Finestone's bodies—while we were strolling through the woods in search of Signora Daphne, you and the count incapacitated my men, removed as many paintings and other valuables as possible so that it would appear that Mr. Brentwood and Dr. Finestone had taken them and escaped. You then concealed them in a place where they would not be found. The originals, of course. The forgeries were still in the countess' secret room where she kept them under lock and key after Mr. Brentwood had completed them."

Things were working to a climax as I was beginning to understand the underlying design. It all made perfect sense. Clive and Finestone were a team of professional forgers and had probably been accomplices for years, which explained the fondness they had displayed for each other from the very first. Clive did the actual painting; Finestone handled the administrative side. By pretending to be such an awful painter, Clive had brilliantly protected his true identity. Who could have ever suspected him of forgery? Racked by debt, both Manu and Amelia, unbeknownst to each other, must had made separate agreements with Clive and Finestone for the sale of the forgeries. Then Amelia had betrayed all three when she had decided to escape with Danilo.

There was one question throbbing in my mind, which in the heat of the interrogation, I blurted out: "But who took the sketch from my room? Clive or the countess, or Finestone or you?" I asked turning to Nigel and then to Danilo. "Or you?"

Manu and Nigel stared as I pronounced these words. Danilo blinked at me in astonishment. I had the feeling that all three knew exactly what I was talking about, but I couldn't be sure. The commissioner turned his cold gray eyes upon me with intense irritation, for I had interrupted his train of thought.

"What sketch?" he asked.

"An old drawing of the Sacred Wood which I found in my room. It later disappeared after the countess was killed. I think it might be valuable."

The commissioner shrugged. To him it was just another piece of missing artwork in Finestone's catalogue.

There was another knock at the door. An officer entered and glanced at the commissioner with a bleak nod, gave us all the Fascist salute, and stepped out again.

With a sigh, the commissioner placed his hands together as if in prayer, closed his eyes for a moment of reflection, and rubbed the bridge of his nose. His face was glistening with sweat. Clearing his throat, he announced, "Signora—Signori, you must now come with me. The graves of Dr. Finestone and Mr. Brentwood have just been found."

On we walked through the Sacred Wood, out the back entrance and up the wooded slopes, in the direction of Le Madonelle, "The Mothers in Mourning," following the trail I had taken just the night before. Tiny pale yellow narcissus and anemones peppered the trail poking up amid the soft, dead leaves blanketing the ground. There was a smell of moss and mushrooms and rotting bark, and the slight taint of death from a decaying carcass of a fox or hare hidden in the leaves. In a clearing up ahead near the great boulders of Le Madonelle, several men in black shirts and a pack of high-strung, whining bloodhounds stood clustered around twin ditches dug at the foot of the niche where I had come with Finestone. To see that spot brought a shiver to my bones. Approaching at the commissioner's side, I saw that the bouquet Amelia had gathered was still in the niche.

Two long forms swaddled in dirty sheets of canvas lay on a carpet of brown leaves and sprouting acorns. I braced myself as an officer reached down to lift an edge of the tarpaulin from one of the bundles, and I flinched in horror as I recognized, with some delay, what had been Clive's face. His beautiful cheek and brow were blue, battered, and swollen. I had to look away.

The commissioner took my arm but I resisted his attempt to pull me away.

"Perhaps I should have warned you that this was not a sight for ladies."

Finestone, bare-chested, with white tufts of hair curling on his breast, instead looked as though asleep, in peace. No sign of violence appeared on his person, for which I was grateful. He had probably been smothered in his sleep.

"I did not mean to kill her," said Manu, taking out a hand-kerchief to mop his brow as we stared down at the two cadavers stretched out at our feet on the upturned earth. "This time it was different. She had—again—that doll in her arms. She had unburied it again. But this time she said she would go away. She would take the doll for remembrance. I had her by the throat. I could not stop myself. How could she leave me for that petty thief! A commoner from the rabble. I let go. I pushed, she fell and hit her head very hard against the fountain."

The doll's head, then, must have been decapitated as it slipped from her arms and fell into the water. In my mind's eye I saw it tumbling into the fountain and sinking to the bottom, nudged by fish.

"The Englishman was there, hiding in the bushes, spying. It was his idea to put her in the fountain and then murder the other two, for the paintings."

"That is a lie! A preposterous lie," shouted Nigel as two officers stepped forward at the commissioner's signal to put handcuffs on both men.

"You shall be hearing from the Consul himself," Nigel shouted as he and Manu were led back through the woods toward the villa.

Danilo was released. Breaking into tears, he collapsed on a mossy stone. We watched solemnly as the bodies of Finestone and Clive were wrapped up again and borne away on stretchers through the trees.

"But where are they? The original paintings and other valuables?" I asked, turning to survey the trails leading through the surrounding woods up toward the cliffs and on to Vitorchiano.

"Oh somewhere hereabouts. In a grotto or a shed. I have no doubt that they will be recovered soon, unless the count has found some more clever way to dispose of them."

"But one thing remains inexplicable. *Why* did Nigel get off the train and return to the villa?"

"We will never know for certain, but it may be related to this," said the commissioner gravely and he handed me an envelope. "We found this in a drawer in the library."

It was a letter to Nigel dated several weeks earlier, before our departure from Paris, from an American film producer in Hollywood. Opening it I discovered that a producer had offered the author of *Signatures*—or her *heirs*—the sum of five thousand dollars. My only heir of course, was Nigel, the executor of my literary estate.

"Then it was Nigel, all along." I mused. The incidents in the bath, in the tomb, in the sulfur spring were now explained. He probably thought he could drive me to suicide again by wrecking my nerves, or perhaps he even intended to murder me, and as literary executor, all would come to him. The morning Amelia was killed, I was still out of sorts from the effect of the drugged wine and the villa was deserted. If Danilo hadn't found me first, Nigel might well have and I was easy prey. *There but for fortune.* It might have been me stretched out dead in the Sacred Wood.

"Nothing supernatural in the solution of this case. It is pure psychology: greed and cruelty."

I looked back at the niche above the spot where Clive and Finestone had been buried, and thought again of the inscription on the drawing "Mothers in Mourning." I could not disagree more with the commissioner's point of view. The path of the future had been clearly mapped on the sketch I had found, which was cluttered with signs and clues, all signatures of what was to come; but I had been unable to read them until it was too late.

We made our way back to the villa, where some food had been brought from a tavern for the commissioner and myself.

"I wonder what will become of Finestone's theory?" I asked, more to myself than to the commissioner, as we ate our bread and ham in the library.

"What theory?"

"Finestone believed he had found proof that the Sacred Wood had been designed by some great Genius of the Renaissance. He never told me who—he said he would be announcing his findings publicly within a few days. It was to be a momentous discovery that would bring him wealth and fame."

The commissioner shrugged. "It seems to have brought him neither."

Seeing his disinterest in the subject, I declined to elaborate any further. It would not do to arouse his curiosity and perhaps inadvertently open up new angles to this case which had just concluded in the best of ways, at least as far as I was concerned.

The villa was to be shut up by the police since Manu was in custody, but I convinced the commissioner to let me stay just one night longer, to prepare my bags and generally myself, for departure the next day. He insisted on leaving a guard at the villa for the night, even though I assured him I felt quite safe. However, I suppose he was concerned about protecting the count's property, now that the villa was empty. Nigel's Packard would be taken the next day to the British Consulate in Rome, and if I liked I could travel to Rome with one of the agents by car. I intended to call in at Thomas Cook's to arrange a trip to the United States. The idea of California appealed to me strongly. But first I would have to stop in at the American consulate to help make arrangements for the funerals of my two friends.

The underlings were still inspecting the villa, searching for the paintings and other valuables in every nook and cranny. Some of the original paintings were discovered rolled up in a niche under the kitchen floor tiles, and the commissioner had these wrapped carefully and taken away. I kept looking to see if the drawing of the Sacred Wood had been found among the other valuables recovered, but it seemed to have vanished. The forgeries were all destroyed, ripped through the center with a knife. Only one was saved, the portrait of Amelia in my purple dress, and the commissioner offered to give it to me as recompense for my assistance in the case. Since I did not care for the subject of the painting, I decided to give it to Danilo, or Sammartino, whatever his real name was; but our Roman friend was nowhere to be found. I suppose he had taken advantage of the general chaos that had followed the arrests of Nigel and Manu to remove himself from future interrogation. I daresay I could not blame him. Not wanting this last trace of Clive to be destroyed as well, I accepted it gratefully and put it with my luggage.

I accompanied the commissioner to his car, and we arranged for my departure next day. "Perhaps we may collaborate again one day," he said pressing my hand warmly before he drove away, and I did not say no.

The sound of an airplane overhead caused me to look up at the sky. A small bi-plane dipped and looped above the gorge, catching a glint of sun on its wing, then leveled itself and headed northward. This intrusion of modernity seemed to say it was most definitely time to leave here.

I went back to my room in the villa, now deserted, and began to pack my things, leaving aside the cedar box of signatures, for which I now had no need, and carefully wrapping my moonstone necklace in a piece of silk. I put my clothes in my suitcase, wrapped my shoes in tissue, adding at the end my few books and writing things, an empty silver box still tainted with the odor of hashish paste, a manuscript of mostly blank pages, and Clive's portrait of Amelia neatly rolled up, my only possessions in the world at this moment. I searched through all the drawers and cupboards again, under the dresser and the mattress, half hoping I might find the missing sketch, but it was most definitely gone.

While I was packing up, the door opened a crack, and the cat crept in, leaping to the dresser to watch me. It followed me downstairs to the kitchen where I gave it some milk and some cheese rinds. The next day one of the commissioner's men would be taking the animal home to give it to his children for a pet, so at least it would be taken care of.

It would soon be dusk; even so, I wished to make a last visit to the Sacred Wood. The little cat followed me there as I made the rounds of the sculptures I had first viewed with Finestone: the sphinx with her unanswered riddle; the ferocious titans; Persephone held captive by her sightless king, awaiting liberation; the tipsy tower that would not topple over no matter how hard you pushed it. I gazed on each detail with a weary eye and recognized them all in some form as *myself.* My knees trembled as I stood before the hell mouth, hoping I need never descend there again.

Whoever designed the Sacred Wood knew this: The mind projects itself upon matter and then comes to know itself through its own reflection. The Monster Park—the Sacred Wood—was just that: a mirror to know the self. But that knowing could only happen by being pulled through the machine of the Wood itself, where its great sculptures marked moments of private revelation: lust, impurity, greed, horror at oneself, hope of innocence and rescue. Each encounter with the Sacred Wood and its sculptures produced a thought, a deed, an emotion, an event in which the mind's deepest urges and desires found expression, satisfaction, and finally, catharsis. More than a great work of art to be contemplated, it was intended to be *experienced* as we all had done, in our separate ways. Each itinerary had been singular, individual, and some had not led to redemption but to death. What great mind could have conceived such a masterful design encompassing these random pathways to self-knowledge? Who was the genius who had guided Vicino Orsini's torch-lit search for Persephone? Now that Finestone was dead, we would never know. Perhaps the sketch I had found concealed a clue to the unknown artist's name, but since the drawing had disappeared, who could say?

I returned to the villa with the cat at my heels. The commissioner had a local girl bring me a basket with my dinner: chicken and asparagus pastries, snippets of salad, and a flask of wine. I ended the meal with some fine cognac from the library liquor cabinet, gave the chicken scraps to the cat and went to bed. This time my sleep was dreamless, and I confess, I felt comforted by the guard's presence downstairs, though he snored half the night. The shrieking of owls and creaking of shutters did not disturb either of us in the least, and no gods, angels, or cats came to trouble me.

In the morning I awoke extraordinarily refreshed, and as the scent of brewing coffee wafted up the stairs as I was getting dressed, I felt marvelously alive for the first time in years.

Staring at myself in the mirror, I fancied I looked younger somehow, despite all I had been through. Walking down the stairs with my suitcase in hand, I realized why I felt so fine. The shadow—that slight umbrage that followed me everywhere, lurking in corners, shading the sun—had disappeared at last.

One by one, I gazed at the few original portraits still left hanging along the corridors, and reflected on Clive's immense talent as a forger. How could I have been taken in so easily? One of the few paintings left was the icon of Michael the Archangel which had concealed the door to Amelia's shrine. It had been removed from the niche and carried downstairs where it was propped against the wall facing a window. Only a handful of portraits remained, probably of Vicino Orsini's friends, lovers, and relatives—the work of minor painters, which Clive had not deemed to be worth copying or stealing. Among such a worldly crowd, this monitory angel seemed out of place. I stared at the winged figure nearly six feet tall, with his strapping, country-boy physique and the golden-eyed serpent coiled round his leg. I still felt that the reptile was in collusion with him; the snake was a necessary part of the angel itself. In the light from the window, it was easier to make out details in the background which had previously escaped my attention due to the insufficient lighting of the niche. Examining it closer, I noted that the landscape behind the angel contained a tiny drawing of the Hell Mouth—so that Michael seemed to be standing guard in front of that cavernous entrance. The letters "Mi. Bo." or "Mi. Bu." were cleverly worked into a mass of foliage nearby, just as they had been on the sketch I had found. I studied the letters again, pronouncing the syllables softly to myself: Mi Bo, Mi Bu.

And then I knew what Finestone had been trying to tell me.

All along he had been inviting me in his own way to solve the riddle of his theory. An illustrious name! A momentous discovery! The proof of which was right before our nose. And what more illustrious name than Michael the Angel? *Michelangelo Buonarroti was the Genius of the Sacred Wood!* Tears stung my eyes as I marveled at the greatness of Finestone's discovery, if indeed it were true. The Sacred Wood of Bomarzo may have been Michelangelo's last work in which nature and art were wed in signatures in stone pointing the way to an initiation into truth. With Finestone's death, the knowledge of this would now be lost again, like the Wood itself had been lost for centuries, buried in the overgrowth of vines. Once again, it would remain hidden until such time when another scholar of Jacob Finestone's astuteness could reassemble the fragments again into a legible pattern.

Was it the name Michelangelo which had cost Finestone his life? Perhaps the sketch I had found *was itself* the legendary treasure of Bomarzo: not only a drawing by Italy's greatest genius, signed with his initials MI BU, and therefore of inestimable value, but proof of his authorship of the Sacred Wood. And what was the Sacred Wood but the model of that artist's own mind, perpetuating itself through time, working through passions, betrayals, nightmares, and quests relived by all those who wandered in his unique creation, compelled by a design not of their own making which yet led them to know their very selves? No greater work of art could be conceived. It was indeed, sacred and yet full of monsters.

The commissioner himself was waiting downstairs chatting with the guard who had brewed me my pot of coffee. A lad from the town bakery had even brought us hot rolls. Breakfast was rushed. I was anxious to travel to Rome at once and to leave the country as soon as the trip should be arranged. While the commissioner and his man inspected the motor of the car in view of the long trip to Rome that awaited us, I surveyed the tall iron gates enclosing the park. I formed a vague farewell in my mind and turned away, but a faint sound arrested my attention. I stopped, listened more intently, and recognized the sound of a child's voice shouting, the bleating of a lamb, and the tinkling of a bell, all coming from within the gates.

Out scrambled a little girl in a ragged pinafore, leading a lamb with a bell around its neck. I recognized her at once: the child who had sold me the lottery ticket! Sophia.

Seeing me, she picked up the lamb and ran toward me through the tall grass, shouting, *"Avete vinto! Avete vinto! Signora.*

L'agnello è vostro!!" You've won! You'v won. The lamb is yours!

I had won the lottery! And she pushed the woolly white prize into my arms.

THE END

Author's note: All characters are invented BUT the park of Bomarzo exists and a daring, recent theory does attribute it to Michelangelo.

Linda Lappin, poet, novelist, essayist, travel writer, and literary translator, was born in Kingsport, Tennessee. She received her B.A. from Eckerd College and her MFA from the University of Iowa Writers Workshop, where she also worked as a translation assistant to the International Writing Program.

A former Fulbright fellow to Italy, she currently divides her time between the US and Italy, where she has taught English in Italian universities for over twenty years. Her essays, reviews, and short fiction appear regularly in US periodicals. Her short fiction has been broadcast by the BBC World Service Radio. She is at work on a second Daphne Dublanc mystery novel, *Melusine*, set in Bolsena and on a memoir, *Postcards from a Tuscan Interior*. Her website is www.lindalappin.net.

Caravel Books, a mystery imprint of Pleasure Boat Studio: A Literary Press.

The Cat Did Not Die * Inger Frimansson, trans. by Laura Wideburg * $18

The Other Romanian * Anne Argula * $16

Deadly Negatives* Russell Hill * $16

The Dog Sox * Russell Hill * $16 * Nominated for an Edgar Award

Music of the Spheres * Michael Burke * $16

Swan Dive * Michael Burke * $15

The Lord God Bird * Russell Hill * $15 * Nominated for an Edgar Award

Island of the Naked Women * Inger Frimansson, trans. by Laura Wideburg * $18

The Shadow in the Water * Inger Frimansson, trans. by Laura Wideburg * $18 * Winner   of Best Swedish Mystery 2005

Good Night, My Darling * Inger Frimansson, trans. by Laura Wideburg * $16 * Winner   of Best Swedish Mystery 1998 * Winner of Best Translation Prize from ForeWord   Magazine 2007

The Case of Emily V. * Keith Oatley * $18 * Commonwealth Writers Prize for Best   First Novel

Homicide My Own * Anne Argula * $16 * Nominated for an Edgar Award

Orders: Pleasure Boat Studio books are available by order from your bookstore, directly from our website, or through the following:

SPD (Small Press Distribution), Partners/West, Baker & Taylor, Ingram Book Company, or Amazon.com or Barnesand-noble.com

www.pleasureboatstudio.com / pleasboat@nyc.rr.com